Also by Susanne L. Lambdin

A Dead Hearts Novel Series:
Morbid Hearts
Forsaken Hearts
Vengeful Hearts

Coming Soon:
Defiant Hearts
Immortal Hearts

VENGEFUL HEARTS

VENGEFUL HEARTS

A DEAD HEARTS NOVEL

by

Susanne L. Lambdin

WYVERN'S PEAK PUBLISHING
An imprint of The McGannon Group, Ltd. Co.

Published by Wyvern's Peak Publishing
An imprint of The McGannon Group, Ltd. Co., 2014

Vengeful Hearts
by Susanne L. Lambdin

Copyright © Susanne L. Lambdin, 2014

Vengeful Hearts / by Susanne L. Lambdin – 1st ed.

Summary: After being exiled from camp, Cadence prepares to lead a group of misfits against the Kaiser to end his reign of terror once and for all.

1 2 3 4 5 6 7 8 9

ISBN-13: 978-0-9854088-7-9

www.DeadHeartsNovel.com

www.WyvernsPeak.com

Dedicated to my sister Lisa, a true survivor.

Chapter One

Snow lay thick across the Cheyenne Mountain Range. As the early sun rose, a sliver of light pushed through an ominous sky. The retort of gunfire filled the air as a small army of zombies stumbled from the north tunnel that led into North American Aerospace Defense Command. Cadence and her team, the Earth Corps, occupied two M-ATV MRAP vehicles firing on the living dead.

NORAD's main gate hung at an odd angle, supported by a single hinge. Remnants of the high-security fence had been forced to the ground. The guard-towers were reduced to rubble. A tank had toppled one tower, and several fire-damaged vehicles littered a nearby ditch. Three tanks blocking the road did not stop the rotting corpses from advancing, driven by an urge for flesh.

Frost-covered zombies staggered forward, black goo oozing from their mouths while their gnarled hands clawed at the air. Less aggressive zombies stood motionless in the road, taken by the sky. Some creatures frozen knee-deep in snow were too weak to break free, flailing their arms like deteriorated windmills.

"They're putting up a helluva fight," shouted Thor, in a husky voice.

Blonde locks hanging past his broad shoulders, Thor stood behind a mounted M60. He gritted his teeth, standing firm as he strafed the front line of zombies. Freeborn, a full-blooded Cherokee, in a worn Army jacket adorned with team patches stitched on the sleeves, knelt and launched a grenade from her M4 carbine. Whisper lay on top of the truck cab, picking off zombies with his sniper rifle. Blaze and Smack knelt beside Cadence, firing M16s as creatures made it through the gate, advancing on their position.

The Dark Angel vampires, Picasso and Lachlan, ran from a Jeep and crawled into the back of a second truck. Xena, Phoenix, and Lotus laid down heavy ground cover in a spraying pattern, blasting the moving corpses. Two furry forms jumped out of the truck bed and raced toward the zombies. Moon Dog, a black werewolf with a white-tipped tail and Sheena, a small, tawny puma, worked together. One by one, the two ripped zombies apart with their sharp teeth, splattering the snow with black ooze.

"The blast doors have to be open," shouted Cadence. "If we're going to claim the bunker, we'll have to fight them hand-to-hand."

Cadence, Freeborn and Thor jumped from the vehicle, boots crunching on the hardened snow as they ran toward a guard shack, attracting dozens of zombies. A loud moan brought a zombie with a decomposed face around the guard shack. It slipped on the ice, breaking brittle bones and crawled toward them, ivory fragments jutting from its flesh. Shambling bodies gathered at the door; mouths opened wide, revealing blackened teeth and withered tongues. Freeborn held the door shut with her boot, shotgun raised as a zombie slammed its head through the glass window pane. She fired point blank, blowing it away.

Thor pointed his revolver at a crawler hanging from the window ledge and shot it between the eyes. He batted his eyelashes to remove a fallen snowflake, pulling back from the window and reloading. "We're outnumbered. Remind me again why zombies won't eat us."

He lifted his gun, another round flying into a zombie outside the window, eye socket serving as a bulls-eye. The creature spun around and collapsed in a snow drift.

"What are we going to do, Cadence? Expend bullets or just let them go?"

"I told you why they don't want to eat us." Cadence raised her Glock, crouched as putrefied hands reached through the shattered window. She blasted a frosty undead captain and the hands disappeared. "When you guys took chameleon blood, it altered your DNA. They don't see us as human anymore because my blood acts as a natural camouflage. I figure there's a chance if we're bitten our blood can cure them, but I'd rather not find out that way."

Freeborn glanced at Cadence. "Even if we get past the zombies, the blast doors may be closed. If there are survivors and they're locked in tight, they might not let us in. I say we pull out and head to Cripple Creek and put distance between us and the Kaiser. We're too close to the Academy."

"The Kaiser has our friends held prisoner at the Citadel," said Cadence. "This is precisely where we need to be."

"Then draw your sword, Commander," shouted Thor. "It's time to go out there and knock a few dead heads together."

Cadence slid a katana from the sheath on her back as Freeborn opened the door. Zombies stumbled forward, falling over each other to reach the three teenagers. Thor whistled and the two young women followed him through a window, pushing zombies aside. Not one creature attempted to bite them, confused as the superhumans ran toward the tunnel. Thor and Freeborn fired round after round, while heads flew from Cadence's sword. She gave a shout for her team to follow. The zombies kept coming close enough to kill, but turned away uninterested the moment they took a sniff of the chameleons. The phenomenon wasn't the same for the therianthropes and vampires, who remained on the dinner menu.

Cadence was thankful for her thick leather coat as she fought her way through the zombies, reaching a tank. She sliced off hands reaching for her and climbed onto the tank, her Glock stopping a zombie intent on climbing up after her. The rest of her team kept close to the werewolf and werepuma, fighting the zombies roadside. Picasso and

Lachlan flew around, appearing in different places as the vampires tore off heads, moving before they could be bitten. Whisper remained behind, firing his M24 from atop the vehicle, taking out the undead at will.

Ammo spent, Cadence returned to using her katana. Gripping the sword with both hands, she dove into the mass of undead flesh and hacked her way through. She glanced up to see the tunnel in sight and caught a fleeting glimpse of Thor and Freeborn following close. The stream of bodies coming out of the tunnel dwindled and remaining stragglers were handled by the Earth Corps.

It grew quiet. Cadence took time to catch her breath, glancing back.

Freeborn stood behind her, holding her shotgun. Over a month ago, Freeborn had been a zombie for a day. After receiving Cadence's blood, she became something else. Chameleons were infected with a strain of the virus that turned them into superhumans. Side-by-side, they entered the tunnel, Freeborn taking out the stragglers.

"This is like shooting ducks in a barrel," she said, firing at a zombie stuck in a draft. The blast splattered black, gooey brains across the snow. "I lost count of my kills and didn't keep my eye on you, so I can't say how many we've killed so far. I do know NORAD houses six-hundred people, and if they brought civilians there's no telling what's waiting inside if we get in. And that's a big 'if,' Commander."

The temperature was below freezing, their breath coming out in tiny white clouds. Neither felt a chill. Thor and the Earth Corps arrived at the tunnel's entrance, holding back to give Cadence and Freeborn time to check ahead.

"Stay behind me," said Freeborn, taking the lead.

Inside the tunnel chunks of cement, granite, and rotting dead lay scattered on the ground. The darkness inside the tunnel would normally require flashlights, but chameleons saw well in pitch-black.

Freeborn growled. "This place is a tomb."

"It could still be a gold mine. We made it this far. Let's keep going."

Zombies moved in and around parked cars, shuffling for the entrance, excited by the noise outside. They took no interest in Cadence or Freeborn, so it was with little effort that Cadence was able to lop heads off with her katana. Freeborn's shotgun boomed with the thunderous echo of a cannon. Cadence froze in her tracks when she noticed a zombie appearing disturbed by the sound of the blasts. Freeborn fired again, and the zombie ducked. Cadence had never seen a zombie act this way before, but her morbid curiosity ended when Freeborn blasted a hole in its head.

"The team's right behind me, Commander," said Thor, appearing beside Cadence. He'd put away his revolver, brandishing a rifle and a lit cigar clenched between his teeth.

"Get to the blast door, Thor," Cadence said. "See if it's open or not."

"You got it!" Thor hurried ahead, pushing zombies out of the way. He gave a loud shout when he reached the blast door. "The door is ajar!"

"Ajar?" Cadence mumbled, glancing at Freeborn. "This is the most impregnable fortress in the country and the blast door was left open. Someone was careless."

Raw granite transitioned into cement toward the back of the tunnel. Pipes, ventilation grills, and electrical boxes dotted the walls. Thor stood beside a blast door made of reinforced steel that looked like something out of a sci-fi movie. Freeborn ran ahead of Cadence and joined Thor. Gunfire filled the tunnel as the Earth Corps brought up the rear, picking off stragglers and crawlers. Cadence spotted a second tunnel leading in from the south, which had collapsed from a previous battle. A tank's turret jutted out of the debris.

"We've got a problem," said Thor. "NORAD is like a small city and it will be crawling with more of dead. A lot more. All we did was clear the zombies left outside. At this rate, we're going to run out of ammo, Commander, so it'll be fighting hand-to-hand once inside."

"Zombies we can handle," Cadence said, examining the gap between the wall and door. A crusty hand reached from the darkness. She lifted her sword and whacked it off. From behind the door came a loud, angry snarl. "You said six-hundred people were here?"

Freeborn nodded. "Give or take. This isn't the only way in." She kicked away the severed hand. "There's a trap door and a secret tunnel that leads into this place, but I don't know where from. I read about it on the internet. A few survivors might have made it out of the bunker."

Cadence glanced back at the Earth Corps. Smack, pigtailed and in a plaid skirt and buckled boots, trailed behind Phoenix. The Dark Angels, Lachlan, and Picasso, walked behind them. The werepuma and werewolf came next, followed by Blaze and Whisper.

"Tunnel is clear," said Phoenix. "What's up here?"

"We're going in," Cadence said. "Freeborn, get that door open."

Freeborn grabbed the door's edge and pulled with all her might, grunting. Despite her strength, she was having trouble opening the blast door alone. Thor shouldered his rifle and gripped the side of the door.

"This is the North Portal," said Thor. "The door weighs twenty-five tons and was made to withstand a nuclear strike. There's a second blast door on the other side, and then four-and-a-half acres to search before we can call this place home."

Blaze stepped forward. Her brows, lobes, and tongue were pieced, and a flower tattoo showed above the neckline of her black, turtleneck sweater. The tips of her black hair were spiked. "Well, open it," said Blaze, annoyed.

"We're trying!" Thor let out a growl. "It's moving, get ready. We're going to release an army from Hell in about five seconds."

With the team standing too close to the door, Cadence knew they would be overwhelmed in no time. While the zombies were not aggressive toward her chameleons, the vampires and therianthropes still remained vulnerable to the zombies' appetite. She had to proceed with caution.

"Set up a defense line fifty yards away from the door," said Cadence. "Chameleons in front. Vampires and therianthropes in the rear." She looked at Lachlan, the tall, red-haired Irish vampire, more worried about him than anyone else. Her attraction to him was growing, a feeling she had not known in some time. She cared more than she should for the vampire. "Don't try to be a hero, Lachlan. Zombies might want an Irish breakfast for a change."

"Not to worry," said Lachlan. He brandished a 13thcentury Irish galloglass broadsword, handed down through the generations by his family. He grinned at Picasso, a bald, serious-looking vampire holding an automatic weapon. Picasso was a former Army Ranger and the one true soldier in the group.

The Corps fanned out. Phoenix, Blaze, and Smack stood in front, armed with AK's. Lotus, the former China Six ninja wore black leather and a scarf over her mouth, holding a razor-sharp katana. Sheena and Moon Dog trotted back and forth, growling and snarling. The Dark Angels stood further back, with Whisper ready to snipe from the hood of an old truck. Thor and Freeborn pulled the blast door with everything they had. The enormous door moved slow, releasing a foul stench. Cadence gritted her teeth and lifted her sword as the door opened wide A single, fat zombie in a general's uniform stumbled forward.

Thor wiped his brow, looking confused. "What the hell? There's just one guy here."

The swollen zombie general and could barely walk. It staggered by Thor and Freeborn. Cadence cut it down without hesitation and entered a gloomy hallway between the blast doors. Her eyes immediately grew accustomed to the darkness. The general had eaten everyone trapped inside with him, leaving behind a mound of clothes, shoes, and bones.

"Check out the next door," said Cadence, stepping aside.

Freeborn and Thor hurried to the second door, finding it open a few inches. At their approach, a cacophony of groans and moans came from the other side, as dozens of hands reached through the gap. The teenagers jerked the door hard, tripping the alarm. A siren blared through the speakers and red lights blinked on the walls. Thor stumbled into Freeborn as they opened the door, releasing an undead army that headed straight for Cadence. She ran out of the hallway and took up position in front of her team.

"They're coming!" shouted Cadence.

The lead zombie wore a colonel's uniform, his empty eyes fixed on Cadence as he stumbled toward her with outstretched arms. Cadence stepped back, pointing her sword at the zombie and waited. When the colonel was within her sword's reach, she sliced off its head. Not having time to bring her sword around again, she was forced to fall backward as zombies surrounded her. The swarm headed for the Earth Corps, eager to taste the vampires and therianthropes. Gunfire and shouting filled the tunnel. Dark Angels darted under the swirling red lights, slaughtering countless zombies. The werepuma and werewolf dragged zombies to the ground, ripping them apart, while Whisper made every bullet count.

Back on her feet, Cadence started swinging her sword, chopping zombies left and right. The swoosh of the sword was one continuous sound as it weaved through the air. Dull, unintelligent eyes gleamed under the red lights.

Hacking her way through the horde, Cadence cleared the second blast door and entered a large room. Zombies lay scattered across the floor, their black goo covering the white walls. Thor and Freeborn left a few stragglers crawling in their wake. Cadence picked them off, aware of gunfire coming from behind and in front of her. When she had killed the remaining zombies, she reached a set of double doors shadowed by an overhead canopy. Above was a sign. *Welcome to the Chey-enne Mountain Complex.*

On the left was an opening in the wall revealing an observation deck on the second floor. Thor came into view firing his weapon. Cadence ran up the stairs, pushed open the doors, and peered into the main lobby of NORAD. The pale lights showed framed photographs of decorated officers and crooked-hanging maps, stained with bloody hand prints. Freeborn was dispatching a zombie with her hunting knife.

"I'm out of bullets," shouted Freeborn, looking up from her kill. "Stay here and wait for the team, Commander. I'm going after Thor. If you can, find the switch and turn off that siren!"

"Wait!" Cadence ransacked a body and found three magazines of ammunition. She handed them to Freeborn, along with a rifle. "Use them wisely."

With a nod, the tall Cherokee headed through the main door to the bunker, leaving Cadence by herself. A small office was visible through a wall of glass, along with several doors in a lobby. Cadence opened the door to find a zombie clerk with half of his face hanging loose, exposing filthy teeth and a gnarled black tongue.

"Are you the one who turned on the siren?" asked Cadence. "Move aside, creep."

A hard push sent the zombie stumbling against a file cabinet. With one eye on the creature, she leaned over the desk, and hit several red buttons. The siren died and the warning lights clicked off.

"That's better. Now for you."

The zombie clerk made a lunge for her. Cadence reacted, slashing from navel to stern. As his organs slid to the floor, the clerk's legs collapsed beneath him, and she finished him off at the neck. The head rolled between her boots. Taking a seat, Cadence stared at the rotting orb, mouth and eyes still moving.

It should feel normal for a zombie to attack, but she had grown used to them ignoring her. None of the dead that came through the blast door had considered her a meal, but this one was different. *No, that wasn't right*, she thought, recalling the zombie in the tunnel. Something was wrong about the NORAD zombies.

The door to the office opened with a bang.

"I thought you might need some help," said Smack. She was covered with black splatter and her skirt had been ripped. Several M16s hung over her shoulder. "I know you told me to stay with Blaze, but when I saw an opening, I took off after you. I'm sorry."

Cadence was fond of Smack. The girl started out as the Fighting Tiger's mascot, but over time had become like a little sister. "Thor and Freeborn are up on the second level," said Cadence. "This guy was pretty aggressive. Maybe it's because I spoke to him."

"Or maybe it's because he's a zombie and that's what they do," Smack said, scrutinizing the body. "Think there's a radioactive leak? Imagine…radioactive zombies."

"Let's hope you're wrong. Did you get bit?"

"No, but a few looked me straight in the eye right before I shot them, so I guess they saw it coming." She spat her gum onto the ground and produced a piece. "You need a new weapon? I picked up a few nice ones."

Smack handed a rifle to Cadence, who checked to make sure it was loaded and turned toward the panel in front of her. Surveillance cameras were set up all over NORAD, and there were a dozen blank monitors. She flipped on several screens and fuzzy lines appeared. Loud footsteps drew Cadence and Smack's attention. Both faced the door as Picasso and Lachlan entered the office. Lachlan's Irish broadsword was covered from hilt to tip with dark stains, Picasso was splattered with brains and gore, but neither vampire appeared to be injured.

"You guys are as a loud as a rhinoceros," Smack said, an impish smile on her face. "Since when do vampires make so much noise?"

A look of concern appeared on Picasso's face. "Since you became a precocious thirteen-year-old, requiring constant supervision," said Picasso. "Whisper has the situation under control in the tunnel, so we came on ahead. I know the layout of NORAD. I spent a summer here on active duty. The emergency generators are still working, but I want to try and bring the main system on line. You two stay here and wait for the team. Lachlan and I will check it out."

"Where are Freeborn and Thor?" Lachlan's Irish accent was thick and charming. He took out his radio and patched through to Freeborn, talking in a muffled voice. "Level 2. Got it." He gazed at Cadence with those hazel eyes. "They've run into another large group and need help. I'm on it. I'll catch up with you later, Picasso."

"There's a map of the bunker on every level." Picasso placed a fresh clip into his rifle. "The maintenance room will be on the lower-level with four underground reservoirs. I want to know the drinking water isn't contaminated. It's marked with a large number one on the door, so you can't miss it, Irishman." He gave a tug on Smack's pigtail. "Stay out of trouble."

Both vampires took off running. Cadence turned back to the console, fiddling with buttons, trying to bring the cameras back on line. Smack chomped on her gum, hanging out at the door and keeping an eye on the hallway.

"I thought you were the only one of us who didn't have super abilities," said Smack. "But that's not the case anymore, Commander. I climbed over a mountain of bodies you killed. Want to know how many I think you killed?"

"Too many," Cadence said in a dismissive tone. "And yet, not enough."

"Lachlan likes you. I know you like him too or you wouldn't turn red whenever he's around. He's, like, years older than you, and a vampire, but I guess he's still dateable. I mean, it's not like you're with Highbrow anymore. You can get cozy with anyone you want. If I was your age, I'd like Lachlan. But I guess I'm stuck with Dodger."

Grinning, Cadence patted her knee and Smack plopped down. The girl laid her head against Cadence's shoulder. Smack's thirteenth birthday had been November 30th, the same day Cadence turned eighteen. They didn't celebrate with a cake, though it would have been nice, and she felt Smack deserved something special. Few kids reached thirteen.

Cadence glanced back at the screen. Three were working and showed Lachlan, Thor, and Freeborn fighting zombies in a large theater. She sat up straight and leaned forward, pushing Smack off her knee.

"Keep your eye on the door, kiddo. I want to get the other cameras running. When Whisper arrives, send him to the second level. Thor may need more help."

"Will do," Smack said, tired.

They were startled by a loud moan. A zombie came through the door, walking toward them. Decay and rot had not set in. The zombie might have passed for a human if it weren't for the deep bite mark in his neck. It was obvious he had been one of the last bitten. Smack gasped, causing the zombie to notice her.

"Poor guy," Smack lamented. "He's so young, Cadence. And fresh. I bet he was the last to hold out. It must have been horrible for him."

The zombie let out a deep, heartfelt groan and reached for Smack. She lifted her hand, meaning to knock him away, but the zombie caught hold of her fingers. A strange expression appeared on the zombie's face that could have been mistaken as human.

"Do you think he understands me?" said Smack. "Do you, Mr. Zombie? I'm sorry you were bitten. You didn't deserve it, nor did all of your friends."

The zombie moaned, responding to Smack's voice. Smack's eyes widened. For a moment, it was as if she could understand what he was trying to communicate.

"We could give him my blood," said Cadence, "and try to cure him. His bite mark isn't that severe. I mean, he's lost a lot of blood, but he was probably bitten a few days ago. My blood worked on Freeborn. Why not this guy? He seems friendly enough."

Smack pulled her hand free. The zombie let out a moan. "We can't. What if he ate someone? You can't cure someone who has eaten a human. He'd feel so guilty, and he would never be normal. Make it quick, Cadence. I don't want him to suffer any more."

The zombie let out an angry groan and reached for Smack's pigtail. She pushed him away, screaming and striking back with her fists. The zombie became frenzied and tried to bite her. Cadence lifted her sword and hacked off his head. It plunked onto the floor and rolled toward her. Flipping the goo off her sword, Cadence looked at Smack and saw tears running down the girl's freckled cheeks.

"I understood him," the girl, with a heavy sob. "He said his name was Jim. Did you hear him, too? I couldn't make out his last name. Something like, Holmes. I'm so sorry I asked you to kill him."

"I didn't hear words," said Cadence. "But he reacted to you. Your radioactive theory is starting to grow on me. I'll have Picasso check out the levels and make sure it's safe to be here. They do have nuclear missiles here."

Smack wiped the tears from her face. "If Dodger was here, I wouldn't be scared. I miss him, Cadence. I miss my family. I want to go home."

"It will be okay, kiddo," said Cadence. "You have a new family now. It's our job to take care of them, so buck up. We've done okay so far."

Sniffing back tears, Smack blew a large pink bubble, sucking it back in before it popped, and chewed with a vengeance. Cadence just smiled. She didn't know what normal meant anymore, but watching Smack blow bubbles was a nice way to try and remember.

Chapter Two

*L*ogan had been under guard at the Citadel for six weeks.

Daily he visited the main lab, staying until twilight to watch Dr. Leopold and his medical staff at work. Several chromatography machines were in use, passing samples through porous material inside tubes, separating liquid into molecular components. There were machines he was unfamiliar with, some antiques and some state of the art. A table held many medieval-looking devices on a metal tray, next to where cell-counters provided test results at ten-minute intervals.

"Learn anything new, Agent Logan?" asked Dr. Leopold, looking up from a microscope. A male assistant stood next to the doctor.

The staff wore lab coats, Latex green gloves, and disposable slip covers over their shoes. Only men worked in the lab, all hailing from Andorra, a country pinched between France and Spain. They looked similar; tall and thin with waxen, yellow skin stretched tight across their bald heads and faces. If Logan didn't know better, he would have thought they were clones.

"When you were a kid, Doc, did you play with a chemistry set?" asked Logan, picking lint balls off his thick green sweater. "Don't tell me. You never married."

Leopold's thin smile revealed a row of small, sharp teeth. "No, I never did. As I was saying, in the initial mutation of the H1N1z virus, the proteins the host produces, and other compounds necessary for cell health, are not produced correctly or in enough of a supply to develop

15

healthy cells. So the host, while not dying, weakens with the fat cells being particularly affected. The host can't store energy like normal, and so is driven to find food more often. Neural pathways, which need fats for insulation, degrade, which is why we have zombies. Degradation prevents cells from properly manufacturing and the infected will die without a constant food source."

"Does that mean you have found a cure?" asked Logan, sitting nearby. Fluorescent lights flickered; the lab had been a former class-room, and while it was kept clean, maintenance wasn't a high priority. "I thought you were working on a way to create an immortal female vampire, so the Kaiser won't be alone. I guess he's taken at least five hundred brides so far. It can't be that bad. When one dies, you just marry another."

"The Kaiser's love life does not interest me. But I am interested in these chameleons. Cadence's blood has adapted to the virus. From the blood samples you provided, I've learned there is no degradation of cells, but the opposite effect. If her blood wasn't toxic to vampires, in theory, I could introduce it into a vampire and create immortals. I believe if Cadence was here, then I could create immortal vampires."

Logan laughed. "Well, I brought all I could get my hands on. I don't think I can steal anymore for you, Doc. Captain Pallaton, nor the Shadowguard, have been able to locate Cadence or the Earth Corps either. Highbrow threw them out of the survivor camp because they are infected. Ironic, considering you want them here for the same reason. If I was assigned to finding them, I wouldn't be combing the streets of Colorado Springs or going from house to house. She's in the mountains, hiding, and I guarantee she's watching the Citadel."

"Five hundred wives is excessive," said Leopold, as he placed a new slide under the microscope. His assistant gave Logan an incredulous look, picked up a tray of vials, and walked to another table to label them.

"What I'm looking at today is lycanthrope blood," the doctor continued. "Those infected with the lupine virus change into wolf-form, but still retain their human nature. It's my understanding you've been to Germany. I'm sure you encountered a few Old Ones there. They're an exception. The virus they are infected with is much older and the host is completely at its whim. The moonlight triggers their change and wipes out any memory of their former selves. I'd like to compare the blood types of these two similar but different animals."

"I'm sure you would," said Logan.

"Human cells can be infected with multiple viruses at the same time, which is what makes humans so interesting to study." Leopold pointed a boney finger at a dead frog, spread out to expose its guts, held open by a dozen slender pins. "A tree frog carries a dangerous slime that when absorbed into the pores of a human can cause a chemical reaction and mutate on a genetic level. If a human is infected with the original H1N1z pathogen, without receiving an antidote, they die and rise again within a few hours. If infected with yet another strain of the virus, they turn into a vampire or a werewolf. However, give a healthy human or a recently turned zombie a single drop of chameleon blood and they can be cured or even transformed into superhumans, although, this I cannot yet be sure of. This extreme evolution of Homo sapiens has happened before, but it is different each time. While we can identify the DNA genome of each separate virus, at this time we cannot identify the acting agent in Cadence's blood…for reasons I do not care to share at this moment."

Logan glanced at the frog. "Thank God, I thought you were going to keep talking. Just tell me what the Kaiser wants to hear and I'll leave. I don't enjoy the time we spend together, Doc."

An ear-splitting scream cut Logan off. He spun around when the lab technicians laughed. Other prisoners watched in horror or looked away, retreating to the back of their cells. Screams erupted once more from a female in great pain. Logan walked over and found Leopold's medical staff hovering around an older captive. They poked her with sharp instruments tied onto the end of wooden poles, cutting her flesh.

Logan considered knocking them aside and helping the prisoner. He was pushed out of the way as a stretcher wheeled in. A mangled werewolf was placed onto a metal table, dead. He assumed it was Huritt, a former member of the local wolf tribe and Chief Chayton's cousin. The lab technicians swarmed the table and commenced with an autopsy. One of the werewolf's front legs had turned back into a human arm and hand. Logan looked away when a lab technician rolled in a table containing a tray of medical instruments.

"You don't approve?" Leopold asked. "Huritt was slain in the arena last night. As for the prisoner, she doesn't deserve your concern, Agent Logan. What you don't understand is that I have discovered the true essence of God. God is science. God is the creation and destruction of particles, atoms, cells, and microbes. God is life and death in its literal translation, not a divine being sitting above, judging who lives and who dies. God is a virus. This virus. And I will discover how to harness this divine power and use it for my own purpose. Tell that to the Kaiser."

The doctor returned to his microscope and Logan looked away, trying not to react when another scream from the victim led to heavy silence. Logan made a huge mistake by betraying Cadence's camp, and by betraying Rose. She was the one person he cared for, and he sabotaged any chance of their happiness together. The Kaiser promised Logan a jet and a pilot, enabling Logan to travel wherever he wanted to, but so far the promise was empty. After spending just days in the lab, Logan realized he valued friends more than anything, especially Rose Standish. Now he was alone in a world full of bloodsuckers.

"This virus you worship is a time bomb," said Logan. "You want to be God? Find a cure before the human race is destroyed. Cadence was infected with the virus and then cured. There's a greenhouse right here. You have the means to create another Cadence."

Leopold offered a thin smile. "Cadence may well have risen from the grave, at least ten times if you believe gossip, but I can't be sure of her regenerative powers until she's here. As for your flower theory, it's ridiculous. If you want flowers, go see Dr. Heston. He's working on that problem."

"Rose said it's the flower," insisted Logan.

"Is that what Rose Standish thinks?" Leopold laughed at the surprised look on Logan's face. "Everyone knows about your secret relationship with the fair doctor. Tell me, Agent Logan, did you come to the Citadel to help the Kaiser or to spy?"

"Both, if you want to know the truth."

"I knew Rose before the Scourge," said Leopold. "She was my student. Even in those days, Rose spent her time in futile effort to cure cancer. Noble, beautiful, and naïve. Always asking questions, challenging my authority. In short, she was a nuisance. What I want to know about regeneration and immortality, I can learn right here, in my own lab."

Logan looked at the autopsy table. The werewolf was sliced down the middle and spread out like the frog. "Butchering shape-shifters and torturing humans is sure to produce results. At the rate you're going, only zombies and vampires will be left. Rose understands that the key to survival is finding a cure."

"Stop pretending you care," said Dr. Leopold, jotting a few notes on a clipboard. "For the record, D'Aquilla has manufactured synthetic blood and will send a large shipment by Christmas. Vampires don't need humans to feed. It is clear you don't know everything, Agent Logan."

Logan crossed his arms. "Yeah? What am I missing here, Doc?"

"Cadence represents a higher biological order. Her chameleon blood is aptly named, for no human infected with her blood has the same super powers. Every night Dragon fights against all manner of opponents, and he always wins. We have several of Cadence's friends imprisoned here; however, Master Dragon alone regenerates at a cellular level that exceeds the healing abilities of vampires and therianthropes. Ironic that he is the one person Kaiser won't let me experiment on. If you want to be of assistance, convince the Kaiser to let me have Dragon, and I'll soon have all the answers he's looking for. Or, bring me Cadence."

Logan looked up at the clock, realizing he had another fifteen minutes before he was allowed out where guards waited. "What happened to the Dark Angels captured at the Cliff Dwellings?" asked Logan. "I haven't seen any Dark Angels fight in the arena."

Dr. Leopold turned, towering over Logan, and gazed at him with calculating eyes. "The Kaiser wanted proof that Cadence's blood is toxic to vampires. Every test subject died when injected."

Logan knocked over a beaker filled with clear liquid onto the tray with the frog. A foul stench rose as the acid sizzled and the frog dissolved. Leopold glared at him.

"Agent Logan, I am not an emotional man, nor some amateur at work with a chemistry set. Dr. Kensington is creating zombie cyborgs to wage war on humans. Dr. Heston is trying to find a cure when he isn't breeding werewolf hybrids, and Dr. Giglio is doing God knows what, but I am doing something for the greater good."

Logan laughed. "You think Cadence is the embodiment of Nietzsche's Übermensch. I assure you, Doc, she's not part of Hitler's Master Race."

"I met Hitler during a brief stint as chief surgeon at Auschwitz," said Leopold. "You see, Agent Logan, immortality is something I'm familiar with, but not something I care to share with others. Despite the Kaiser's tedious demands, I have no intention of bestowing immortal life on vampires. My interest here is the survival of my own species. We lack physical prowess and that is what I'm after. If you tell the Kaiser that I've sabotaged his efforts from the start, I will make sure your friends kept prisoner here are killed in the arena. I might even have Rose Standish turned into a cyborg."

Logan imagined taking a scalpel and shoving it through Leopold's eye. He would do the world a great service. Until he figured out what species Leopold and his staff were, he would put off killing them. It wasn't prudent to kill something he knew nothing about. As far as Logan could tell, Leopold could be a vampire. A scalpel wasn't the weapon he needed when he killed him and his gruesome staff.

"When I was a boy of six, I saw my mother murdered," said Logan. "A vampire came to the door dressed as a cop. She let him inside. He sucked her dry and then turned on me. 'Do you want to live forever? I offer a life free of pain, heart break, and remorse. You will be my son, and we will travel the world together, taking what we want, when we want, with no regret.'" His eyes grew dark as he recited the memory. "When my father found me, I was hiding under the bed. He believed me, and for the next twenty-five years we hunted down and killed supernatural creatures. The vampire was the Kaiser. One day I will repay him for what he did to my mother. That's why I came here. I intend to kill him."

"Then we have an understanding based on honesty" said Dr. Leopold. His eyes turned black as ink. "You'll tell the Kaiser nothing, and I'll continue what I'm doing. Still, I can't help wondering which of us most resembles the virus, feeding off its host."

"Oh, it's you Doc. You're a monster. I just don't know what kind yet."

Leaving the lab under guard, Logan decided to spend some time watching the Death Game fighters practicing in the basketball arena. As long as he didn't talk to the prisoners, Logan could spectate. He climbed the bleachers with his two guards and took a seat on the top row. The Kaiser owned the most fighters, but the best belonged to Captain Pallaton and had at one time been at Cadence's camp. Barbarella and Luna were werepumas, both deadly in the arena. Red Hawk was a werewolf from Chief Chayton's tribe, while Cricket, Dodger, and Xena were chameleons.

The ultimate fighter was Dragon, owned by Salustra. She was a sexy Vampire Maker who Logan suspected of siring most of the Dark Angels. Salustra avoided Logan, but he was desperate to ask her about Rose. She was present and sat several rows from Logan, watching Dragon train by himself. There were no other fighters on the court. Bare-chested and arms covered with dragon tattoos, he moved around a large mat, practicing karate.

"How much money have you made off Dragon?" asked Logan. He climbed down to where Salustra sat and joined her. The guards remained vigilant behind him. "I know we aren't well acquainted, but it's no fault of mine. Do I have bad breath?"

"You're human," said Salustra, as if this explained everything. She wore a mink stole around her shoulders. A blue velvet jacket, a skirt, and high-heeled boots completed her ensemble. Perfume clung to her like a second skin, her skin being so pale it was white under the lights.

"Would it make a difference if I was a vampire?" Logan leaned toward her. "Just what do you do all day in your room with Dragon? Does he get bored, or do you entertain him?"

Salustra flipped back her long black hair and pointed a cool gaze at Logan. "I keep Dragon safe in my room. However, you smell Agent Logan. You've been in Dr. Leopold's lab. Did you learn interesting things today?"

"Yeah, he cut open Huritt and removed his spleen, pancreas, liver, and kidneys. Then his assistant ate him," said Logan. He laughed when her eyes widened. "Okay, maybe he didn't eat him. But what do they eat? Leopold never leaves the lab, nor do his assistants. I assume they're vampires because I've never seen them eat solid food. Care to enlighten me?"

Dragon spun around on the court, gaining speed and moving so fast he seemed to turn invisible. The guards located around the court didn't seem worried, since vampires could follow Dragon's moves, while Logan only saw impressions on the mat left by the fighter's feet.

"You're asking me to reveal Dr. Leopold's species." Salustra remained still. "I'm here to watch Dragon. I don't think the Kaiser wants me to advise you on the origins of his medical staff. It's obvious you know they are not human, so let's leave it at that."

"Let's not," said Logan, pressing. "Let's say you and I are close friends, and I would no more tattle on you than you would me. For instance, what if I told you I'd like to get a message to Rose Standish at Seven Falls. To tell her Leopold isn't working on a cure. In fact, he's nowhere near finding out what he desires most. Not until he gets his hands on a chameleon fighter, like Dragon. Your fighter is by far the superior fighter and what Leopold wants is superior strength for himself and his little helpers."

"Then as your friend, I'd tell you to be more careful. I'd also tell you that Rose doesn't trust you, nor has she forgiven you for breaking her heart. You allowed Pallaton and Aldarik to enter Seven Falls, killing and capturing her allies. It's because of you that Dragon came here and was captured. Of course, if he wanted to leave bad enough, he could. No one is as fast, strong, or clever as Dragon."

"Maybe if someone convinced Rose that I've had a change of heart, she might think better of me. She might even forgive me, that is, if someone told her I'd made a horrible mistake and would like to redeem myself." He waited for Salustra to respond, but she said nothing. "I guess you're not the real leader of the Dark Angels, after all. You might not be in communication with Rose, but if you were, I'd hope you would tell her what I said."

"Like all humans, you're boring. Please go away. I have no intention of doing anything you suggest or providing you any information. But if I were you, I wouldn't provoke Dr. Leopold. As I said, he isn't human. He's nasty if you get on his bad side, something you don't want to do. Now, goodbye."

Logan stood up and Dragon appeared on the mat, gleaming with sweat. The Asian teenager glared at Logan and could have cleared the distance between them in one jump. The look of hatred was apparent in Dragon's eyes.

As Logan left the court to return to his own room in an adjoining building, he wondered if Dragon could escape whenever he wanted. If that was the case, why was the legendary swordsman sticking around? Did it mean Dragon remained with intentions to kill the Kaiser?

Get in line, thought Logan.

Chapter Three

Snow was falling as the limo pulled up to Miramont Castle in Manitou Springs. With the red stone draped in giant Christmas lights and a large wreath on the door, it looked like an old man's Christmas miniature. A squad of guards dressed in Renaissance costumes with spears, stood beside torches looking like Christmas nutcrackers. Pine boughs with red ribbons adorned the staircase and hung over every interior door. A large Christmas tree stood in the center of the entryway, completing the festive atmosphere. As Raven, Pallaton, and Salustra entered the mansion, a servant in Renaissance garb received their cloaks. Captain Pallaton led both women to a large living room, styled with furnishings fit for a king.

Twenty or more vampires, adorned like royalty, lounged on lush couches, drinking blood from silver chalices while listening to a string quartet. Raven sat beside a roaring fire, watching as Pallaton set a gift on a table covered with stunning presents. Salustra removed a small card from her bodice, set it among the gifts, and drifted off to socialize with the guests. The captain joined Raven on the couch.

"You look upset, Raven," said Pallaton. "Your first time out of the Citadel and it's supposed to be a birthday party, not a funeral. Try smiling."

"I didn't bring a gift. I was so excited to come here, I forgot to get something."

Trumpet fanfare and loud applause announced the arm-in-arm arrival of Queen Cinder and Lord Cerberus. The girl's red hair piled high, circled by a jeweled crown. A black gown and rouge-brushed cheeks gave life to her pale complexion. Lord Cerberus, a dark-complexioned child of eleven years, strutted forward in a silver doublet, black hose, and polished, buckled shoes.

"Good evening, ladies and gentlemen," said Cerberus, in a voice deeper than his appearance suggested. "Welcome to Miramont Castle! Come. Pay homage to your Queen!"

A woman in a green brocade dress knelt before the vampire children. The queen and lord extended their hands to be kissed. The woman moved aside, allowing another guest to gesture the same. Pallaton gave Raven a lopsided grin, rose, and stood in line. When it was his turn to kneel, Cinder rushed forward throwing her arms around his neck. The girl kissed the captain right on the mouth, giving every impression that her body, while young, contained a maturing mind.

"Must you?" Cerberus asked in anger. "Pallaton is old enough to be your grandfather. Shall I kiss every woman here?"

The tiny queen tossed her head and laughed. "This is my party and I will do whatever I please. Put me down, Pallaton. I want to see Raven."

Queen Cinder ran over and plopped beside Raven. Taking hold of Raven's hand, she pressed it to her cool cheek. "You're the prettiest one here, sweet Raven," she said. "I've wanted you to visit us for ages. What do you think? Too many decorations, or not enough?"

"Your home is beautiful," said Raven. "I'm impressed."

A large, white wolf trotted over and sat at the queen's feet. Raven had seen him in the queen's company at the Citadel, but never in his human form. Everyone knew the story of Cerberus jumping into the arena at Cinder's command. He helped the lone werewolf fight a small horde of zombies. The Kaiser awarded her the beast following the victory.

"His name is Stephan," said Cinder. "I know what you are thinking, of course. How does the man look? But I forbid Stephan to ever change back into his human form." She smiled. "Do you recall when we first met? I'd strayed too far from my patrol, the Little Leaguers, and was being pursued by a nasty zombie. You killed the zombie, picked me up, and carried me all the way home."

Raven remembered, but never imagined that months later the same girl would become vampire royalty. "Of course I remember. You were brave. And I didn't carry you. We rode back on my ATV."

"I was a child then. Now I am a queen. It's because the Kaiser is so generous. I was terrified the first time we met, but now we're all one big, happy family. I guess that makes you and me sisters, Raven." She laughed. "No, that's not good enough. From now on, you will be known as Duchess Raven in my home."

Giving a gift to Cinder was important. Raven couldn't be the only guest who came without a gift to the party. The one suitable thing she had was her diamond necklace. Though she regretted it at once, she removed the Hope Diamond and placed it into the girl's hand.

"Happy Birthday, Queen Cinder."

"*Le bleu de France!*" cried out Cinder, as she slipped the silver chain over her neck. "The largest blue diamond in the world! It is said to be cursed. Every owner has died wearing this jewel. It's the perfect gift for a vampire." She glared at her guests. "No one else has given me anything this unique. Stephan!"

Raven laughed when the werewolf laid his head in her lap. Her fingers tingled when she ran them through his thick, softer-than-silk fur. The queen smiled with approval as Raven kissed Stephan on the head.

"You're magnificent," whispered Raven. He let out a soft growl and thumped his tail. "I want my own werewolf."

"I shall make sure you have one sired by Stephan," said Cinder.

"Did you hear that, Stephan?" Pallaton's words were thick with sarcasm. He nudged him with the tip of his shoe. "You must set out to find a bitch suitable for breeding and present your Queen and Lord with a litter of pups. Not good for anything else, are you?"

The wolf snapped. Cinder swiped her hand across Stephan's nose. The beast dropped his head and let out a regretful whine.

"Don't be mean, Stephan," said Cinder. "If I didn't like you so much, Captain, I'd let Stephan bite you."

A servant rang a small bell. The little queen jumped up, ran over to grab Cerberus's arm, and in a grand procession, the vampires gathered in the dining room.

Colorful flags bearing the mark of a boar, a unicorn, and a dragon hung over a long table covered by a silver cloth, set with gold plates and jeweled chalices. Antlers covered one wall, while a large stag's head peered out with marble eyes above the main door. Gold candles surrounded by green wreaths lined the table. Hand-written, gold placards marked with elegant, silver-inked names topped each plate. The musicians took position in the corner of the room and became a soft backdrop of entertainment. Raven sat next to Pallaton at the end of the table, near Cinder, the wolf at her feet. Lord Cerberus seated Salustra at the far end beside a silver-haired vampire. Spreading his arms, he commanded the party's attention.

"Thank you all for coming here tonight. A few of you are residents, however most have traveled great distance to celebrate Cinder's 10th birthday. My Queen has ordered a special menu be served this evening. Our humans were fed a single item for one week to give each dish a savory taste. It will be your task to discover what it was." He motioned a waiter as he sat. "Serve the first course, and make sure my guests have champagne!"

Warmed blood was served in a gold bowl with a sprig of mistletoe in the center. Raven tried the soup, finding it spicy from hot peppers, feeling the tip of her tongue burning. She wondered if the human who ate the peppers had lived the seven days.

"Tell us about the Holiday Games, Captain Pallaton," Cinder said, dabbing her spoon into the thick soup. "We were dismayed the Halloween Games had been canceled. Will they never catch that outlaw Cadence and her band of mutants?"

"She's like Robin Hood," said a woman with glitter in her hair.

The silver-haired vampire lifted his glass of champagne. "You're growing lax, Pallaton. But I offer a toast in your honor. To your success in locating Cadence. May you find her before you're replaced by someone with more zeal."

Raven noticed Jean-Luc's eyes turn bright violet, marking him as one of Salustra's offspring. In response, Pallaton's eyes shone vibrant amber, fangs sliding out over his full lip. The two vampires glared at one another. Violence was imminent, but Cerberus tapped his spoon against his bowl, shushing them both. The boy's eyes became an intense shade of blue, his own fangs piercing holes in his bottom lip, causing blood to dribble into his soup. Pallaton leaned back, calm, and returned to his meal.

"The soup is delicious, Lord Cerberus," said Raven. The dark lord perked up and gestured for her to continue. "I'd say this human ate nothing but chili-peppers. I should know, since my family came from Mexico."

"Are you aware," began Jean-Luc in a snide voice, "that peppers are from the nightshade family?"

Cerberus thumped the table with his hand. "Raven is correct. But do stop showing off, Jean-Luc. You may live here, but Raven is our guest of honor. Besides, the ladies are always right in this home, regardless of their answer. Isn't that so, my queen?"

"You are wise," said Cinder. "Hurry everyone. Eat! The next course is coming."

Throughout the seven-course meal, Raven marveled how human blood could be prepared into so many different textures and tastes. Her favorite was dessert. Raven guessed correct that a young girl had eaten spearmint leaves. Following dinner, the guests retired to the parlor. The next hour passed playing cards, drinking champagne, and nibbling on deep-fried blood nuggets with chocolate filling.

"Would you care for a tour of the mansion, Duchess Raven?" asked Cerberus, rising from the table. He pulled Raven's chair back. "Poker can be dull."

Pallaton, Salustra, Jean-Luc, and three male vampires sat around the table. Jean-Luc was shuffling cards, his hands moving so fast it took mere seconds to shuffle the deck numerous times. Other guests gathered in the library, listening to Cinder play the piano.

"Get back here, Cerberus," roared Pallaton. "I want to win back my money!"

Cerberus flashed a mischievous smile. "We're playing for rubies, but don't worry, I have an ace up my sleeve." He motioned to a red-haired servant girl. "Frances, give the Duchess a tour. I must return to the game." With a stiff bow, Lord Cerberus returned to the parlor.

The girl led Raven through the mansion, pointing out antiquities acquired by Cinder and Cerberus. By the time they reached the third floor, Raven was envious of the children's palatial estate. One door at the end of the hall seemed to be off-limits when Frances turned from the door and gestured for Raven to follow. Raven ignored her tour-guide and tried the latch, finding it locked. The girl let out a shriek and backed away, trembling hard. Raven pressed against the door, listening for any sounds.

"Who's there?" called a male voice from behind the door.

"Rafe? Is that you? I had no idea you were the Queen's prisoner. I thought you were dead."

Laughter came from behind the door. "Not yet. Are you enjoying Cinder's birthday party? She invited you tonight to earn favor with the Kaiser. Cerberus' gambling has gotten out of hand. The feast cost a fortune. We'll be starving by the end of the week, unless Cinder convinces you to ask the Kaiser for more humans. The little monsters have a voracious appetite."

"I don't believe you," said Raven. "Cerberus has won a pile of rubies from Pallaton. He can buy all the slaves he wants at the downtown market. Are they feeding you well?" She never liked Rafe, but she was curious.

"I'm not the one you should be concerned with. While you've been living in your little dream world, Raven, the Shadowguard has been searching for Cadence."

"I know. So what? She asked for it."

"Your ex, Thor, is with Cadence. Heimdall and Baldor are dead, and Loki is in Italy. They were Vikings. If you no longer care for them, you must still care about Luna? Wasn't she your true love? I don't understand why you haven't helped her at least. She fights in the arena, yet you could ask the Kaiser to give her to you. I'm sure he would."

Behind the door she could hear the clank of chains as Rafe moved.

"Everyone wants something from me," said Raven. "I have no power. I'm watched day and night by the Shadowguard. I can't even leave the Citadel without permission."

A fist hit the door, causing a crack in the center. Raven jumped back.

"Listen, you little fool. The Kaiser isn't who he pretends to be. He's a demon, Raven, and when I say demon, I mean he's a vampyr. We were created in his image, but we are not like him. He isn't a Maker. He's been spinning a story to make you sympathetic to his cause, but we're not immortal, as I'm sure he told you. We're not supernatural, but he is. You and I are just infected with a virus he created. Why? To create an immortal female to spend eternity at his side, and it's my understanding you're to be his wife."

She placed her hands against the door. "How do you know this?"

"This comes straight from Rose. Salustra and Pallaton were chosen by the Kaiser and were the first infected. They are Vampire Makers, not the Kaiser. Rose was Salustra's first, but she saw things differently. The Dark Angels fled Denver and came here, but Rose didn't expect the Kaiser to follow. He thinks Cadence is the key to what he's been searching for, the one special ingredient to make vampires immortal. However, you know her blood kills vampires. What sets Cadence apart from the rest of us is that she's immortal. Ask Pallaton if you don't believe me, though he still may not tell you the truth."

"No, you're lying, like you always do," said Raven.

She knew she should not linger. There was a reason Rafe and Jean-Luc were being kept at Miramont Castle, and she had a feeling Cinder and Cerberus were under close surveillance. The Shadowguard had eyes and ears everywhere. She looked up and down the hall expecting to find cameras, and felt no comfort when she didn't see any. Raven ran from the door.

"I wish we could keep driving," said Raven, tucked away in the corner of the limo. "We should drive south, to the sea. Go somewhere where we can bathe in sunshine, enjoying tropical breezes, and live our lives without being told what to do."

"Did Jean-Luc say something to upset you?" Pallaton sat across from Raven and Salustra. "I told you he is a troublemaker, Salustra. The only reason he lives is because the Kaiser is fond of you."

"Jean-Luc is tame," Salustra said in a cool voice. She put her hand on Raven's arm. "I think there's another reason for this outburst. I suspect Raven found Rafe. Is that what happened? Did you speak with Rafe?"

Raven pulled her cape around her body. "They're keeping him imprisoned in an upstairs room. Cinder and Cerberus are broke, and they will starve unless I beg the Kaiser for a loan. They need more humans, but what has me upset is Rafe. He said the Kaiser is a demon. A vampyr. He said we're not immortal, but the Kaiser is."

Bloody tears trailed down Raven's cheeks. Salustra wiped them away with her handkerchief. The captain sat up, giving them both a disapproving look.

"This is madness," said Pallaton. "Tell no one you spoke to Rafe. No one."

Salustra patted Raven's shoulder. "What would you have us do? Run away? We'd be signing our own death warrants. Put this behind you, dear, and don't think of it again. We can't help anyone but our-selves."

"Not exactly true." Pallaton leaned forward, keeping his voice low. "Jean-Luc was right. I haven't been doing my job, so the Kaiser hired bounty hunters to track Cadence. These hunters survive by tracking their own kind, humans. They'll find her, too. Something I couldn't, or wouldn't, do."

The revelation that Pallaton was helping Cadence by doing nothing gave Raven a spark of hope. He was risking his own life by admitting it, which she found admirable. He trusted her. It was obvious in his dark, brown eyes. A soft hand landed on Raven's arm, and she turned away from the handsome captain.

Salustra offered a weak smile. "The Kaiser isn't a Maker, my dear. He can't make vampires, not with his bite. He can, however, with a virus. We will grow old and die, but what can we do? Most of the Dark Angels are dead, and I don't want to be next. Doing nothing is what we must do."

"Please. Let's not go back," said Raven. "Ask your brother to hide us, Pallaton. The wolf tribe would protect us. He's your twin. We could live in the mountains or just run until we can't run anymore. I don't care. I'm too young to be this miserable."

Salustra took hold of Raven's hand. "All you need do is put on a brave face and accept the Kaiser's marriage proposal. Everything will be fine. I promise."

"Never. I'm not going back. If you don't stop the limo, I will open the door and jump. I'll find Cadence and tell her everything. You can't force me to marry a demon! Stop the car!"

Pallaton hit the back of the seat. "Dammit Raven, be reasonable! We can neither run away nor rush to the aid of your friends. Just do what Salustra says and stop tempting fate. There is nothing you can do to change things, except obey the Kaiser."

The limo pulled onto Interstate 25, heading north. Abandoned vehicles on the side of the road were hidden by large snow drifts. The fierce wind and sleet hammered against the limo, requiring the driver to drive at a slow pace.

"Please don't be upset, Raven. I can't tell you what you want to know. I'm trying to protect you," said Pallaton. "I care about you."

"If you care about me, then you would tell me the truth."

Pallaton and Salustra exchanged a quick glance, the female Maker nodded.

"Very well. What I am going to tell you is never to be repeated to anyone. Ever," said Pallaton. "Every plague in history was designed to create a race of immortal vampires, but the Kaiser's doctors have always failed in their purpose. Zombies were an accident. So is Cadence. The virus has a way of determining what its host will become and a few, like Cadence, developed special abilities. Zeus, Poseidon, Odin, and Isis were all infected with the virus, but it changed them into superhumans, not into vampires. Great wars were fought by ancient gods and goddesses in futile attempts to defeat the Kaiser, but he cannot be defeated. He's so single-minded in his purpose to create an immortal wife he doesn't care who he kills along the way. He's killed millions. A handful of teenagers can't defeat the Kaiser. If Zeus couldn't, neither will Cadence, nor is there any way to help them. The Kaiser is indestructible."

"Forget all this, darling," said Salustra. "Play along like we do and you'll be fine."

The limo turned onto the road leading to the Citadel. Raven felt

34

an overwhelming fear spread through her body. She latched onto Salustra's hand, panicking. It was too soon to return to the Kaiser after the night's events. He would know her secrets the moment he looked at her. *Play the game*, she told herself as they pulled up to his mansion.

There he was. A short, bald man dressed in casual attire for the evening stood in the open door, casting an enormous shadow on the wall. As Raven walked up the steps, the shadow separated from the Kaiser. As it left him, she saw a large horned, winged beast reflected on the snow.

"Welcome home," said the Kaiser, holding out his hand. "Come, my dear. The sun will soon rise, and you must retire."

Raven smiled and took his grasp. As she followed the Kaiser upstairs, she said a silent prayer for herself, and then one for her friends.

Chapter Four

Captain Highbrow stood on the battle deck. He gazed through night-vision goggles at a herd of zombies, frozen stiff in the winter wasteland beyond the perimeter. Since Cadence's departure, Highbrow had earned the respect of his soldiers for his honesty, by-the-book protocol, and by keeping the camp safe despite the Shadowguard and endless zombie hordes. The living dead made target practice easy for the teenage patrols stationed in guard towers. Now and then, the crisp retort of gunfire sent another zombie toppling into the snow.

"When the storm lets up, send a team to clear out the zombies," said Highbrow. "Let's not waste bullets when a club or bat will do. See to it, Sterling. Have the bodies burned where they lay. It's too cold to make a funeral pyre."

Lieutenant Sterling, a dark-complexioned man in his late-thirties had served in the U.S. Army, and had earned Highbrow's trust for his dependability and effectiveness in combat.

"Nomad is coming up the stairs, Captain Highbrow," said Private Destry. He and several other soldiers were trying to get warm around a small propane heater. The new siding and windows kept the wind out, but the inside remained frigid.

"Hot cocoa, coming up!" Private Odin handed out plastic cups. His gloves made it a difficult task and he spilled a little on Highbrow's coat. The captain took the cup without complaint.

The door to the battle deck swung open, allowing icy gusts and snow before it slammed shut. Nomad's voice boomed as he shook off snowflakes and stomped ice off his boots. "It's cold as a witch's tit! Got the Beast up and running, sir. If you want to clear out those zombies, I volunteer to run them over with a snowplow. I'll check on Betsy after it's done. She's tending to a bunch of sick kids with runny noses and coughs. Guess Betsy is better with the little kids than Ginger. No one wants a nurse with fangs."

"It's flu season." Highbrow handed the hot cup to Nomad. "I'd rather have vampires attending to the ill since they don't get sick. But whatever Dr. Rose thinks best."

Nomad grinned. "Betsy does a fine job rubbing Vicks on hairy chests, too."

"I didn't need to know that," Sterling muttered under his breath.

Both Highbrow and Nomad laughed. Nomad was the only man at camp Highbrow considered a true friend. He had been a biker before he was a scavenger, but since coming to camp, he had taken over maintenance and the garage. Big, bearded, and rugged as they came, Nomad was trustworthy, which made him invaluable. Nomad finished his cocoa and set aside the cup.

"Is Rose stocked up on medicine?" asked Highbrow. "If not, I'll ask Tandor and Micah to go out and find fresh supplies."

"I believe the Doc has everything she needs." said Nomad. "Isn't Tandor overdue at Cadence's camp? I hate thinking of those kids out in this weather. The storm doesn't seem to be letting up."

Highbrow offered a stiff smile. "Cadence will be fine. Get out of here, Nomad. I'm sure Betsy is eager to see her husband."

One of the pleasures of being in command was performing wedding ceremonies. Highbrow felt good knowing he had performed the ceremony for Nomad and Betsy a week earlier. Their honeymoon had been a party in the mess hall.

"You should be aware, some of the Dark Angels are sneaking out of camp at night." Nomad leaned forward. "Micah and a few others left hours ago. They take the same path every night. You can see it from the garage. I guess that makes me an old snoop."

"No, it's makes you responsible. You should be in uniform, Nomad, not in mechanic's overalls."

"Not happening, son." Nomad thumped Highbrow on the back and left the battle deck.

"This isn't good, lieutenant," said Highbrow. "We have cameras on every angle of this camp. The monitors are right here. It doesn't get easier than this. The Dark Angels have no business leaving camp. Go with Destry, check out the path Nomad mentioned. But I want those zombies cleared out before lunch."

After saluting, Sterling left, Destry and the soldiers in tow. Highbrow glanced over at his young bodyguard at the door. Odin was a former Viking, but he proved loyal. In his uniform and military coat, Odin looked like an Academy cadet. He caught the captain staring and came to attention.

"At ease, private," said Highbrow. "We'll go as soon as the War Gods arrive." He looked at a red button on the control board. Nomad and Micah had set up a warning system. With one push of the button, sirens would alert the entire camp of an invasion. He was thankful he hadn't needed to use it.

"You ever get tired of it, sir?" asked Odin. "I mean, killing zombies?"

"Zombies rule the planet, and every last one needs to be killed. I can't afford to get tired." Highbrow gave Odin a hard look. "I realize it's been difficult without the Vikings, but you're in the Freedom Army now. Not growing soft on me, are you?"

The private shook his head. "No, sir. I'm one hundred percent ready to kick ass, sir!"

The door opened. Lieutenant Kahn of the War Gods entered accompanied by his team. He was nineteen and showed gumption. Highbrow had promoted Kahn a month earlier after the last skirmish at the walls. Kahn had killed three Shadowguard, an amazing feat. Vampires were fast, difficult to predict, and even harder to shoot. Patience and accuracy were two qualities Kahn possessed.

"I left the Jeep running, sir. Figured you needed some shut-eye," said Kahn. He was olive-skinned with a unibrow running over his dark eyes. "Dawn patrols are out, sir. Snipers posted. Camp is quiet." He motioned for his team to settle in for the morning.

Highbrow pushed Odin toward the door. "A few Dark Angels left the compound without permission," he said. "Private Destry is check-ing into it. Sterling will handle the zombies, so if he sends your team out, keep your eyes open. I'm counting on you."

A stocking cap on his head, Highbrow descended the stairs with Odin. A blast of freezing air sent snowflakes swirling into Highbrow's eyes. He tucked his head until he reached the Jeep. Climbing in pas-senger-side, he waited for Odin to join him in the warm interior. High-brow's bodyguard slipped on the ice, but kept his feet and crawled in.

"Got to be ten below," said Odin, slamming the door shut. "You ever wonder if werepumas get cold? I mean, I know they have fur and all, but…"

"Why do you ask?" asked Highbrow. "Are you curious about werepumas, or is there a particular one you have in mind?"

Odin nodded. He didn't say more, leaving Highbrow wondering just who the young man was crushing on.

The mile back to the camp wound through tall, snow-laden trees and cliff walls that rose and fell in a winter wonderland. Passing the barracks at the former tourist office, they curved around the narrow road, arriving at the site where dozens of R.V.s sat. Sentries stood guard in shacks, shivering. A patrol with mufflers and fur coats marched by, as the Jeep came to a halt outside the hospital.

Highbrow and Odin started toward the building, but paused when the sounds of a heated argument from a nearby R.V. caught their attention. The wind had eased and the sleet had turned to light snowfall. The lights in the Buccaneers' R.V. were on and the front door was open.

"Stay behind me, Private," said Highbrow, drawing his pistol and entering the R.V.

A Buccaneer lay on the floor, his head covered in blood, while two teens stood in a tight section of the kitchen fighting over a butcher knife. Highbrow pointed his gun in their direction. They turned and stepped apart, dropping the knife to the floor.

"Drake is infected," said Black Beard, panicked. "Ranger and Calico Jack, too." He pointed at the big teen on the floor. "But I didn't hit him. Drake did."

Drake stood with his arms at his sides, bloody knuckles curled into fists. Highbrow aimed his gun at Drake as Odin's tall frame filled the doorway.

"I called for backup, sir," said Odin. "Lieutenant Sterling is on his way."

"What's this about?" Highbrow addressed the team leader.

"Saber's in the hospital with the flu. When I came back here, I found these two acting funny. Ranger took off a while ago. He said he was meeting Hawkins. I think they stole chameleon blood from the lab."

"You're a liar and a thief," snarled Drake. "Tell the captain the truth so he'll stop pointing his gun at me. You stole my cigarettes. Jack found where Black Beard was hiding them, sir, and then this son-of-a-bitch took a bottle of whiskey and cracked it over Jack's head. I don't think he's dead."

A carton of cigarettes lay on the kitchen table, but it was the bloody butcher knife that concerned Highbrow. Dribbles of blood trailed across the table to the floor where Calico Jack lay. The young man had not been hit. He had been stabbed.

"Get something around Jack's head. Stop the bleeding, if you can,"

Highbrow instructed Odin while keeping his eyes on the two teens. Odin found a towel, wrapping Jack's bloody head. "Is he still alive?"

Odin nodded his head. "He's lost an ear, sir. But he'll live."

"Take a seat on the sofa, Black Beard." Highbrow waited for the team leader to scoot past Odin, plopping on the couch. "Drake, get your ass over here and sit at the kitchen table." He kept his gun aimed at Drake. "Put your hands flat on the table where I can see them. I suggest you don't reach for the butcher's knife."

Drake sat. "Black Beard is lying! I didn't start the fight. He did!"

Walking over to the table, Highbrow pulled the knife free. Drake was sobbing. Black Beard remained quiet.

"Calm down," said Highbrow, his voice laced with anger. "You're both drunk. You know the new rules. No alcohol in camp and no cigarettes!"

The R.V.s were small, living spaces cramped. Each patrol had six members, and had to share everything. It was clear the Buccaneers weren't handling their small space and few belongings anymore.

"I'm responsible for the whiskey, Captain." Black Beard pointed at the bedroom he shared with Saber. On the bed was a busted bottle of Cutty Sark. "When you had all liquor destroyed, I kept a box. I know that means demotion, but I swear I had nothing to do with Drake or the others going to the lab. Ranger must have the vial of blood."

"Did you see the vial?" asked Highbrow. "I ordered Rose to get rid of all of it. So saying your team stole a vial means you're accusing the Dark Angels. Is that what you're implying, Black Beard?"

"No, sir. I never saw Drake, Calico Jack, or Ranger drink blood. I heard them talk. I'm not saying the Dark Angels are involved, but it's my fault I can't control my team. I apologize. I didn't mean for this to happen and take full responsibility."

"We believe you, Black Beard." Highbrow turned to Drake. "You've always been a pain in my ass. In a short amount of time, you've racked up more demerits than everyone else combined. If you don't want to be disciplined for your infractions, then you'd best come clean. What did you take from the lab, and what the hell did you drink? Are you infected?"

Drake looked scared.

"Who gave you the blood?" said Highbrow. "One of the Dark Angels?"

Drake shook his shaggy head. "No, sir. We stole it out of the fridge when the vamps were tending to the sick. Everyone in camp wants chameleon blood, so we took what we could find and drank it back here. Just a drop, sir. Honest."

"Micah wasn't involved? Did any Dark Angel know?"

The teen shook his head again. Highbrow sensed he was protecting someone.

"So you just selected a vial of blood without reading the label, stuck it in your pocket, and came back here to drink it? Didn't you consider it might be zombie blood?" Highbrow watched him turn pale. "Then you're as stupid as you look, Drake. A week in the brig will do you all good. Sorry, Black Beard, but this falls on your shoulders."

"I understand," said the team leader. "A week sounds about right."

"There's no way I'm spending a week in a cave!" Drake glanced at a rack of knives beside the sink. "I could overpower all of you if I wanted. No one is stronger than me. Tell him you cut Jack or I will cut out your eyes, Black Beard!"

"Both of you shut up," Highbrow said. "It's the booze talking, not super-blood."

A commotion at the door caught Highbrow's attention. Lt. Sterling entered the doorway, supported by the Bull Dogs. Drake gazed at the table wanting to disappear. Black Beard looked relieved and stood at attention. Sterling wasn't impressed.

"Problem, sir?" asked Sterling, giving both Buccaneers a stern look.

"Take Black Beard and Drake into custody and toss them into the brig." Highbrow put away his gun and stepped back so the Bull Dogs could carry Calico Jack out on a stretcher. "Find Jack's ear and put him in the hospital, under guard. Saber is there. I want her questioned about whether or not she was involved in the theft of a vial of blood. Hawkins and Ranger are on the loose. Find them and take them to the brig, too. Best to keep them separated in case they're infected, lieutenant."

"It'll be crowded in there," said Sterling. "I just hauled in the Panthers and Razorbacks for inciting a riot at the garage. They tried to take the Beast out for a joy-ride and cracked Sturgis over the head with a wrench."

The Buccaneers were cuffed and escorted out by two M.P.'s. Odin found the severed ear and handed it to Sterling, while Highbrow grabbed the box of booze. The captain took the alcohol outside and broke each bottle against the side of a frosty metal trash can.

The snow had stopped and the first rays of dawn were creeping over the cliffs, but Highbrow sensed it was going to be a bad day. A Bull Dog placed yellow tape over the closed R.V. door, while the rest of the team carried the stretcher to the hospital.

Lt. Sterling blocked Highbrow's path. "The Captain would never have tolerated this infraction. He would have lined up the Buccaneers before the entire company and given them twenty lashes. The same should be done with the Panthers and Razorbacks. Discipline must be maintained, sir. Make an example out of Black Beard and Drake, at least. A serious example for a serious offense."

Highbrow didn't whip people as their former captain had, nor did he want to start. If Sterling doubted his ability to command, others might too. But he was not going to change his mind, which would look worse.

He placed his hand on Lt. Sterling's shoulder. His father, Senator Powers, did the same thing when talking to a subordinate. The older man looked surprised, his hardened features softened.

"Do what's necessary to get the truth lieutenant, but no floggings.

Cut rations for anyone in the brig. An empty belly is just as effective." He dropped his hand.

"Yes, sir," said Sterling, saluting.

Highbrow walked back to the hospital. Odin fell into step beside him. Sensing his follower, Highbrow glanced over his shoulder. The lights in the Buccaneers' R.V. were still on and it was empty, yet he saw a shadow move across the window. Someone was still inside. Thinking it odd, he turned back to Odin and again glimpsed a flash of darkness drift past the private, gliding over the snow toward the hospital. Highbrow figured he was just tired and seeing things, so he didn't mention it.

The new hospital was built on the location of the original, near the mess hall. Aurora and her Valkyries were on guard duty. The all-female team was formidable in battle and always followed orders. The young women were tall, athletic, wearing blue capes over metal breastplates, and helmets with painted wings. Aurora carried a sword, no gun. Her team carried spears and battle axes, with guns strapped to their hips. Spotting Highbrow, Aurora held up her blade in a salute. Odin waved back, grinning like an idiot.

"I like her," said Odin. "Whisper, Aurora, and I went to the same high school, but they were a year ahead. She was the captain of the cheerleading squad. We came to the Peak together. Both saved my life more than once."

An M.P. marched out of the mess hall, dragging an Amazon who was cursing up a streak, hands tied behind her back. Under the lights it was easy to see a nasty bump on her forehead and a bruise on her cheek. Aurora opened the door for Highbrow and Odin, but didn't follow. Calico Jack was having his ear reattached by a Dark Angel. The Bull Dogs stood at the door, guarding the injured Avenger.

"Dr. Rose? A word please," said Highbrow.

The vampire doctor was caring for a little girl with a bloody nose. The child held a doll saturated with blood. Ginger assisted, keeping the hysterical girl confined.

"In a minute," Rose said, in an agitated voice.

At another table, Betsy was examining male twins. Nomad's wife placed bandages on their foreheads. Both had identical cuts above their right eyebrows. Nomad sat against a wall, holding a small boy in his arms who was coughing hard. Saber, the Buccaneer's sole female member, was a pretty sixteen year old with a ponytail. She lay on a cot, under a blanket, sneezing and blowing her nose. There were a dozen beds, each one holding a sick child or teenager. It reminded Highbrow of the initial outbreak during the Scourge. The room was warm, having several heaters.

The Bandits, a former Latino street gang, helped tend to the sick, wearing Latex gloves and surgical masks. They were the toughest group in camp, having found a new calling.

Highbrow walked over to Dr. Rose, waiting while she finished with her patient. The slender, pale-haired vampire wore a white lab coat splattered with blood, looking exhausted. She left Ginger to hold a cloth against the little girl's bloody nose then turned and shook her head at Highbrow.

"What's going on? We've never had this many children sick or injured at one time," said Highbrow. "I just broke up a knife fight at the Buccaneers' R.V. The Razorbacks and Panthers are in the brig for rioting, and I don't see Sturgis in here. Where is he? He got whacked on the head."

"It's been this way all night," said Rose. "Most kids came in with the flu. Typical during this time of year, but we're running out of beds. The worse cases are in our R.V. Tandor is tending to them. Most symptoms I can treat with antibiotics and aspirin. If I didn't know better, I'd say these kids are suffering from anger and resentment."

Pulling off his cap, Highbrow stuffed it into his coat pocket. He lifted his hand to wipe it across his nose, sniffing. Rose caught his arm and squirted disinfectant gel into his palm.

"Come on. Is it that contagious, Doc?"

"Infection is never good, captain. Last thing we need is you falling sick. But in my medical opinion, apart from the flu, these kids are going stir-crazy being snowed in. They're fighting over dolls, arguing over stolen caps and socks. I have a boy here who swears his dead mother told him not to eat his dinner or he'd die. He ate something that didn't set well and he's been throwing up in the bathroom for an hour now."

"Where is Micah?" Highbrow asked, looking around the hospital. Rose lowered her eyes. "Are you aware Micah and a few other Dark Angels have been leaving camp at night? I thought I made it clear that no one leaves without my approval."

"There's a new nightclub in Colorado Springs called the Graveyard," said Rose. "It's a big hit with the younger vampires."

Highbrow snorted. "Do they drink human blood at this club?"

"Another good question that deserves an honest answer." Rose went to Ginger and drew her to the captain. "Did your boyfriend go back to the club, Ginger? Don't make excuses for Micah. He was told not to leave camp."

"He better be at the Graveyard. If Micah is cheating on me, I'll break his neck," said Ginger, sweeping her long, red hair from her shoulders. "Micah says the Shadowguard hang out there and get loose-lipped when they're drunk on champagne."

"When Micah gets back, tell him I want to see him," said Highbrow.

Ginger walked away to help another patient. Rose remained beside him.

"The Buccaneers stole a vial of blood," said Highbrow, trying not to sound accusing. "I thought we destroyed it all."

Rose's cheeks turned bright red. She was the only vampire Highbrow knew who still blushed. "We did," she said. "The only things I'm keeping are a few samples of the flu outbreak. The Buccaneers are infected with the flu, nothing else."

An older female vampire was singing to the sick children in French.

Some knew the song, *Alouette*, and sang along. For a moment, the hospital became brighter. Highbrow nodded to Rose and headed toward the door. Odin went to talk to the Valkyries, leaving Highbrow alone with Rose. They walked down the path and came to the waterfall, frozen mostly, a small trickle still feeding the pool.

"You're sure there are no more vials of Cadence's blood?" Highbrow asked again.

"There isn't any chameleon blood in camp," said Rose. "It was destroyed. I think these kids are homesick. It's Christmas, and this isn't a cheerful place."

"Maybe I'm jumping to conclusions, but I'm worried the Kaiser is behind this outbreak."

Rose laughed, the sound soft. "Let's not jump to conclusions. Eliminate possibilities. Cross-reference evidence. Solve the mystery. But if you want your doctor's medical opinion, a few hours of sleep will let you see things more clearly."

He took Rose's advice and went straight to HQ. Odin entered as he was turning on the cabin's small heater, laying on his cot and tossing a wool blanket over his legs. The soldier fell onto the couch, producing loud snores within seconds. Sleep for Highbrow wasn't far behind.

Chapter Five

*F*reeborn toppled her king. "How many games is that?"

"Forty-eight wins for me. Zero for you," said Picasso. "I've played for thirty years, so don't be disappointed. You must have contempt for your opponent if you ever hope to win."

Cadence stood inside the doorway of NORAD's small control room unnoticed, watching Freeborn and Picasso play chess. The pair had not played a match in days. Earth Corps had been working around the clock clearing the bunker of bodies and debris, setting up a functional operations center.

Computer stations dotted the room, each with operational flatscreens hanging on the walls, showing ground-based radar and satellites tracking objects through space. Two-panel glass walls separated the control room from the battle cab, an interior room for high officials to gather in case of a nuclear strike. It was as impressive as Cadence had expected. Enormous, boasting private quarters, a gym, a theater, restaurants, stores, a library, and an armory.

"Shame we can't launch an air strike against the Citadel," said Cadence. She walked between the cubicles and took a seat. "What's going on over there, anyway?"

Picasso brought a world map up on the center screen. Five monitors revealed images of the Citadel. The Shadowguard were unloading supplies from a plane; an armored convoy was driving the main road to the former campus; vampire soldiers were drilling in the courtyard, and clearing out carcasses from the football stadium; and one screen showed a hallway with a large door being guarded.

"They're guarding the Kaiser's bedroom," said the Dark Angel. "The plane came out of Los Angeles, but I haven't seen a bird in the sky or any movement at sea. The Shadowguard appear to be in a hurry to launch another attack on the camp. Fortunately, the Kaiser is also preparing for the Christmas Eve Death Games."

"Dragon will be fighting," said Freeborn. "We have to get him out of there before he's killed in the arena."

Cadence nodded. "And we will, Freeborn. I promise." She pulled the brown, leather journal from her coat pocket. "This belonged to Captain Richard Mallory. It gives a detailed account of NORAD before and after the Scourge. A general brought the virus in, and they weren't able to evacuate quick enough. Some of the journal is written in Latin, so Lachlan might read it when he has time. I need someone to hack into the computer in my room, too. I can't figure out the password and I want to know what's on it."

The vampire leaned back in his chair. "It wasn't easy breaking into Skylab, but the security codes here are even tougher to break. Tandor can do it. He was a computer technician for a big Japanese corporation. Good news is the bunker's secure. Everything checks out, except for the last underground reservoir, which we still need to look at. The surveillance cameras aren't working at the fourth lake, the one used for the cooling system. When Lachlan is available, we'll go get things running."

"Sounds good," said Cadence. "Have you reached our military bases? Any luck getting anyone to respond? I'm eager to find other survivors and make contact."

"I've sent messages to every military base worldwide including Cape Canaveral, as you asked. If Senator Powers is there in a think-tank, he's off the grid. I did manage to pick up S.O.S. broadcasts from Atlanta, London, Honolulu, Rome, Hong Kong, and a few others. I can't tell how long they've been playing, though one from Vancouver says any survivors are going to the Aleutian Islands, off the northwestern coast of Alaska."

"What about locating survivors? Can satellites track them from space? Are you able to distinguish between the living and the dead?"

Picasso hit a few buttons and black, red, and green dots appeared on the map. He gave her a quick rundown. Most of the countries were blacked out and occupied by zombies. Italy was lit up in red for vampires, along with London, Paris, Denver, Colorado Springs, New York City, L.A., and Vegas. Smaller amounts of green scattered throughout the continents like tiny ants, appearing and disappearing at random. The greatest number of humans was congregated at Seven Falls.

"The satellite I'm relying on the most orbits the earth eight times a day, so we should hear something back if anyone is listening," said Picasso. "You wanted me to focus on what's going on at the Citadel, and I have an update."

"Freeborn, I'd love a cup of coffee. You mind?" Cadence didn't want her present when they discussed the prisoners. Freeborn and Dragon were an item. The less Freeborn knew about Dragon's current situation, the less she had to worry. "Lotus and Smack are in the restaurant. I'm sure you need a break anyway, so take your time."

"Can't it wait?" Freeborn hesitated. "Fine. I can tell when I'm not wanted." She grabbed her coat from the back of the chair she was occupying, and marched out of the control room.

Taking a seat beside Picasso, Cadence gazed at the screen. "I'm impressed with everything you've shown me so far. What have you found on prisoners at the Citadel? I'm sure we've lost quite a few, but who's left?"

The screens reverted back to images of the Citadel. One brought up footage of the Death Games aired the previous night. Images of Dragon, Xena, Dodger, Luna, Barbarella, Cricket and Red Hawk appeared.

"All the chameleons exhibit supreme skill," said Picasso. "Dragon is the strongest and fastest. From what I can tell, Dodger and Xena are the Dynamic Duo. Let me show you last night's footage and you can verify who the masked ones are."

Cadence watched as a tall young man in black, with metal shoulder pads and leg-guards, wearing a Batman cowl, stepped into the arena carrying a sword and shield. Three fighting areas divided the arena; he fought in the south end. A young woman dressed in a silver breastplate, greaves, and a gleaming mask joined him. She held both an axe and a sword. Five vampires wielding chains and spears appeared to fight them. The vampires looked clumsy and slow as the humans launched an immediate attack.

"It's Dodger and Xena, alright," said Cadence. "I haven't seen Dodger use a sword before, but his body size is right, and his attitude. I'd recognize Xena anywhere."

Dodger was flung across the cage and collapsed to the ground. He lost his sword. A vampire jumped on his back and sank his teeth into the teen's neck. Within seconds, the vampire fell over dead. Dodger reclaimed his blade and returned to the fray. Xena hacked up an opponent before being wrapped in a chain. Two vampires then dragged her to her knees and as they bit her, they collapsed to the ground. Dodger stabbed another opponent from behind. He crumpled, convulsing, before Dodger whacked off his head.

Applause roared from the vampire audience with fervor. Many waved small black flags with two silver serpents entwined, displaying the letters "DD" in the corner.

"I can't believe what they're being made to do, but at least they're alive," said Cadence. "Smack will be relieved that Dodger is okay, for now. What about Cricket? Has she been fighting this week?"

"No, she hasn't, but I'm told Cricket is training with the werepumas and werewolves for an upcoming event. Dragon has fought every night for the last two weeks. What's interesting is that he's developed the ability to turn invisible. They throw everything imaginable at him, but Dragon always wins. A fight has been arranged between him and Aries of Athens for Christmas Eve. It's being broadcast worldwide."

Dragon appeared onscreen dressed as a ninja, ascending the stadium stairs. He carried two swords and jumped into the arena. Two animated, fire-breathing dragons—one green and one red—appeared on the arena jumbotrons, breathing his name in fire: Master Dragon. . He bowed and faced his opponent, a tall vampire in chainmail holding a spiked mace. A bell rang cueing the warriors to begin.

"Aries is supposed to be indestructible," said Cadence. "We have one week to get our people out before Christmas Eve. Can your inside-man help us? And we're not talking Pallaton, right? He's not to be involved. I don't trust him."

"Pallaton isn't the only Dark Angel at the Citadel, nor does he know the identity of my source. Plans are in motion to get our people out."

"We'll be putting our eggs in one basket. I'm not sure I like that."

"The Dark Angels are the only ones who can move close enough to get them out. Have a little faith, Commander. This plan will work. Now, if you don't mind, I need food. Deer blood might not be my favorite, but it's available."

"Patch me in to Highbrow before you go."

The vampire clicked a few buttons and brought up Private Destry who was staffing the controls at Seven Falls. Pleasantries were exchanged before Picasso left the control room. She waited, nervous, unsure what to say to him until he appeared on the monitor. Bundled in a heavy coat, cap, and scarf, he looked tired.

"Cadence? When Destry said I had a call waiting, I expected the landline. Looks like Picasso found an easier way for us to communicate. Are you able to see our entire camp through the surveillance cameras?"

"Yours and the Citadel," she said. "But I called because I wanted to tell you we've found other survivors all over the world. We sent word to your dad and every military base, but so far we haven't received a response. I figured we'd dig in deeper and wait it out until we hear from Senator Powers. It's only a matter of time before he arrives with the entire U.S. Army and Air Force. We're not alone."

Highbrow looked relieved. "You have no idea how good it is to hear that, Cadence. I wanted to contact you the other night. Before you say anything else, I have to apologize. What happened between us was my fault. I had no right to take command and send you away. You might hate me now, but I'd do anything to take it back. It was a huge mistake based on fear and stupidity. I'm so sorry."

Cadence wasn't sure she heard right. "Huh?"

"I said I'm sorry. Big time." Highbrow smiled wider. "Say something."

"Well, you are stupid...and I'm sorry, too."

Laughter came swift between them, ending as sudden as it had started. For a moment, they sat staring at one another, caught up in their own emotions. Cadence spoke first.

"It would help us if Tandor came here. He's overdue. Picasso needs his ability with computers. This place is good, Highbrow. We have plenty of room, fresh water, supplies, even entertainment. It's safe, and I mean, vampire proof, but I can't say more."

Fingers near the screen, as if he could touch her face. "I've been such a jerk, Cadence. I still love you." He paused when she did not respond. "Of course an apology doesn't fix what I did, and I appreciate your offer, but I've got to stick it out here. I hope you understand. We're doing okay."

Cadence knew Highbrow wanted more. She did not feel the same. Too much had happened to forget what he did. Their relationship could never be the same again, but she didn't have the heart to tell him.

"Highbrow..."

"Okay, I lied," he said, exploding with pent up emotion. "I'm miserable. The camp is awful. I don't know what's worse, everyone coming down with the flu, the recent thefts and fights, or this ache in my chest. I don't know how to make things right. We need help, and I'm at a total loss."

Cadence watched Highbrow stare at his hands, struggling to say what was on his mind. His biggest fault was his pride. It wasn't easy for him to admit he needed help. Maybe he had changed for the better.

"Of course I'll help," she said. "We have everything Rose needs to handle a few stuffy noses and sore throats. I can send it right over. But that isn't what's upsetting you."

Highbrow looked up. Worry lines appeared across his forehead. His eyes showed concern. "The Shadowguard has left us alone for a month now, but I'm seeing signs of extreme violence in the younger kids. The brig can't hold everyone and house arrest isn't helping. Would the Kaiser stoop to using chemical warfare on us? It's horrible, Cadence, and it's not the Christmas blues that is making everyone act crazy. Do you think it could be black magic? It sounds lame, but I'm not sure what else to think."

Cadence sat back, chewing her bottom lip. "You're not describing anything out of the ordinary. It's snowing. Morale is low. And you're locked in a box canyon with a bunch of kids who are homesick. Nothing more."

A frown appeared on Highbrow's face. "It's more than that, Cadence."

"Well, I suppose the Kaiser has the means to gas your camp or poison the water. But I don't think its black magic. If you want my true opinion, I believe you should bring the camp here. It's the only solution I can offer short of coming there and kicking butt."

"I can't," said Highbrow. "It's not personal, Cadence. I'm in charge now, and if you bail me out of this, they'll see me as weak."

"Then change what you've been doing. Have the older ones assume duties and keep the younger kids under surveillance. Separate the sick from the healthy and let the vampires care for them. Sedate those who are violent but don't resort to the Captain's methods of discipline. Hold a camp meeting of the team leaders, tell them the situation. Meanwhile, I'll try to learn what the Kaiser is up to."

Highbrow smiled. "Thanks. I'd appreciate it, Cadence."

"Sure. I still think you're not telling me what's got you so down. I've never seen you like this. Is Sterling giving you trouble?"

"It's not that. Micah ran into Pallaton last night at the vampire club. I hate being the messenger, but Pallaton gave him a message I was asked to pass along."

Cadence laughed without humor. "This ought to be good. What is it?"

"This isn't easy for me to say," he said, "so just know that I don't agree with it. The Kaiser has promised to leave our camp alone if you turn yourself in. He's hired bounty hunters from Texas to find you. Human bounty hunters. They'll come here first, but we're ready for them." A long pause followed. "Well? What should I tell him?"

"Tell him to suck eggs," Cadence said, her tone betraying her anger. "Here I am feeling guilty I can't do more and you're ready to sell me out to save your own hide. Pallaton can tell the Kaiser to sit tight and wait, because when I'm ready, I'll slide down the chimney and kill him myself. As for your camp, figure it out, Highbrow. You seem to be holding all the cards."

"I told you not to shoot the messenger," Highbrow said, looking flustered. "Why do you have to assume the worst about me? I don't want you to surrender. I wish you were still here. I wish we were..." He glanced at the door to his office.

An argument was happening outside, raised voices becoming audible.

"I've gotta run," said Highbrow. "I'll relay your message to Pallaton and hold the fort. We'll talk later, okay?"

The transmission ended.

Cadence stared at the screen for several minutes, processing everything she had just heard, including Highbrow's last ditch effort to save his own skin. He had sacrificed her again to protect his camp. Knowing how he felt didn't make her warm and fuzzy inside.

Chapter Six

"The Kaiser requests your company at dinner," said the guard.

A sneer spread across Logan's dark, handsome face as he attempted to move around the Shadowguard. He wanted no part of the Kaiser or his smug little friends tonight. Logan intended to watch the Death Games at the arena. The Shadowguard carried a new M16, and while Logan had a pocketknife to protect himself with, it would do the trick if a vampire tried to suck him dry.

"Dragon is fighting," Logan said. "I'm going to the arena. What happened to my old guard? I haven't seen you before."

The Shadowguard had olive skin, nearing middle-age. Beyond that, he resembled every other guard in a black trench coat and black shoes. Logan walked around the guard, experiencing a rush of irritation when the guard appeared in his path.

"The dining hall is in the opposite direction, Agent Logan."

"Are you deaf? I'm going to the arena. Dragon is fighting." Logan made a quick decision. "Why don't you come with me?"

The vampire smiled, revealing long fangs. "This might be the first time I've been assigned to guard you, but I know you. Maybe you gave other guards the slip, but I will be your shadow."

"Good," said Logan. "You can buy me popcorn."

The old jock dorms where Logan lived sat near the football stadium. The vampire followed him downstairs and into the lobby where two Shadowguard stood, grinning like idiots flipping through a Playboy Magazine. Logan's guard opened the front doors, catching up with him on the shoveled sidewalk. The night was clear, stars were bright, and loud cheering came from the arena. A stocking cap over his shaved head, Logan stuffed his hands into pockets. He felt around for his game-pass until it brushed against the fingers of his hand.

"You don't like vampires, do you?"

Logan thought it an odd question. Wasn't it obvious? "Gee, where did you get that idea?" he said with his usual sarcasm. "Am I giving off that kind of vibe?"

"It's curious that a woman as intelligent as Rose Standish is interested in someone like you."

The vampire had a Middle Eastern accent, but Logan could not discern the dialect.

He continued, "You look surprised. There's little that goes on at Seven Falls we don't hear or see. I was with Lieutenant Aldarik when we attacked the survivors' camp. Rose killed one of my friends."

"Well, she's a Dark Angel and she doesn't like the Shadowguard. A good way to my bad side is to keep talking about her. Whatever relationship I had with Rose Standish is none of your business. But I'm glad to know she killed your friend."

The wind picked up and Logan hurried forward, joining the line of vampires standing outside the stadium. A large banner hung over the side of the building, reading *DEATH GAMES*. Vendors sold souvenirs behind tables, just as they might at an Air Force Academy football game. He picked up a *Master Dragon* sign that someone had dropped, brushed away the snow and grinned at his guard.

"I'm a big fan of Dragon's," said Logan. "That kid has killed more Shadowguard than the entire Freedom Army. I'm not sure why, but it makes me happy. So if that means I don't like vampires, then you're right. I don't."

"Rose Standish was my friend, too."

The guard stood behind Logan in line, but being chatty would not win him over. Logan's breath came out in white puffs, setting him apart from every man and woman in line, and he received more than a few looks from other fans. Vampires needed air but they were immune to the freezing temperature.

"Mind changing the subject?" Logan asked. He waved his banner. "I'm here for the entertainment, so let's not get friendly. I don't want to be friends."

"Maybe I could be one," said the vampire, keeping his voice low. "My assignment as your guard isn't a coincidence. I arranged to be closer to you, upon Rose's request. My name is Bechtel. I'm a Dark Angel. And I need to know if you're willing to help us?"

Logan thought about reaching for his pocketknife. "Bechtel, is it? Let's not pretend you know Rose, or that she cares about my wellbeing. I am whatever you've heard about me, plus a hundred and ten percent more mercenary than you could ever imagine. I go to the highest bidder, and right now, the Kaiser owns me. What's your deal? Did Pallaton put you up to this? Forget it. I'm not your man."

"Rose told me you'd react this way," said Bechtel. "But she also said she forgives you. She knows you regret what you did and thinks you may want to make amends. She also knew you wouldn't believe me, unless I gave you something of hers that had meaning to you." He reached into his pocket and produced a solitary brown acorn.

While an unimpressive specimen, the acorn had significant meaning to Logan. After he caught Rose off guard in the lab with that first kiss, she demanded he bring a fresh basket of wildflowers to study. Instead, he brought her a handful of acorns. No one else knew.

Even if Bechtel was a Dark Angel, Logan wasn't sure he wanted to get involved with the people he had betrayed. Rose was assuming too much.

Taking the acorn from Bechtel's hand, Logan pocketed it and marched through the gate. He gave his ticket to the attendant and entered the stadium, threading his way through the crowd to reach the concessions, giving himself time to think. The odor of popcorn sat heavy in the air. It took a while to get a box, as it was a snack vampires could digest. Logan heard the music signaling intermission, ushering a crowd from the tunnels.

Bechtel kept up as Logan shouldered his way into the arena. "Is there a problem? Rose needs your help. She needs to know what the Kaiser is planning. You're with him every night. He must have mentioned plans in front of you. Rose is worried about her camp, and about Cadence. If you can tell us anything at all, it would be appreciated."

Exiting the tunnel, Logan stood looking up and down the bleachers, trying to find his seat. He moved as a young couple holding hands rushed up the stairs. Bechtel put his hand on Logan's shoulder, bending to whisper in his ear.

"Will you help us?"

"Is this a trick or some crazy female way of finding out if I care?" Logan headed toward his seat. "I'm not one to be pumped for information. Not my style. And I'm not sorry for what I did, either."

Out of instinct, Logan checked under the seat for a surveillance camera before taking his place among the vampire crowd. Squished in on all sides, it felt like he was sitting in an ice locker. The only thing vampires were good for was providing a wind block. Logan passed Bechtel the popcorn as he stood up, waving his banner in the air and handing it to a pretty girl sitting in the row ahead of him. He sat back down and considered Bechtel from the corner of his eye.

"Does forgiveness hold any value, Agent Logan?" asked Bechtel. "Because to some it means nothing, but to others it may be priceless. How about you?"

"Does she want to hear that I love her? Is that what she wants? What she needs to answer is why she still loves me. I'm not worth it. She knows it. I turn on the flip of a dime. You're putting your life in jeopardy by telling me any of this. The answer is, 'No.'"

During intermission a lame werewolf was released into the arena, along with fifteen zombies dressed like sheep. The wolf tried running from the zombies and when surrounded, he fought for his life. Seconds later, the wolf was torn to shreds. The crowd laughed as another prisoner stumbled out. This time a human appeared, dressed in a tattered business suit stained with blood. He carried a briefcase as a weapon and killed one zombie before being swarmed. The scoreboard counted down the final ten seconds before game time. The crowd cheered, "*Dragon, Dragon!*"

A large screen hanging over the arena displayed animated red and green dragons, twisting around each other with open jaws. The lights dimmed. A red beam spotlighted the middle of the court. The wolf and human bodies were removed, but the gore remained. More red beams hit the eastern tunnel. Expectant vampires erupted as Dragon became visible.

Master Dragon, dressed as a ninja with traditional face-covering, carried two Japanese swords of different lengths. In one leap he cleared the expanse between the tunnel entrance and the middle of the arena, landing in a crouched position. Rising as the stadium lights brightened once more, Dragon lifted his swords, revving up the audience until the cheers were deafening.

From the western tunnel, three cyborg-zombies entered the arena, outfitted with flamethrowers on one arm and chainsaws on the other. In support, twenty berserker-zombies dressed in Falcon football uniforms appeared, wearing helmets with antennas. Somewhere in the press box, a doctor sat holding a remote control. Ten vampires riding motorcycles roared into the arena, driving in circles around Dragon, all carrying spears.

The berserker-zombies headed straight for Dragon. The cyborgs spread out, shooting flames toward him, as the vampires continued circling.

Dragon moved into action. He was faster than any vampire, vanishing and reappearing in the center of the zombies, swinging his swords and lopping off heads. The three cyborgs advanced on Dragon, spewing fire from their arms, keeping him occupied as the vampires headed toward him. With a leap, Dragon unseated a vampire, confiscated his motorcycle and zipped around the field.

"This is new," said Logan. "I didn't know Dragon could ride a bike."

A vampire in front of him spilled her bottle of blood and turned to wipe her chair. The man seated next to her shouted in excitement, jumping and knocking her over. Logan caught the bundle of blonde hair and curves, and helped her back to her seat. The excited fan glared at Logan.

"Thanks," she said. The blonde stood up and yelled, "Dragon! I love you!"

Dragon leapt off of the bike, letting it slam into a cyborg causing both to explode in flames. Blood splattered the crowd as Dragon eviscerated another cyborg with his long sword. A stroke of his shorter blade beheaded the third, sending its head flying. The audience screamed Dragon's name as he pursued the motorcycles on foot. The vampires tried to outmaneuver Dragon, but he was too fast. Using his invisibility, he kept everyone guessing where he would appear next, striking fear in the vampires and raucous fervor in the fans. One after another Dragon destroyed the bikers until he alone remained standing. The crowd erupted in riotous fanfare, chanting Dragon's name.

"Next week, on Christmas Eve," said the male announcer over the speakers. "Our very own Master Dragon will face his most lethal opponent yet, Aries of Athens, the Cyborg from Hell! Place your bets early, folks. It's happening right here at the Citadel's Christmas Eve Death Games!"

Dragon collected bouquets of flowers and a giant white teddy bear tossed to him by fans before he waved at the crowd and disappeared into the tunnel. A full squad of Shadowguard accompanied him. Ecstatic fans tried to follow and were clubbed to the ground by guards, ending any riot before it began, as new contestants entered the arena.

"Christmas is overrated," said Logan. He stood and motioned at Bechtel. "Come on. I don't want to see the grand-melee. You can only watch so many zombies die in a night. Pit Dragon against the Dynamic Duo and you'd have a real fight."

With Bechtel in the lead, they headed toward the exit. The crowd cheered as zombies were let onto the field. Logan quickened his step. Bechtel caught Logan by the arm, dragging him past the concession stands and vampires toward the Falcon's old baseball locker room. He handed a program to Logan.

"Have a souvenir, my friend. Let's see if Dragon will sign it for you."

Logan flipped it open. The program's headline article featured the upcoming Christmas Eve match between the champions. The stats told how many opponents each had killed, and both fighter's strengths and weaknesses. Dragon had no weakness, but Aries had lost both arms in a prior fight. His new arms were made of titanium and the man looked like a tank. Logan placed the program in his coat pocket as he approached a blue door with a large red star. Dragon's name was beneath the star in black.

"Why are we doing this?" asked Logan. "I'm not that big a fan. Dragon doesn't like me and I don't want to give him a chance to cut off my head."

"We're going," said Bechtel. "This is business."

A line of fans waited to meet Dragon, ladies first. Guards were posted outside the fighter's door. Bechtel held out a gold pass. He and Logan were ushered in without question. An oriental theme dressed the locker room. Banners with dragons hung from the walls, red carpeting covered the floor, and a gold table and chair sat against the far wall. Dragon autographed black and white photographs for his female fans.

A group of self-indulged vampires were drinking champagne, lounging on red couches, acting like common groupies.

"Hold out the program," said Bechtel. "Have Dragon sign it for you."

"You want his autograph? Fine. I'll get it for you."

Logan pulled out the program. A fan gave him a dirty look. It was evident the vampires all revered Dragon as a celebrity. When it was Logan's turn in line, he stuck out his program to the star.

"Hey, Dragon," said Logan. "Can I get your autograph? I'm a big fan."

Dragon lifted his head. Shirtless, his tattoos exposed a red dragon inked on his right arm, and a green one on his left. He was damn good-looking. Logan offered a glancing smile as Dragon caught his eyes. Hatred reflected back at Logan as the top-ranked fighter yanked the program from his hand. With a gold pen, Dragon scribbled onto an interior page and thrust the program back at Logan.

"I love you to death, Master Dragon," said a woman, pushing Logan out of the way. "Would you sign my program?"

"Let's go," said Bechtel, grabbing Logan by the arm and leading him out.

Once outside, Logan breathed in the crisp, fresh air. Vampires were leaving by car or in tight pedestrian groups, chatting away about the fights.

Bechtel pointed at the program. "What did he write, Agent Logan?"

"I can well imagine what he wrote." Logan opened the program, flipping through the pages. He frowned. "'*Make it happen.*' I'm not sure what that's supposed to mean," closing the program. "Does that mean something to you?"

"You aren't as bright as Rose claims. It means he's ready to leave. You have a reputation for making things happen. This is our sign that Dragon agrees to leave. You'll have to plan something fast. We are running out of time."

"Me?" Logan grimaced. "How the hell am I supposed to arrange for that?"

The idea was ridiculous. Dragon was the most powerful fighter in the arena. Being asked to help someone who could turn invisible seemed stupid. Dragon didn't need help to leave. Logan wanted to tell Bechtel what his true thoughts were about any such plan, but kept his mouth shut. They walked back to his building in silence.

"I thought you agreed to help?" Bechtel was angry. "Dragon trusts you more than you think, Logan, or he wouldn't have written that message. We've been waiting for this for quite a while. Now you're on board we should be able to make it happen."

"Look, pal, you've come to the wrong man. I never agreed to anything."

They arrived at Logan's building. Bechtel put his hand on the door, keeping Logan from entering.

"The fight is rigged," said Bechtel. "Dragon is meant to die. I can't do this alone, Logan. I need your help. Dragon needs your help. So does Rose."

Logan tried to push Bechtel out of the way. It was like pushing on a boulder. "Do you mind? We're through here. I'm not the guy to rescue the champion. If Dragon wants out, he can just leave. Will you move?"

"You owe Rose," said Bechtel, stepping aside. "And Dragon."

"I'll think about it and let you know tomorrow, okay? Right now I just want to go to my room, open a bottle of scotch and drown out my thoughts of Rose. It won't make me feel any better, but I need to get her off my mind. She's one woman that knows how to get under a man's skin."

Bechtel patted Logan on the back and opened the door. "Go on up. I'll see you tomorrow night. The Dynamic Duo are fighting. I can't wait."

"Bloodsucker."

Logan nodded at the guard posted to his room, went in and made a beeline to his desk. He grabbed a bottle of scotch and poured a drink. Instead of downing the drink, he changed into pajamas and slippers. Who did Rose think she was, asking him to plan the escape of three people who hated him? Three fighters who were popular with both their fans and sponsors. Logan had no idea how to make it happen. He needed a diversion, yet no matter how many scenarios he thought up, he was always the weakest link. He was human, after all.

Standing by the window, Logan pulled aside the curtains. His building was "L" shaped and he could see Salustra's window. Her drapes were open. Salustra was wearing a red silk robe, appearing to be talking to someone behind her. Dragon was Salustra's fighter and lived with her, so Logan assumed he was there. She spotted Logan. He lifted his glass, mouthing the words, *Hey there, pretty lady.* The drapes closed.

Spot lights swung toward their building, lighting up Salustra's window revealing a large, monstrous shadow. Logan watched it slither across the side of the building, darkening frosty panes of glass, then vanishing around the corner. Either his eyes were playing tricks on him, or he had seen the shadow of a winged, horned demon.

Chapter Seven

Raven sat in the middle of her canopied bed, flipping through books from the library, reading up on vampires. Across the room, Star watched her from a chair.

No matter how nice the Kaiser had been, Raven couldn't stop thinking about what she learned after the party. It was the third night in a row she left dinner early to retire to her room. Most of what she found was fiction, and despite the recorded sightings of vampires in history, nothing was mentioned about a vampyr named the Kaiser. Raven didn't think it was his real name, but she knew he was a demon and wanted to send word to her friends.

"It's not here," said Raven. "I can't find a thing on the Kaiser. Why have you stopped looking? We have a dozen more books to go through, Star. If we want to learn what the Kaiser is we can't stop."

"Are we talking now?" Star pulled her legs up and rested her head on her knees. "Just because you've confided in me, doesn't make us best friends. I'm still your slave and you're still the Kaiser's mistress. I thought you were going to send for Luna. Are you aware they keep her in a cage and don't let her change back into human form? It's cruel and inhumane."

Raven closed the book. "I feel horrible for how I've treated you and for what's happened to Luna. Must you remind me every second that I'm a total bitch? I said I was sorry. All I want is to find something useful about the Kaiser. If he's as old as they say he is, and fought against the gods, there must be something about it in these stupid books."

"Don't forget, you're relying on what you were told by vampires," said Star. She pulled a book out from behind her. "I'm not blaming you for being turned, Raven. But you haven't talked like a real person in weeks, and now you tell me all of this crazy stuff about the Kaiser. I don't care what the Kaiser is. He's sent bounty hunters to capture Cadence and we have to get word to her."

"Just keep looking for something helpful. If we kill the Kaiser, Cadence will be fine." She glanced at the book beside her on 'Ancient Culture.' It seemed irrelevant so she closed the book.

"We can kill him later. I'm worried about protecting Cadence right now. Can you imagine what Dr. Leopold intends to do with her? You said Logan goes to the lab every day, but you can't get close him. I want to know what they plan to do."

"Logan is a backstabber, plain and simple," said Raven. "I hate him. He was never nice to me. Besides, I'm not allowed to talk to Logan. Not about Cadence, and not about the Kaiser. It's a shame, too. He's so rich and powerful."

Star hurled a book at Raven in disgust, just missing her head. "So what? The Kaiser doesn't love you. He's using you. Thor loved you. Luna loved you. Demons aren't capable of love." She sounded exasperated. "The book on demonology I read listed the name of over forty different demons. Nothing on vampyrs." She lowered her voice. "For all you know, the Kaiser is Lucifer."

"No. He can't be. It's just too terrifying to consider."

"Maybe he serves Lucifer," said Star, grinning. "The Scourge was the end of the world. Then the dead rose, just like it says in Revelation, and the Kaiser is certainly evil."

Raven rolled her eyes, throwing her head back on the pillows staring at the canopy. "Well, Cadence isn't some Savior. I wonder how many battles were fought against the Kaiser. It's a rather weird name to choose. Maybe he's the real Kaiser, you know, the German leader in World War I? Hitler, too. They were both short. So was Napoleon."

"This isn't helping," Star groaned, massaging her face. "All we have to do is get close enough to stab him in the brain and heart. It's best to do it while he's sleeping. We could kill him today."

"Pallaton says he can't be killed, and I trust him. Until we're sure how to do it, we just keep pretending to be obedient servants."

"Then try the Kaiser himself. Use your charm to get close to him. In a moment of passion, he may reveal something we can use to kill him. It's not that difficult, Raven."

"Yuck," said Raven. "Yes, it is. He has nose hairs. And bad breath."

"Is this about Pallaton? I've seen how you stare at one another when you think no one is watching. Keep it up, the Kaiser will catch on." Star slid out of the chair and picked up books, placing them in a large plastic container to be returned to the library. "Did you forget, he's the one who killed Cadence? There's nothing nice about that guy."

"Cadence didn't die. Don't be so judgmental."

"Don't be so stupid."

Raven and Star looked at one another and laughed. They never got along at camp or even hung out back at Pike's Peak. Funny how trying to kill a demon-vampire-lord could bring people together.

A knock made both girls scream. Star ran over to the bed, ducking behind it, leaving Raven to deal with whoever it was. Raven pulled on a black silk robe and walked to the door.

"Who is it?" asked Raven.

"Room service." A man's voice.

Annoyed, Raven unlocked and opened the door. A Shadowguard stood holding a tray with a pitcher of blood and a bowl of limes. A champagne bottle stuck out of a bucket of ice. With contempt, Raven tossed back her silky black hair and pulled the tray from him.

"I asked for this two hours ago. What took you so long? Never mind. Back to your duties and stop bothering me. I'm busy."

The guard opened his mouth, closed it, then stepped back. Glancing down the hallway, he flinched. Raven acted as she always did and pushed the oaf out of the way, charging out into the hall, prepared to throw a fit.

Pallaton was standing there, dressed in a black suit. He dismissed the guard and gave her a frosty look. "You've caused a great gossip with this sudden interest in books. What are you up to? The Kaiser has serious doubts about you, Raven. He thinks you're playing games with him. He's looking elsewhere for a new wife."

"Good," said Raven. "I don't want to marry him. He's bald. And he's too old."

"Shh! Get inside, you stupid girl. We need to talk."

The Captain of the Shadowguard was fast as a serpent, sweeping forward, catching Raven and slamming the door behind them. Pallaton sent her tumbling to the floor and towered over her, a dangerous look distorting his pale face. Star didn't make a peep.

"You asked the Kaiser to give humans for that little queen and her moron consort?" Pallaton glared at Raven as she gathered herself. "Right now the Kaiser is putting men and women on a bus and sending them to Miramont Castle on your behalf. Whatever happened to helping people? You said you wanted to help. You were talking through your fangs, as usual. It didn't even cross your mind what will happen to them. A silly request by a silly girl with no idea how the real world operates."

"Me?" Raven asked, incredulous. "How many humans have you killed in the line of duty, Pallaton? Your Shadowguard attacked the camp several times, and people died. You're the reason Star and I are here. In fact, it's your fault Luna is in a cage and the Vikings are all but dead." She wiped bloody tears away. "Why are you so angry? You don't care about me, so stop acting like you do. What are you doing here anyway? You're not allowed in here."

Pallaton scoured the room furious, reaching for a priceless Egyptian vase, hurling it against the wall. The clay dust showered over the bed and Star peeked from behind the bed.

"How dare you!" Raven stood up hissing, exposing her fangs.

Without warning, Pallaton gripped Raven's arm and pulled her against his body, leaning in to kiss her. He changed his mind, giving her a push and sending her flying backward. The bed caught her, scattering books across the floor. Her hand found a heavy volume and she threw it at his head. Pallaton knocked it away. His fangs released and his eyes glowed, turning bright yellow. Raven launched another book, striking him in the head.

"Will you stop that? I'm here because I care, so stop being childish."

"Leave my room this minute," shouted Raven. "Get out!"

Star appeared in a flurry of motion, setting upon Pallaton. She spun around and kicked the tall vampire in the chest, knocking him across the room. Before Pallaton regained his feet, she pulled a spear from a ledge and threw it at him. He ducked. The spear pierced the wall behind him, but Star had another weapon in hand. The vampire threw a chair in her direction and moved for the door, but she was too fast.

Raven watched in amazement as Star attacked with lightning speed, hammering at Pallaton's chest and stomach with blows that broke his ribs. Pallaton fell back, angry and in pain, unable to defend himself. Desperate, he reached for his gun. But Star was quick, low-kicking his legs out from under him. Pallaton lost the gun and Star jumped him, holding an Egyptian khopesh to his throat.

"Touch her again, bloodsucker, and I'll kill you. I'll kill your guards. I'll destroy anything that holds meaning for you." A savage look raged in her eye.

Pallaton laughed. Star pressed the blade of the sword into his skin.

"Stop laughing, or I'll slice you open and let you bleed out."

"You should be in the arena with Dragon," Pallaton said. "I had no idea you were a superhuman. You acted so demure and obedient."

Star's smile was cold. "You're nothing but a coward, Pallaton. Your yellow streak twists up your spine. I should cut it out of you."

He swallowed hard. With an angry scream, Star hauled Pallaton to his feet and tossed him into a gold, wing-backed chair. With a sweeping move, she ripped cords from the drapery and tied him to the chair.

"Please don't hurt him," Raven shouted. She climbed off the bed, running over to sink beside the chair. "He didn't hurt me, Star. It's a misunderstanding."

"He shouldn't be here," said Star. "I won't have him hurting you."

"That wasn't my intention. Are you going to kill me or give me a close shave?" asked Pallaton, his voice smooth as honey.

Star looked at Raven. "I know you care about this filth, but you shouldn't love someone so much when they don't feel the same."

Pallaton caught Raven's gaze. "The only reason I'm here is because I love you. Having you marry the Kaiser is better than seeing you his slave. I don't want you harmed. If I can protect you…"

"Are you my Maker?" Raven cupped Pallaton's face. "It's you, isn't it? You're the one who turned me. The Kaiser can't make vampires. Those with yellow eyes aren't his offspring. They're yours, and so am I."

"You weren't supposed to know," Pallaton said, in a gentle voice. His eyes returned to a normal dark-brown as his fangs retracted. "I loved you the first time I saw you, Raven."

Raven's heart leapt to her throat. Not caring if Star watched, she threw her arms around Pallaton and kissed him. He fought at the cords wanting to break free and hold her. She sat on his lap, pressing her nose against his, while she laughed and cried.

"I love you too, Pallaton. I wasn't sure…I've been so confused, but I've never felt like this for anyone before. It doesn't matter who knows and I don't care what they do to us. Just knowing you feel the same makes all this bullshit worthwhile."

"No, it doesn't," said Star. "How can you say this after what's he's done? How do you feel anything but hate and revulsion? This man raped you. He made you a vampire against your will, forcing a life of bloodsucking, day-sleeping, and oppression on you. Let me kill him, we'll leave for camp together."

"I'm going to untie him," Raven said. "He won't hurt us."

"Star may be right." Pallaton lifted his head as Raven untied the cords. "I'm leaving for Seven Falls and I'll bring Highbrow back. They'll put him on T.V. and demand Cadence turn herself in. By the time Highbrow is begging for her help, I doubt there'll be much left to save."

"Leave him be," said Star. "Let's get out of here while we still can."

"When do you leave?" Raven finished unfastening the cords and dropped them to the ground. "If it's tonight, then Star and I have plenty of time to reach Seven Falls and warn Highbrow."

Standing, Pallaton kept Raven between him and Star. "Straight away. My team is waiting outside. I need to change clothes first. I'm a bit over dressed for an assault."

The sound of glass breaking spun Raven and Pallaton toward the window. Star had ripped the drapes from the wall and used a chair to break the window. She jumped onto the ledge barefoot, wearing a thin negligee.

"I've got to go, Raven," said Star. "You want to stay here with this guy, it's your call. Try to help Dragon and Luna, if you can. I'm out of here."

Star fell out of the window, vanishing as the morning light spilled into the room. Instead of shouting at her, Pallaton held Raven in a passionate embrace and kissed her, blocking everything from her thoughts.

One moment Raven was in Pallaton's arms, the next she was laying on the bed. Confused, Raven saw that Pallaton was no longer there. He exited through the window. The bedroom doors splintered inward. The kiss, and Raven's dreamlike state, was over. Figures sped through her room like hornets repairing the windows, replacing the glass, and vacuuming the carpet with vampire-speed. New drapes hung from the windows, cutting off the pink and purple glow of dawn. It was as though nothing happened.

Raven sat up and spotted the Kaiser in the doorframe, donning his smoking jacket. He wore a look of disbelief and anger. The cleaning crew scurried out.

"Your slave escaped," said the Kaiser. "I wasn't aware Star was superhuman. All this time, we had one in our tender care. What was I thinking? How careless of me to place you in such danger, my darling. Please, forgive me, Raven. My poor child."

The Kaiser removed his jacket to cover her, a thin negligee clinging to her body. His eyes were dark and filled with hunger as she placed the coat around her shoulders. The doors closed on their own. Raven shivered with renewed fear.

"You must choose your friends with more care, my dear," said the Kaiser, his voice anything but cruel. He made no move to touch her, yet she had never been more terrified. "Star will not get far. Pallaton, even now, makes his way to Seven Falls. Cadence refuses to give herself up, so I must take more drastic measures. By collecting the young captain and bringing him here, she will have no other choice but to concede to my demands."

"You don't know Cadence well if you think she'll surrender."

The Kaiser sat on the edge of the bed. "Oh, but I do know her. Cadence will always come to the aid of her friends. Her true friends. It's clear she does not consider you one, but I do. Which is why I sent a delivery of children to Queen Cinder. In exchange, she has returned the Hope Diamond to you." He leaned toward her. "It's right there in my pocket. Go on, Raven. It's meant for you, not a child."

With no other recourse, Raven reached into the Kaiser's pocket and removed the large blue diamond. There was a trace of blood on it. "Did you kill Cinder?"

"Not yet. I'm helping her, as you asked."

Movement at the doorway lifted Raven's eyes. Along the wall she saw a shadow creeping toward the window and she grabbed the Kaiser's arm, a look of alarm on her pale face. He glanced back at the shadow and let out a deep chuckle.

"It won't hurt you, my dear. Not if you agree to be my wife. This is the last time I ask. Marry me, Raven."

"Yes," said Raven, gulping. She would promise anything to save herself. "I'll marry you, my lord and master. I'm sorry to give you cause to doubt me. Nothing stands between us and…happiness."

"Everything is forgiven, my dear." The Kaiser slid a strand of black hair behind her ear. "Forget these books, and I will teach you whatever you desire to learn. From now on I shall protect you, comfort you, love you, and be at your side."

Raven didn't say a word. The shadow stopped at the foot of her bed. It was so dense and dark she couldn't see through it. Dread filled the room and she moved closer to the Kaiser, putting him between her and the strange darkness.

"Reach into my other pocket, Raven."

She did as she was told, fingers closing around something small and plush. His arm slid around her waist as she withdrew and held up a purple, velvet box.

"Accept this sign of my love. We shall one day leave this place and go where the sun is warm and the sea tranquil. You will be a goddess and forget these friends and any misery you've ever known. And I shall love you, alone. Always."

Raven's eyes widened as she opened the box. Inside was a large white diamond, grasped by tiny gold claws on an ornate band. The ring was alluring with an ancient flair. But there was something else. Something wrong.

Her first inclination was to hurl it across the room and run. The shadow gave a shudder and loomed over the bed, blocking any escape as if it could read her thoughts.

"Put it on. Let me see how it looks on your hand."

Raven placed the ring on her finger, and a sudden dizziness overtook her. She swooned against his body, felt his warm lips on her neck, and the world slipped sideways in her mind. Her worries, feelings, and doubts vanished in an instant. The room danced with bright colors, candied sheets and walls made of silk. The lights became as glowing crystals.

"You are more beautiful than Helen of Troy or Marie Antoinette," said the Kaiser, his voice deeper and richer than she had realized. He kissed her cheek, the soft brush of lips causing her to shiver with delight. "You are by far the fairest creature I've ever encountered, and now you are mine, Raven. Truly mine."

A red flame danced within the diamond, holding Raven transfixed. She heard the Kaiser speaking to her, but stopped paying attention. The ring alone held her interest, until at last, he grabbed her arms, pulling her back and gazing into her eyes.

"Never remove the ring, my dear. Gaze upon it a while longer, and then say, 'Yes. I am yours, Prince Balan,' and everything will be perfect."

"Yes, I am yours, my love."

Raven leaned against her master and kissed him on the mouth. The shadow creature stirred, but she paid it no attention. She only cared about her fiancé.

"Never tell my true name to anyone, Raven. It's our secret. Tomorrow night, I will announce our engagement at a reception. I'll be sure Pallaton and Luna are present, and anyone else who would take you away. They will all understand that you are mine."

She silenced him with a deep, passionate kiss.

Chapter Eight

*T*he camp sirens blared as an army of zombies advanced on Seven Falls with unprecedented eagerness. Bodies sizzled and sparked as they came into contact with the tall, electric fence. With uncanny resilience, the undead scrambled over the growing mound of bodies, trying to reach the top, and found themselves hindered by razor-sharp barbed wire. Echo and her team of Blue Devils used flamethrowers to remove zombies from the chain-link. The Panthers and Monster Squad were stationed in the forward towers and lobbed grenades into the throng of moving corpses. More zombies were marching over the road, as if under the control of an aggressive puppet master.

"If the generator fails, Captain, we're in for one helluva battle," shouted Sterling. "That fence will topple right over without electricity to keep them back."

The stationary guns riddled the zombies with bullets through the front windows of the battle deck. Everyone old enough to fight, including those from the brig, stood on top of buses at the barricade, firing at the enemy. The only ones absent from the battle were the sick in Rose's care, hidden inside of a tunnel. The Bull Dogs were stationed outside to protect them. Tandor was the single vampire present in the battle. The remainder of the Dark Angels patrolled camp.

"These zombies are cyborgs," said Tandor. "You can see the metal in their skulls and a blinking red light. They're under control of the Shadowguard."

Highbrow stared hard at the zombies. He could make out red blinking lights on their heads, but Tandor's vision was impossible to match. The Dark Angel wore a black racing suit, with a katana strapped to his back and a 9mm pistol on each thigh.

"I should have known the Kaiser never meant to respect a treaty," said Highbrow. "You were right about this being a ruse, Tandor. Even if Cadence agreed to surrender, they had every intention of attacking us."

Tandor headed for the door. "You've got Micah in charge of the Dark Angels at Midnight Falls. The Shadowguard won't find it easy to come in that way, but they're here, Highbrow. I think I'll take the path Micah has been using and make sure the Shadowguard aren't flanking us."

"Go ahead, but be careful. You're just one man."

A smile cracked on Tandor's face. "I'm a vampire. Don't worry about me. Nobody is coming through that path, except me." He tucked his head and left.

Lt. Sterling held up his radio, listening. "Nomad and Destry are in position with rocket launchers. Should they fire, sir?"

"Affirmative. Have them concentrate on the zombies coming up the road. The flamethrowers can protect the fence. If it falls, set the safe-zone on fire. There's enough kerosene in those pits to burn for hours. I want the battle tanks in position behind the buses to send in as a last resort."

Highbrow watched the battle, his confidence rising until Private Caesar of the War Gods came rushing up the stairs and through the door. The young man had one arm in a sling and carried a pistol.

"Sir, the Shadowguard broke through to Midnight Falls. I just heard from Micah. The Dark Angels have gathered at the Moon Tower, but he's asking for reinforcements. The War Gods and Razorbacks are ready to move out, if you are?"

"I'll be right there," said Highbrow. Caesar ran back out the door.

"Tandor had to have run into trouble on the ridge. Contact Picasso and tell him to send in the Earth Corps. There's not a moment to delay."

Sterling paused. "Sir? We've got this. We don't need the mutants."

Highbrow bristled. "You heard me! Make the call! They can be here in minutes!" He headed to the door with Private Odin. "Take command, Lt. Sterling! Don't let the zombies through our lines!"

With Odin at his side, Highbrow ran to a battle-truck and jumped onto the side. Odin and Caesar climbed into the back with the two teenage patrols. The truck accelerated over the winding, snow-covered road. As they passed the R.V.s, the sound of gunfire and shouting was thick. The truck came to a halt outside the mess hall. A swarm of vampires in trench coats was pouring in from beyond the stairs at the waterfall and into the campgrounds.

Micah and the Dark Angels were no longer in the Moon Tower, but fought close-combat with the Shadowguard in front of HQ. A fire at Midnight Falls had moved into camp. The small HQ cabin was ablaze and casualties from both sides lay in the snow.

"Razorbacks to the tunnel," shouted Highbrow. "War Gods with me!"

The young soldiers climbed out of the truck. The Razorbacks raced to the left, heading toward the tunnel where Rose and the children were hiding. An elevator at the back of the tunnel led to a lookout point, where the Buccaneers held an advantage for sniping. The Bull Dogs fought shoulder to shoulder at the entrance, firing at anything that moved, proving more dangerous than effective. A Dark Angel lay on the ground shot by friendly fire, blood pooling.

Highbrow charged forward, flanked by Odin and the War Gods, to support the Dark Angels. The Dark Angels and Shadowguard fought with swords and traded gunfire. Ginger ran forward, firing a large-caliber automatic rifle, heading for the stairs. The War Gods took cover behind an overturned golf cart, firing over the top and in opposing directions. They held their position, waiting until the Shadowguard moved from their cover before firing again. It was an effective way to kill vampires, resulting in several enemies scattered in the snow.

"We need to get to cover," shouted Odin, standing back-to-back with the captain.

A rush of wind passed in front of Highbrow, alerting him that a vampire was close. He fired in the direction the breeze was blowing and a Shadowguard tumbled to the ground. Highbrow shot the vamp in the head and through the heart. He grabbed Odin's arm, hauling him to the mess hall where the Bandits were keeping the Shadowguard at bay.

"Betsy and the kids are inside," a Bandit called out. "We found them hiding in the hospital, but couldn't get them to the tunnel in time."

Highbrow spotted Odin kneeling behind an over-turned trashcan. The private took out a vampire, but more were coming. The Shadowguard swarmed around the golf cart where the War Gods stood in tight formation. Caesar just escaped the mass of struggling bodies. An explosion sent the golf cart and countless bodies flying into the air. Caesar fell yards from Highbrow, a section of the cart's fender sticking from his back.

Another explosion lit the hospital in a huge fireball. A teenager burst through the front door engulfed in fire, screaming in agony before falling to the ground. The Bandits reformed their defensive line outside the mess hall, as roaring flames from the two buildings turned to clouds of black smoke in the sky.

"Odin, go help Betsy." Highbrow had to shout to be heard. "You've got to get those kids out before they set the building on fire. Try to reach an R.V. and stay out of sight."

"Me?" said Odin in a panic. "I can't do it alone!"

There was no time to argue. Highbrow pushed Odin toward the mess hall and took position behind a cement park bench, leaving the Bandits to defend the doorway. Micah appeared in the center of the battle, swinging a sword. His opponent was missing an arm, but continued fighting with a knife. Highbrow aimed at the Shadowguard and fired, striking him in the temple before Micah was lost in a surge of bodies in trench coats racing toward Highbrow.

"Get the Captain," commanded a vampire, tossing a mangled Bandit into the snow. He drew a small blade and marched for Highbrow.

A Bandit team leader broke rank and ran toward his captain, but was stopped short. A husky Shadowguard blocked his path and sent the Bandit sailing into the flames on the hospital roof. Amber-colored eyes locked with Highbrow's as a vampire stepped in front of him.

"The Kaiser wants you, Captain," said the vampire, in a menacing voice.

Highbrow kicked snow up into the Shadowguard's face and dashed toward a discarded AK-47 laying in the snow. Hurling himself forward, Highbrow slid on a patch of ice toward the rifle. The remaining Bandits came to his aid, encircling him and swinging their machetes as the dark figures closed in.

Odin stood at a window in the mess hall, picking off vampires trying to reach Highbrow. His steady, accurate gunfire kept the Shadowguard back, but reinforcements appeared around the side of the burning hospital, overwhelming the exhausted Bandits. Breaking through the mass of bodies, Highbrow made it to the door of the mess hall, continuing to fire at figures in black coats.

"Get in here," shouted Odin. "We can go out the back door!"

Highbrow used his rifle as a makeshift club fighting off two more vampires trying to get inside the mess hall. Betsy and the children gathered in windows, shooting back at the incoming vampires. Highbrow grabbed the latch to the door. Someone yanked his cap off and spun him in circles. Another push sent him stumbling forward as a sharp object sliced across his face. Unable to determine how many Shadowguard surrounded him, Highbrow swung his rifle back and forth as unseen hands pushed him. Laughter came from several directions as they apprehended him, lifting and tossing him into a snowdrift.

As Highbrow struggled to rise, a dark-haired young woman in a negligee appeared out of nowhere and rushed the Shadowguard. She vanished from sight, leaving countless bodies missing their heads. The Shadowguard retreated to the waterfall.

"What the hell?" Highbrow rose to his feet, dazed and confused.

"Protect the Captain," shouted Micah. The white-haired Dark Angel hurried over to Highbrow, along with the remaining six members of his team. "We won't let them get you, sir."

The snow turned red from the mess hall to the waterfall, as dozens of Shadowguard soldiers were dropped in twisted, freakish positions, every one missing their head.

Odin opened the door. "Are you alright, sir?"

"I'm fine, now the Earth Corps has arrived. Micah, come with me. The rest of you stay here with Odin and protect the children."

Highbrow set off with Micah toward the tunnel where the sick children were hiding, passing a familiar figure in the snow. A Dark Angel lay face down in the snow, bright red hair spread out in chaos. Micah let out a pitiful sound, stumbling. Ginger was dead.

Fighting continued at the mouth of the tunnel. The Bull Dogs were trying to hold back a large force of Shadowguard gathered at the entrance. Buccaneers leaned over the side of the lookout point, taking shots at whatever moved on the ground. Micah moved ahead in fury, attacking the enemy from behind, leaving Highbrow to take cover behind a tree. The captain fired at the Shadowguard scaling the cliff, some of them converging on the Buccaneers. Shots from the team ended. The Bull Dogs' line broke and Shadowguard entered the tunnel. The sounds of screaming children echoed in the darkness.

Highbrow ran forward determined to rally the Bull Dogs and stop the slaughter, but a hard form knocked him off his feet. He watched from the ground, stunned as the Shadowguard were being hurled out of the tunnel without their heads. Micah and the Bull Dogs formed a line at the tunnel, fighting off members of the Shadowguard who had yet to scale the cliff. Few vampires reached the top, with heads and corpses landing below.

"Anyone injured inside the cave?" asked Highbrow. He joined Micah and the Bull Dogs, standing inside the entrance to avoid splattering blood and falling bodies.

Micah shook his head, morose. "No serious injuries. Minor cuts and scrapes." He paused as a petite figure drenched in blood appeared. "Sir, it's China Star!"

In disbelief, Highbrow ran to her. Star locked her fierce gaze on him and fell to her knees. He dropped his pistol and pulled Star into his arms, hugging her while she pressed against him, trembling.

The sound of gunfire and screams ended, the camp was still. There were no signs of Cadence or the Earth Corps. Every last Shadowguard lay dead, and Star stood alone.

"She did that?" asked Micah, joining them. "How is it possible?"

"Get on the radio, Micah," Highbrow said. "Check in with Lt. Sterling. You Bull Dogs hurry to the lookout point and see to the Buccaneers."

"I just came from there. The Buccaneers are dead," said Star, pulling back. "One of the Shadowguard had a remote control, but he and the cyborg zombies won't be causing any more trouble. Pallaton's already retreated back to the Citadel. I doubt he'll return soon."

"How did you get here?" asked Highbrow. "I thought you were a prisoner?"

Star was barefoot and her lingerie was shredded. He removed his coat and covered her slender shoulders.

"I came here to warn you about Pallaton and his troops. I had the lead on him, so I dealt with the zombies, and then came to find you."

Her smile flashed white amidst the blood. "They didn't stand a chance against me. Won't the Kaiser be surprised when Pallaton returns with his story? I'm sure he'll make something up or be disgraced."

"You arrived just in time. I sent word to the Earth Corps and thought they answered the call, but that was you. I don't know what else to say. Thank you. Thank you for coming here. You saved us, Star."

"I had help. Your camp fought well, Highbrow."

Rose stepped out of the cave, holding a child in her arms. The doctor was injured protecting the children. Micah took the child from Rose and led the rest of children to the mess hall where Tandor waited, his body suit and face burned.

"It's a miracle you got here when you did, Star," said Rose, walking over to Star. She looked her over, satisfied she was uninjured. "You do not understand how relieved I was when you appeared in the tunnel. I'd given up hope. Many children would be dead if you hadn't arrived. But how did you become a mutant?"

"Mutant?" Star laughed. "Dragon gave me his blood and turned me. I'm a Chameleon, Doc. Not a mutant."

"Will you be staying, Star?" asked Highbrow. "I will not pretend I don't need your help, when it's obvious I do. At least until we get things under control."

She nodded. "For a while. I'll help with camp repairs and security, but then I'm leaving to join Cadence. I want to see her and Thor." She slid her arms into Highbrow's coat and zipped it up. "Come on, Rose. I need to get cleaned up and find something else to wear. Keep me company, will you? I have so much to tell you."

"Then report back to me! Both of you!" Highbrow watched the two women depart before walking to the mess hall.

By late evening, order was restored to the camp and repairs to the Moon Tower were in progress. The front entrance required snow ploughs to remove hundreds of zombies and body parts. Those fallen in battle included the War Gods, Buccaneers, Bandits, Monster Squad,

Blue Devils, most of the scavengers, and over half the Dark Angels. A mass funeral would be given at Midnight Falls.

Highbrow returned to the Freedom Army barracks and claimed the command center as his new quarters. He sent Private Odin to fetch cots and blankets. Tandor sat behind a desk, attempting to bring up the surveillance cameras. The cameras, landlines and shortwave radio, were all down making it impossible to contact Cadence.

"The Shadowguard knew where to strike," said Tandor. His dark eyebrows hung like thick feathers above his alert brown eyes. Smudges of filth covered his body suit and his right arm looked like someone used a rake in an attempt to remove the material. "Pallaton won't be greeted with open arms by the Kaiser for yet another failure to take this camp. Micah and Rose put too much trust in Pallaton. He may believe he's doing the right thing by not destroying the entire camp, but I left him with a permanent reminder that I no longer consider him a friend."

Highbrow noticed a few missing parts from the radio. Tandor had taken it apart and rebuilt it, without favorable results. "Can you get the radio to work?"

"It works, but something is blocking our transmission." Tandor turned up the volume and static filled the room. He was disgusted after trying every channel, and turned it off again. "There has to be a source close by that is causing this interference. The Citadel or another military base, I don't know. Until it's located and destroyed, though, we're not contacting anyone."

"Then the only alternative is to send someone to Cadence's camp. She asked for your help. They must be experiencing the same problem, and may have an idea what's causing it. Go pack your gear, Tandor. You're leaving."

Nomad and Micah appeared in the doorway. Both men had been busy making repairs. Splotches of soot and blood covered the biker's coat and face. Micah's white hair was in tangles, his jacket torn, and his features were gaunt. There were bits of dried blood where Micah had been crying. Nomad gave a quick account of their progress before the two sat down.

"It's snowing." Nomad stretched out his legs. "Star is anxious to head out to Cadence's camp. I could take both Star and Tandor in the Battle Beast. I wouldn't mind Micah going along in case we run into any more Shadowguard."

"You will if you drive," said Highbrow. "Tandor can leave on foot, but I need Star here. Both of you get something to eat and then make sure the generators are in working order. The Kaiser has been providing our camp with electricity because Colorado Springs has it, but once he cuts it off, we're in deep. I don't want those kids freezing to death."

Tandor stood up and hoisted his sword belt off the back of the chair. "While I'm gone, I suggest you reconsider moving this camp, Captain. Cadence can offer protection and safety for these kids. The only reason everyone's still alive is because the Kaiser doesn't know where she is, and he's hoping someone will leak the information. Another reason I can't have Nomad and Micah going with me."

"I have a good idea where her camp is," said Micah. "But don't worry. I'm not saying. Ever since she's left, I feel like this camp is being watched from the inside. I'm even beginning to doubt my own shadow. Be careful going over the mountains. The trails will be watched."

"If I can send help back," said Tandor, "I will, Captain. But you'd best keep guards at your door, day and night, in case they come back for you."

Rising from his chair, Micah saw Tandor out. Nomad unzipped his leather coat and pulled out a bottle of bourbon. He took a sip and stood to hand the bottle to Highbrow.

"You did good today. I'm proud of you, son."

Highbrow shook his head. "I don't deserve any credit. I lost five patrol teams and most of the Dark Angels died trying to protect me. Star is the only reason Pallaton failed. She showed up when we needed her most, but Raven let her go. I can't figure out either Pallaton or Raven, whether or not they're on our side or not, or why they remain at the Citadel."

"Because we need inside help. Without them we're in the dark."

Nomad lit up a cigar and sat down, puffing like a dragon. Highbrow found the smoke comforting, though he had stopped smoking after banning cigarettes from camp. It was a habit he didn't want the younger kids picking up. Micah returned long enough to see that guards were standing outside the door and left again.

"I can't figure out Micah either," said Highbrow. He sat in a chair behind his desk and took a sip of bourbon. "Vampires don't think like we do. Rose can't be any different, but she puts on a good act. I don't want to doubt their loyalty, but…"

"Then don't," said Nomad. "The man just lost his girlfriend, Highbrow. Ten Dark Angels survived the battle. There used to be thirty of them and they gave their lives defending this camp."

"I keep thinking all we have to do is hold on until my dad and the Army arrives, and I know they will. Even Cadence is confident they are coming. When my dad gets here, I want him to be proud of what I've accomplished. What we've accomplished. Maybe I should have let Pallaton take me and not fought back. I'm the one responsible for the lives of everyone here. I let them down today."

"Son, you need to stop carrying the weight of the world on your shoulders," said Nomad. "This isn't just about you. We're in this together. Say what you will about Pallaton, but if he'd come in here with Black Hawks, there wouldn't be anyone left alive."

"And if I hadn't kicked out Cadence? Would we have been better off? Say what you will, Nomad, but I made a big mistake. I shouldn't have sent her away. I know I should move the camp, but how can I when most of the children are sick or acting strange?"

Nomad reached into his coat pocket. He pulled out a stack of folded paper. "Betsy wanted me to give these to you. The little kids drawing the same thing over and over, and it's got my wife spooked." He tossed the stack over to Highbrow. "Take a look and tell me what you see."

Highbrow set aside the bottle, unfolded the paper and looked through dozens of children's drawings. They looked like nuclear missiles. Some had stars and stripes, some polka dots, and a few had weird shapes and symbols, shaped more like columns than nukes.

"Bombs? I can't think of any place around here where they have bombs. The Air Force fields are overrun with zombies, and without fighter pilots we can't get any planes off the ground."

"I thought it looked more like one of those big stones at Stonehenge. But if you say it's a bomb, maybe it is. Only place 'round here with bombs is NORAD. Cadence is a smart girl. If that's where she's relocated, she has bombs at her disposal. You said Picasso can contact survivors around the globe and you need satellites to do that. Skylab was amazing in its time and if I was her, it's where I would have gone. Of course, that means NORAD didn't survive the Scourge and the doors had to be wide open for them to get in."

Highbrow put aside the drawings. "The equipment went on the blink a few days ago, around the same time Cadence left Chief Chayton's camp and found a new home. Tandor said something is causing interference with our gear and it's close by. NORAD isn't far from here. It won't take Tandor long to get there even in this storm, or to figure out what's blocking our signals."

"Why are you keeping Star here?" asked Nomad. "Why didn't you let her go?"

"For protection. She's the fastest and strongest fighter in camp. If I had another dozen Stars, we could hold the fort a while longer. But I don't know if she's a Maker, and to tell the truth, I'm not that desperate to infect others. Not yet."

"Yes, you are. You need a volunteer, so I'm volunteering. Let's get over to Rose and at least ask her about it. Star isn't going to stay here forever, not when she's dying to go see Thor. If we're staying, we need stronger fighters."

Highbrow grabbed his gun and headed for the door as Odin appeared dragging in two cots and blankets. "Forget that for now, private. You're driving us to the hospital. I need to talk to Doctor Rose."

Once in the Jeep, Odin started singing *Jingle Bells*. He was off key, but no one cared. Nomad joined in with an impressive singing voice. Christmas was near, thought Highbrow, whether he was ready or not. He joined the singing.

Chapter Nine

*T*he dream weighed heavy in Cadence's mind.

She walked through a graveyard on an ancient path. The path stretched through a meadow lined with rock walls and yellow flowers. Passage of time eroded names etched on the tombstones. A tall, slender monolith carved from black stone stood prominent. It rose over twenty-feet with carvings of Celtic symbols adorning it. Rings of smaller white stones surrounded it, and bodies of dead rodents lay within the circle. At its base sat numerous human skulls in perfect rows.

The scene changed and Cadence found herself in a cavern looking at a crystal coffin looming in shadow. Inside laid a body holding a spear. She approached it and stared at the spear. She had seen it somewhere before and felt it meant something to her. When she placed her hand on the coffin it vibrated and a strange humming filled her ears.

Cadence heard a loud buzzing. The sound woke her and she looked at her bedside table. A digital message read 3:00 a.m.

The witching hour, she thought. At the same time for the past three nights she had the same dream. Each time she woke feeling scared and alone. She often had nightmares and this was no different. A clap of her hands and the lights turned on. Cadence rubbed her face. Her cheeks were cold and she could smell the odor of earth on her skin. A journal belonging to the room's prior tenant fell from her lap as she stood up. She must have dozed off while reading, however she couldn't remember much. A hot shower helped revive Cadence's spirits. She dried off and got dressed. No one kept normal hours anymore and she was relieved to find some friends having an early breakfast at the bunker's western-themed restaurant. Music hummed from an old-fashioned jukebox.

Lotus and Smack were in the kitchen while Blaze and Phoenix sat at the counter sipping their coffee. Cadence slid into a booth and scanned a menu. Lotus was a good cook and responsible for rebuilding and maintaining the kitchen. Smack enjoyed acting the waitress and hung out at the restaurant because it felt familiar to her.

Phoenix raised her coffee to welcome Cadence, and Cadence returned the nod. Coffee would do her nerves good and warm the coldness gnawing at her stomach.

Her eyes a little clearer now, Cadence noticed the journal on the seat beside her, sprinkled with blood. She didn't remember bringing it with her. This was the journal of Captain Richard Mallory. Cadence found him in her room, lying on the floor with both a revolver and this journal next to him. It gave a harrowing account of the months leading up to his death. The writing was archaic, too formal even for the military and the penmanship was flowery, with big loops and fancy letters. She only read a few pages each night, but his writing was so powerful she felt she knew him.

Among his clothes she found a jeweled dagger. She also found a gold pendant with a Celtic cross on a long chain. Both items looked like they came from a museum. She began carrying the dagger in her boot and wearing the necklace. She found no mention of either item in the journal thus far.

Flipping through the pages, Cadence came across a drawing of a spear labeled, *Spear of Destiny*. She frowned. There was a quote from the Bible when Jesus was pierced by a Roman spear while hanging on the cross. Someone had circled the word 'spear' with blue ink, and had written a note about the blood of Christ being on the spear.

Before the Scourge, she had read about Hitler searching for the

Spear of Destiny. Hitler thought he could use the spear to win the war. After World War II, it was reported the Americans had found it and returned home with it.

Cadence jumped when a shadow fell across her table.

"Steady there," said Thor. "Didn't mean to startle you."

Cadence smiled, tucking the journal away. "Sorry, I haven't been sleeping much. Sit and keep me company. Coffee is on its way."

Thor slid in across from her. "Waitress! We're paying customers! Some service over here!" He laughed when Smack revealed her single, middle finger in his direction.

"Must you be so loud?" Cadence winced.

"Sorry. I get a kick out of pretending to be an annoying patron. It makes it feel like an ordinary day in the 'hood.'" He picked up her menu and looked it over. "Sometimes I wish we had meat other than venison. Guess I'll go with pancakes."

"What do you know about monoliths? I've been dreaming of the English countryside and a giant monolith in a graveyard. It doesn't make any sense."

At that moment, Smack came over and placed two mugs and a pitcher of coffee on the table. She smacked her gum and gave Thor a once-over. "Whatcha want for breakfast, hot stuff? Oatmeal or pancakes?"

"Scrambled eggs and four strips of bacon, sweet thing," Thor said, placing his arm on the back of his seat.

"No eggs or bacon. Canned soup, oatmeal, fried rice, or pancakes. It's what we have. What about you, commander? I also made butterscotch pudding. They had no shortage of pudding here, but no canned-beef or tuna. The pudding has a shelf life of like, forever. And of course we have beans. Baked beans. Lima beans. Black eyed-beans. And green beans. But if you ask me, I'd go with the pancakes."

"Pancakes!" Cadence and Thor declared in unison.

Smack skipped across the room to the kitchen, bundled in an oversized sweater pulled over black tights. Tall boots met the sweater at the knees. Her reddish-blonde hair swung in braids across her back.

"Underneath that chipped fingernail polish and bubble gum is one tough little kid," said Thor. "Speaking of tough, Star escaped the Citadel. Tandor got here a little while ago with news that the Kaiser sent zombie cyborgs under the control of the Shadowguard to attack the camp. Star showed up just in time to save their butts."

"Wait a minute. Were there any casualties during the attack? Highbrow is lucky he wasn't captured and his camp wiped out. They should come here. I told Highbrow to come here, but he's being stubborn."

"Yeah. They lost a lot. Highbrow has asked that you to send help. Do you want to go with me? I was hoping you would. I could care less about Highbrow, but I want to see Star. Plus, while the Dark Angels are at the Citadel getting our people out, we don't have to plan a rescue, so you've got time."

Thor had changed since the days at Pike's Peak. He was a bully then, but now was one of her most dependable team members. She understood his desire to see Star. She wanted to see her too. Leaving NORAD after the camp had been attacked with news of incoming bounty hunters seemed like trouble. She baptized her coffee with sugar. It still tasted awful.

"I don't think I should leave. Take Whisper and Lachlan."

"If Whisper goes, Blaze will want to go," said Thor. "I'd rather take Phoenix. You ever notice Phoenix talking to animals? She can coax a deer right to her, which is why we have venison."

"Smack can talk to the dead. I saw her do it the other day. Phoenix and Smack both have new gifts. Heck, even I'm getting stronger. I might be slow to develop my skills, but I've noticed a change. I feel more in tune with everything these days."

"Maybe I should take Smack in case we run into zombies on the way, she can tell them to attack the Citadel." Thor grinned. "You look tired. I'll deal with whatever is going on at Seven Falls. Stay and get some rest." He noticed the journal and reached for it. "Now I know why you're not sleeping. You're keeping a diary."

"It belonged to Captain Mallory, my room's previous steward. I read a little each night before bed, but a lot of it is in Latin." Cadence pushed the journal toward him. "I was hoping Lachlan would show up. He speaks Latin. It might have valuable information. Like a government conspiracy."

"You sure you want Lachlan to go with me? Maybe you and he should read this in bed together."

Cadence laughed. "You need to mind your own business."

While Thor flipped through the journal, Cadence watched her friends at the counter. Phoenix was downing a stack of pancakes. Lotus served Blaze a bowl of soup. And Cadence noticed she showed no interest, spinning her spoon around the bowl.

A subtle gasp from Thor caught Cadence's attention. He was pulling a folded piece of paper from a slit in the spine of the journal. Thor offered her the paper. She opened it and was shocked at what she saw. It was a detailed picture of a monolith.

"Now do you think I'm crazy?" asked Cadence.

"A little. I don't believe in coincidence. Wonder what that is and why Mallory drew it? And no, I don't read Latin. You need the Irishman."

"Here you go!" Smack returned with two plates of pancakes. "No eggs. No bacon. No toast. There's syrup, and plenty of it."

Thor pushed the journal aside and dug into his food with gusto. Cadence took her time cutting the pancakes into tiny pieces before taking a bite. She kept looking at the drawing. She lifted her fork for a bite, missed her mouth, and dripped a glob of syrup on the picture. Annoyed, she tried wiping it off with her finger and smeared one of the runes drawn on the stone.

"Will you eat?" asked Thor. "Stop worrying about it. People dream about the last thing they see at night. Trust me, it's not a government conspiracy. That type of crazy thinking stirred everybody up when the Scourge broke out. People said the government released the virus, when everyone knows it was..." he paused, "a virus picked up by a soldier in Afghanistan who returned and spread it here. Yep. Must be a government conspiracy, just not ours."

"I've never seen this drawing before, Thor. You just found it."

"Then eat up, show Lachlan, and figure out your little mystery. Maybe you can speak to the dead, too. Maybe Mallory's ghost is visiting you at night." Thor stood up.

"Where are you going?"

"To find Lachlan and Whisper. Then I'm off to see my girlfriend!"

Thor headed out. He brushed past Sheena and almost knocked her over. The petite teen entered with Moon Dog, a tall, lanky Navajo with a white streak marking his long, black hair. Wearing simple jeans and sweaters, it was rare to see them in human form. Blaze left without saying a word. The new arrivals sat on either side of Phoenix.

"We need a team meeting," said Cadence. She slid the journal into her coat pocket and brought the dishes to the counter. "There's been an attack at the camp. Thor is heading over there with Lachlan and Whisper. Is Blaze okay? She took out of here fast. What's up?"

Sheena spoke up first. "Whisper was out all night. He and Lachlan went to the fourth lake around midnight. I think they were hooking up surveillance cameras down there. Blaze went to find them and you know how pissy she gets when Whisper isn't at her beck and call."

"What time is it?" asked Cadence.

Phoenix glanced at her watch. "About 4 a.m. You want me to head Blaze off before there's trouble in Love Land?"

Cadence looked worried. Yeah, go check it out and tell Blaze I want to see her. Lotus and Smack, you two go see if Lachlan and Whisper are in their rooms, or at the arcade. I'm going to talk to Tandor about the attack."

Smack saluted. "Yes, sir. I mean, ma'am." She headed out with Lotus.

"I overheard you talking to Thor," said Phoenix, intuitive. "I've been having the same dream too, but then I've got a poster of a monolith on my bedroom wall."

"Okay, now I'm worried," said Cadence. "I don't believe in coincidence."

Moon Dog and Sheena glanced at one another, stripped, and transformed into animals. The tawny werepuma and midnight-black werewolf trotted toward the door. Phoenix whistled at them and they shot through the door together.

Cadence was right behind them. She picked up the light scent of perfume in the corridor and knew it belonged to Blaze, but she wasn't headed toward the lakes. Following the scent down the hallway, and turning several corners, she arrived at the armory. She opened the door and turned on the lights. Blaze stood in the middle of the room staring off into space, holding her M4 carbine, with grenade-launcher. Her behavior was anything but normal.

"You okay?" asked Cadence. "What do you need that for?"

Blaze spun around and pointed the weapon at Cadence. "Stay out of my way, Whisper needs my help."

Cadence jumped behind a table, and Blaze bolted for the door. Rolling to her side, she pulled radio and contacted Freeborn.

"We've got a problem," said Cadence. "Blaze just left the armory locked and loaded. She said Whisper needs her help, and she seemed spooked. Tell Thor to meet me at the lake. The rest of the team is already on their way."

The radio fuzzed.

Cadence ran toward the stairs leading to the underground lakes. She didn't think she was running fast enough, but when she caught up with Freeborn and Thor on the next level, she took pride in her speed. Another flight of stairs led into the heart of the compound, with loud generators and pipes running across the ceiling and walls. They came to the last door in the hallway. *No. 4.*

Thor removed the rifle from his shoulder and opened the metal door. "Ladies first."

The lights were still out. Phoenix, Moon Dog, and Sheena stood beside the lake. Red flares around them created an eerie glow. Phoenix tossed another flare to the opposite side. The black water rippled, as if something lived beneath its surface.

Cadence broke into a nervous sweat. On the far side of the lake stood a monolith, hidden by shadow. Hundreds of dead animals surrounded it and lined the lakeside. The cavern reeked of death and decay.

"Are Lachlan and Whisper here?" Cadence asked, keeping her voice soft. "Where is Blaze? I thought she was coming here?"

Phoenix lit another flare and tossed it toward the monolith. A figure stood next to the stone, illuminated by the red flash. A monolith resembling the one in Cadence's dreams was exposed too, but it was not the same one from Mallory's journal. The cut of the stone was at an angle reaching to a point, while the drawing reflected a flat top.

Blaze was standing in front of the stone monument. She held her rifle close and stood motionless.

"What the hell is Blaze doing?" asked Thor. "Blaze? What's your boggle? Get over here. Can't you see all of those dead animals?" His voice echoed through the chamber, causing large ripples to move across the surface of the lake. Something disturbed the water, drawing his gaze. A long, spiked tail slid beneath the top of the water. "Are there eels in the lake? 'Cause I just saw a big one."

The werepuma and werewolf crouched low, tails held straight out, their attention fixed on what stirred the water.

"Forget about the eel," said Phoenix. "I want to know what's up with the giant rock. This must be one of those supernatural objects the government collects. Like in Indiana Jones. I bet that rock caused the death of those animals. Shouldn't someone get Blaze away from it?"

Thor turned around and shouted. "Blaze, you damn fool! Step clear of that rock. It's poisoning the air or something. Do you hear me? Move aside!"

The monolith hummed and the ground trembled. It opened at the center, allowing a green light to spread. Freeborn and Thor moved forward, but Cadence wasn't about to let them be harmed. She pushed through them and ran toward the monument as fast as she could.

Blaze was bathed in a strange glow of red and green light. She screamed.

Cadence launched herself through the air, tackling Blaze and slamming into the cave wall. She lifted an unconscious Blaze over her shoulder, standing.

A voice shouted a warning. Cadence spun toward the great stone, as if apprehended by an invisible hand being pulled toward its widening center. Light spilled out, surrounding Cadence and Blaze as they were sucked inside the stone. Everything turned black. Cadence felt her body spinning and had the sensation of falling. She screamed as she landed on soft, wet ground.

Cadence opened her eyes and realized she was lying on a grassy knoll. The breeze was cool on her face and the scent of rain hung in the air. A storm was approaching and she heard the sound of a tower bell in the distance.

"Maybe you should get up," said Blaze.

Scrambling, Cadence stood and assessed the damage from the fall, found everything in-tact, and brushed off. The journal remained in her pocket, and her sidearm was still in its holster. "Where the hell are we?"

"How should I know?" Blaze sounded pissed. "The last thing I remember was Whisper contacting me on the radio to say he and Lachlan had found a big, creepy stone at the fourth lake." She picked up the heavy gun off the ground. "I wasn't going to shoot you back at the armory. I just didn't have time to explain what was going on."

"All you had to do was tell me about the monolith," said Cadence. "I've been dreaming about one for three nights and now I know why. This isn't a government conspiracy, but they were using the monolith for something. I guess that's what we have to figure out now."

Blaze nodded. "Whisper and Lachlan must be here. We have to find them and another stone monument and maybe we can get back home."

Cadence saw a castle in the distance and a nearby graveyard. They were close to the sea. She could smell the ocean and noticed sea gulls flying low.

"This place looks just like my dream. There's the church and the same graveyard. That's where the monolith was. Let's head to it and try to get our bearings."

"You want to go to a graveyard? This place could be crawling with zombies." Blaze held up her rifle and looked through the scope. "Nope. No zombies."

"I think we're in England. But there are no telephone lines or paved roads. The castle doesn't look like it's in ruin, and the graveyard has seen recent use." Everything seemed surreal, insane even.

Blaze was ready to throw a fit. "Well, that's just great. You don't know where we are, or what we're doing here, and it's going to rain soon."

"All I can think is the monolith is some type of displacement device that Mallory was studying."

Blaze eyed her commander. "Displacement? As in…teleportation?"

Cadence shook her head. "I'm taking about time, Blaze. We aren't in the right time. Not anymore."

"That's impossible!"

"Can you explain what we're seeing?"

Blaze huffed, for once lacking a response.

"Anyway," Cadence continued, "we need to find something else to wear. If I'm right and we meet anyone on the road, they'll be suspicious. Our clothes, weapons, and accents don't exactly fit in. The last thing I want is to be tossed into a dungeon or burned at the stake."

"I can handle myself if we run into Sir Mordred."

They walked through tall, wet grass to a path thick with mud. Fresh graves with simple wooden crosses and older moss-covered gravestones dotted the yard. Celtic crosses marked most graves, with skulls and angels holding roses marking others. A deteriorating stone church stood next to the graveyard. A murder of crows flew out of the failing roof at their approach, startling both young women.

"There's a lot of fresh graves," said Blaze, pausing to get a close look. Her shoulders slumped. "Okay. Maybe you were right."

Cadence came to look over her friend's shoulder. "Well, this is interesting. 1318, 1332, 1344, 1344, 1344. Must be a popular year to die," quipped Blaze. "Wonder what they died of? Or if they'll rise when it gets dark. It's almost dark."

Cadence could hear the desperation in her chattering. She patted Blaze's shoulder. "We'll be okay. The Scourge hasn't happened yet, remember? So no zombies. We'll get through this. Besides, if you're right and Whisper is here, we need to find him first."

The sun set with a finality that filled Cadence with dread. Gazing at the newest graves, she placed her hand over her chest and felt the cross beneath her sweater. If anything catastrophic were to happen, it would be at night. A thunderclap announced a sudden downpour. Glancing at one another, they ran through the graveyard, sliding in the mud. They were soaked when they reached the church. Hoping they would not find trouble waiting inside, Cadence opened the door and led the way in.

Chapter Ten

"*T*he Kaiser will see you now. Enter and wait for instructions."

Logan glanced at the robot-like guard and wiped his sweaty palms on his long, wool coat. He wasn't sure he wanted to enter the Kaiser's throne room. Once known as the Cadet Chapel it was the most impressive building on the campus. History and tradition gave way to the Crystal Palace, serving the vampires' need for flair.

Lacking any crystal in its construction, it was a slender, triangular structure built of aluminum, glass, and steel. Stained glass adorned its walls, and it was crowned with seventeen pointed spires. The doors opened wide and Logan stepped inside. He brushed snow off his wool coat before handing it to the guard.

"Have a seat in back," the guard said. He closed the doors and returned to his post.

Vampires filled the chapel. Renovations morphed the Protestant chapel, being stripped of its religious icons and transformed into something dark and macabre. Thirteen mahogany pews lined the room. Black candles sat aflame on iron stands towering behind an altar. A gold throne christened a round dais, raised high enough to overlook the assembly. The pews were backed by World War I propellers, reassembled to look like crossed swords. The pinnacled ceiling soared 99-feet-high, with stained glass windows between the tetrahedrons. A golden gargoyle perched on a ledge above the altar. The gray-white terrazzo floor was covered with black rugs or animal pelts, and several ancient statues stood as sentinels against the walls—grotesques, with giant wings and sharp claws.

Shadowguard occupied the first row. Logan sat alone on the last row. He leaned forward and tapped the shoulder of a woman in a red cloak. Her silver-haired companion glanced at Logan as he whispered into her ear. The woman spun and flashed her fangs.

"I just wanted to know what was going on," Logan whispered. "Is there a wedding?"

"Silent. It's a ceremony. New recruits are being inducted into the Shadowguard." The woman gave Logan a hard look. "I don't know why the Kaiser wants you in the Shadowguard. I know who you are, Agent Logan."

"Yep, I'm the 'Man of the Year.'" Logan sat back and crossed one leg over the other.

The Kaiser entered through a side door, wearing a blood-red robe covered with symbols Logan recognized as demonic. The winged shadow followed behind. Master and shadow came to a halt before a sleek marble altar.

The audience remained quiet as the Kaiser claimed the throne. He clapped his hands and twelve vampires in black trench coats filed in and knelt before the altar. A bald priest robed in black followed the initiates. The priest placed a jeweled goblet on the altar beside three human skulls and an assortment of bones. The priest faced the twelve vampires and spread his hands out across the altar.

"Tonight, you will take your oaths to join the Brotherhood of the Shadowguard. Each of you will swear faithful service to the Kaiser. To him alone you will offer your worship as the one true power on Earth. To him alone you will offer your lives in sacrifice. To him alone you now belong from this day forth, until your last. Now repeat the oath."

The vampires repeated the priest's words. The vow ended with, "We will not lie, steal, or cheat, nor tolerate among us anyone who does."

Logan had seen those words printed in many places around the

Citadel. It had been the motto of the Air Force cadets. The priest approached and offered the jeweled goblet to each vampire, who partook. With every initiate, he dipped his finger in the cup and traced a symbol upon their foreheads. Each one stood and bowed before the Kaiser, then exited the chapel.

The silver-haired vampire turned to glare at Logan with bright, violet eyes. The color of his eyes marked him as one of Salustra's children. Logan remembered meeting Jean-Luc at one of the Kaiser's dinner parties.

"You were to have joined the new initiates," said Jean-Luc. "Refusing to be turned vampire will not win you any friends here, human. You get one more chance. Don't blow it."

Logan didn't need to be reminded he was the only human present in the chapel. The side door opened once more. Two guards in red ushered in a girl in her early teens, dressed in white. They forced her to kneel at the altar. The priest approached her with the goblet, and stroked her head. Logan did all he could to restrain himself when the priest slashed her throat with a dagger. Blood splattered on the altar. The guards held the girl's body as the priest filled the goblet with blood.

"Bring me the virgin's blood," said the Kaiser, in a deep, masculine voice. He sat forward in his chair, reaching for the goblet. The priest offered it to his master. "In my name, I accept this blood sacrifice." He slurped from the goblet, sending drops streaming down his chin. He handed the goblet to the priest and waved him away. "Now, bring me the next recruit."

"You're next," Jean-Luc said, turning around again to annoy Logan. "You are to become a vampire tonight. I came here to watch."

Logan felt far from polite. "Up yours, pal."

A man in a red, hooded robe appeared at the end of Logan's row and motioned for Logan to follow. He stood attempting to get a look under the hood. Logan flinched when he saw two gleaming green eyes. The cloaked figure remained at his side, silent, terrifying, and smelling worse than sewage. Logan stood at the altar as the priest approached him. *They are mistaken if they think I will drink from that goblet*, Logan thought to himself. He lifted his head higher when he realized he was taller than both the cloaked figure and the priest.

"I suggest you wipe that smirk off your face," said the priest.

Logan looked beyond the priest and met the Kaiser's gaze. "You fixed the place up real nice." His smile widened. "Trick or treat?"

The Kaiser jumped off his throne. Someone in the audience gasped—their master never left his throne to address a subject. "Kneel!"

The figure in red moved fast, twisting Logan's arm behind his back and forcing him to the ground. The priest faced Logan, holding the knife and goblet.

"Take another step, friend, and I'll break your neck," said Logan.

"What's that?" The Kaiser came from behind the altar to stand before Logan. He leveled his gaze with Logan's. "This is a Maker. He will turn you tonight. Isn't this what you wanted, Logan? To be a Shadowguard?"

"I changed my mind."

"If you refuse to join my army and become a vampire, then what further use are you?"

Logan looked at the cloaked figure. "Mind letting go, pal? We're talking here."

The Kaiser nodded and the hooded figure released him. Logan scrambled to his feet. The Kaiser was shorter than Logan, but his dark shadow much taller, an ominous cloud behind its master. Logan reconsidered his options, and for once remained quiet.

The Kaiser laughed, and the congregation joined him. The crowd grew silent when the Kaiser stepped forward and slapped Logan across the face.

"Other cheek too?" Logan asked, unable to hold his tongue. The next blow knocked him on his back. He pushed up on an elbow.

"You try my patience, Logan. Since you were a boy I have dreamed of this night, but you've grown cynical and churlish. Now get up, I'm weary of your games. Why do you insist that Dr. Leopold study flowers? Does a flower hold the answer I'm looking for, Logan?"

The red cloaked figure pulled Logan to his feet at the Kaiser's nod. The shadow hovered over the altar, blocking light from the candles and plunging the chapel into complete darkness. Logan knew he was experiencing pure evil. Glowing eyes and clouded stars above offered the only light.

"Perhaps it's my fault for indulging you all these years. Perhaps I'm at fault for not making expectations clear. However, a wise ruler does not slaughter those who may yet be useful." The Kaiser held out his hand. An onyx ring, carved with a circle encompassing two curved arrows, engulfed his left index finger. "Kiss my ring and all will be forgiven."

Feeling sick, Logan sucked it up and kissed the ring. The strange shadow backed off, sliding behind the throne, revealing light from the candles once more.

"All better now," said the Kaiser. "You will learn obedience, Logan. If you ever dishonor me again, I will put you in the arena. Now get out. Return to your cage."

Logan turned and walked the aisle. A Shadowguard waited for him at the last row. He felt his luck change. It was Bechtel. "Am I to go with you?"

"Keep your mouth shut, and follow me human."

A black Cadillac waited outside. Bechtel entered the passenger side after shoving Logan into the backseat. A young female vampire was driving. Adorned with pink lipstick and a French manicure, she was the prettiest Shadowguard by far.

A stern look from Bechtel kept Logan from making any jokes. As they drove away from the Crystal Palace, he hoped they would keep going. Disappointment set in when they drove down a street, made a few turns, and ended up back at the science building.

"Oh, come on. I wasn't that rude. You saw them murder that poor girl. Like I'd want to wear the trench coat after that," Logan said. "It's not that I have higher aspirations, but I don't want to be a vampire. I enjoy eating steak and a fine salad. All you guys eat is popcorn and drink blood."

"You're an idiot," said the driver. "Now get out of my car."

"Who is she, Bechtel? She's bossy. I like her."

"Get out." The female driver turned toward her companion. "Bechtel, please. I know all about this human, and I might bite him. He's rude."

"Yes he is," said Bechtel. "I'll take him."

Bechtel refused Logan her name, but he grasped her arm with affection, like a close friend. A very close friend, Logan noted when the woman leaned over and kissed Bechtel's cheek. Bechtel pulled back, though he was smiling when he got out of the car. Logan jumped out and slipped on the ice. No one caught him. He clung to the door, until he gained his footing, glaring at Bechtel.

"This is the lab. Why did you bring me here?"

Logan steadied himself and traversed the sidewalk with caution as Bechtel accompanied him to the front door. He opened the door and stepped inside. The vampire followed as they walked toward the lab.

"You don't approve of my methods, I get that. But I am consistent. Rude, unpleasant, and I tend to make jokes at inappropriate times," Logan stated.

"You said you'd help us," said Bechtel. "It's obvious you're not serious, nor do you care you jeopardized everyone's safety by mocking the Kaiser. You have three days, Logan. On the third evening, I need you to create a distraction. Hold the attention of the Shadowguard long enough so I can get you and Cadence's people out of here. If you want to stay, tell me now and I'll do this alone."

Logan removed his wool coat and draped it over his arm. "This isn't personal, Bechtel. I didn't mean to make you mad. I'll figure out a way to provide a diversion for you, but make sure you don't leave me behind. After tonight, I don't think I have many more days to live as a human. I want out of here."

"Blow up the lab," said Bechtel. "You know the ingredients to mix and have everything at your fingertips. Just remember it's not to blow until Friday, three days from now. Around dinner time would be perfect. Then, I'll help you escape."

"Won't be a problem. I have a knack for blowing things up."

The vampire smiled, revealing tiny fangs. "Be careful. Dr. Leopold and his kind dislike humans. Every demon does. They are cunning and clever. Do not underestimate the vescali, Logan."

Logan wanted to run in the other direction now. "Are you serious? You know what they are? They're a myth, and far worse than any vampire. If the Kaiser is depending on them, it's no wonder he never gets what he wants."

Bechtel caught Logan by the collar. He was furious. The vampire slammed Logan into the wall, who laughed as he noticed the guards watching. Bechtel said nothing and stormed off. The guards stopped laughing. Logan threw his shoulders back, gave his neck a jerk and opened the door. The stench was overwhelming.

Worse than usual, thought Logan. He tossed his coat over a chair and slid on a white lab coat.

Several lab attendants looked up as Logan meandered around the room. He studied labels on bottles and boxes, mentally rehearsing the ingredients needed to construct a chemical bomb. He pocketed a watch, some wire, and a few other items before approaching a group in the back of the lab, as they peered into a cage.

"Logan? Is that you?" asked the female occupant.

Barbarella crouched at the far side of the cage. She held a blood-splattered lab coat against her nude body. The attendants stared at Logan, muttering to each other when he gave them a dirty look. They moved away and Logan scanned Barbarella, assessing her injuries. Her arm was injured and several fingers were missing.

"You have to help me. Pallaton is no longer my guardian. That bastard Bechtel now owns Red Hawk and Cricket. I don't know what they did with the Dynamic Duo. All of Pallaton's fighters were given to someone else, but they won't tell me why. Tell these idiots I can't regenerate missing fingers." Barbarella held out her injured hand. "They think I can regrow fingers. But you know I can't do that!" Her voice cracked with desperation.

"What about Luna?" asked Logan. He was fond of the werepuma.

"The Kaiser gave her to Raven as a pet." Barbarella inched forward. "I heard the guards talking. They said Star escaped last night. You have to help me escape."

"I'll figure something out. Wrap that rag around your hand so you don't lose any more blood. These demons aren't interested in a naked woman. Trust me."

Logan turned around and glared at the medical staff, wishing he had a gun. He would shoot every one of them.

"Where is Dr. Leopold? Haven't you idiots figured out by now you can't slice up modern-day therianthropes and expect them to regrow a limb? This isn't the motherland, gentlemen. Maybe you're used to seeing regeneration, but she's not an Old One."

An ugly man with a skinny neck and wrinkled skin glared at Logan. He appeared to be in charge. Logan had not seen him before, not that he paid close attention to Leopold's people. Under the fluorescents, he could see blue veins bulging near the surface of his skin. The lab assistant was bald, like all vescali, and possessed no pupils in his black eyes. Logan felt the same disgust when Leopold glared at him.

"I've just returned from the Crystal Palace," said Logan. "The Kaiser isn't pleased with your lack of results. I revealed to him that Dr. Leopold is stalling. You'll make him an immortal vampire wife before Friday, or you will be punished."

"You're lying," said the ugly vescali. "I'm Trotsky. I'm in charge here."

"Then maybe you'll listen when I say the key to controlling the virus is a flower called foxglove, also known as dead man's fingers. In small amounts, it can kill a human, but used with care, it can save lives. It contains cardiac glycosides and during the ingestion phase it produces sugar and aglycones, affecting the heart muscles. I believe this is the flower the bee that stung Cadence collected nectar from, and it altered her metabolism. Of course I'm not a scientist, but I do read books," he said, on a roll. "I also object to your treatment of that werepuma. Take another finger and I'll cut your balls off. That is, if you nasty little goblins have any."

Logan expected at least one of the vescali to take interest in foxglove, but not one blinked. He gave up trying to educate them and wondered if giving Trotsky a beating might be what the doctor ordered.

"The girl is ours to do with what we want," said Trotsky.

"Barbarella is a Class B fighter," said Logan. "Pallaton is her guardian."

"Pallaton doesn't own slaves anymore." The monster eyed the teen, gleaming. "He lost that right when Captain Highbrow defeated his army this morning. He's yet to return. It's assumed Pallaton is dead, so his slaves were given to Bechtel. Bechtel didn't want this one. You know how vampires are."

"If you creeps had any brains, you'd keep her as a fighter and make money. Money have any interest to you? Don't you like to buy things? Booze, drugs, women? You don't care about a cure."

Trotsky hissed and curled his hands into fists. A vein in his forehead turned bright purple and throbbed. "What we do with the werepuma is our concern. Things you find valuable do not interest us, Agent Logan. Only science holds any interest to our kind. We have given her a new serum to see if she can now regenerate. If it disturbs you so much, I'll inject her with a synthetic version of chameleon blood and see if you like her as a little cat. One drop to a therianthrope and they never turn human again."

Logan had heard enough. He grasped Trotsky by the throat, catching the demon off guard, and squeezed with all his might.

He had to know what demons were capable of. There were dozens of species of demons, but the vescali were not known for strength. The demon's eyes bugged out of his head and his cheeks turned bright purple. Feeling something pressing against his ribs, Logan looked down and noticed a scalpel sticking out of his side. It wasn't deep. Releasing the demon, Logan stepped back and pulled the scalpel out. As the demon's cruel eyes glinted, Logan threw off his lab coat, reached into his pocket and wielded a small knife. With a flick of his thumb, the blade discharged. Logan snarled as he sliced into the demon's throat. Blood spewed as the demon screamed.

"Do...something," Trotsky gurgled to his companions.

Logan flashed his knife and a vicious smile. No one came near him. They surrounded Trotsky, watching with fascination as he collapsed to his knees. Logan landed a kick in the side and reveled in the demon's groan.

"Go pick some flowers, you little imps. Chameleon blood covers this blade. It's toxic to vescali. Then again, let's just watch him die, shall we?"

"Interesting," chimed one of the attendants. "One of you get a blood sample from Trotsky and analyze it. And someone locate Dr. Leopold. Tell him we have a breakthrough. We should have tested this on Trotsky days ago."

The demon attendant looked at Logan and smiled, not at all upset. Logan stared at the rest of the workers in the lab. Each one turned toward him and smiled, revealing mouths full of shark-like teeth.

Logan kept his knife raised. "I take it you don't like this guy?"

"Not really. He's a brownnoser," said the attendant.

"Yes, a brownnoser," they all repeated.

Trotsky stopped moaning. His face turned a blotchy red, and he appeared to be running a fever. Lifting him from the floor, lab workers carried Trotsky to an operating table and swarmed him, leaving Logan unattended. He rushed to unlock Barbarella's cage.

She sobbed into Logan's chest. "Thank you, thank you."

Logan put his knife arm around her and helped the injured teenager stand. No one bothered them. A scream came from Trotsky as an excited giggle rippled through the room. Logan glanced over his shoulder in disgust as he walked Barbarella through the lab doors.

They reached the front doors of the science building. Two Shadowguard watched, but made no move to stop them.

"Turn into a werepuma and head for Seven Falls," said Logan, thankful it was dark and no moon was cast. "Rose will take care of you. Tell her I'm doing what she asked."

"I don't understand. Why are you helping me?"

"Because you asked. Don't cross the courtyard. Go around the building to the forest. Stick to mountain trails and avoid the roads. They may come looking for you."

Wasting no time, Barbarella morphed into a large, black werepuma, bolted forward and vanished around the side of the building. Search lights hit the front of the building and Logan walked back inside. A lab attendant waited for him.

"It's a miracle," said the bald man. "You must come back, Agent Logan. Trotsky…he's changed into his true form, but he can't change back. It's precisely how it was for all the therianthropes injected. He's unable to turn back into his human form. It's incredible. Please, you must come back with me."

"What for?" asked Logan. "I cut the guy's neck open."

"And we thank you. I'll care for your wound. Trotsky had no right to harm you. We're furious with him for doing so. I promise no one is angry with you, Agent Logan. We're so excited about the results. We wanted to tell you before fetching Dr. Leopold. We'll do whatever you want, even if it means picking flowers."

Logan was dumbfounded. "I helped you guys out?"

"Oh, yes. It's because of you we've progressed in solving the riddle of chameleon blood. Hopefully, Trotsky will live and be stronger than ever."

This was not what Logan wanted to hear.

Chapter Eleven

*T*he Night Market cuddled into the city's former Fine Arts Buildings like a stuffed bear in the arms of a spoiled child. It was a marketplace for vampires to barter for goods, ranging from slaves to fine art. Building-sized, purple and black banners featuring various gargoyles extended from the roof on long poles while torches flickered in the snow-laden courtyard. Guests in fine apparel arrived to attend the slave auction in the theater.

Raven walked hand-in-hand with Salustra from the limo to the glass-walled building. They accompanied Queen Cinder, Lord Cerberus, and Jean-Luc. The little queen and lord dressed like a fairy-tale princess and prince, in elaborate costumes stitched with gold thread and matching crowns. Cinder led Stephan on a leash. The golden-eyed werewolf trotted at her side, snarling at anyone who approached his queen.

Not to be upstaged, Raven donned a lengthy, crushed-red velvet opera cloak over a midnight-black dress followed by her new pet, Luna. The werepuma wore a collar with diamonds and trotted close to Raven's heels. Escorted by Captain Bechtel, the disgraced Pallaton's replacement, Raven sauntered forward. A dozen Shadowguard followed.

"Tonight was to have been my engagement dinner," said Raven, as they ascended the stairs to the entrance. "I'm sure the Kaiser has his reasons for the delay. I intend to spend lavishly on a new fighter. His money. My bag is filled with diamonds."

The lobby illuminated red and purple as the crowd filtered into the theater, taking their seats. An elevator delivered Raven's entourage to a private box on the second floor. Bechtel removed Raven's cloak and remained standing while his men fanned out and framed her companions. The two therianthropes lay at their mistress' feet casual and uninterested.

Bechtel offered Raven a playbill. "The auction will begin soon, Duchess. If you would like to purchase a fighter, nod and I will make the bid."

Jean-Luc leaned across Salustra. "Duchess, these slaves hail from all over the world. Vampires are expensive and to be sold last. They will start with zombies, then advance to therianthropes, cyborgs, humans, and vampires."

"I can read," snapped Raven. She flipped through the playbill, reading each fighter's bio. She found one that looked interesting.

Loki was from Italy, and had once been a fellow Viking and friend, but that life was far removed from her now. His owner, Salvatore D'Aquilla, was selling the champion for one-million in valuable jewels, or traded for one-hundred humans. The fine print listed two more fighters being auctioned by D'Aquilla: Skye and Monkey, who Raven also knew from the survivors' camp.

"I want Loki," said Raven. "He's a chameleon, which is why he's so expensive and why I want him. A wedding gift for the Kaiser. He likes mutants."

Salustra leaned toward Raven. "Why not someone else? Several fighters from Greece and Germany are appealing."

"Because I want a winner, not a loser. Did you see the photos of those cyborgs? They are disgusting. I won't own a common zombie cyborg. You can pick them up off the street and outfit them with a computer. As for humans, they don't last long in the arena; they are food. Nor do I wish to own a tarnished vampire." She leaned down to pet Luna on the head. The werepuma let out a soft purr. "You're a good girl."

"It's starting," said Salustra.

Vampires filled the auditorium. A European power-metal band performed from the orchestra pit, creating a dark, lusty atmosphere. A vampire served Cinder blood and champagne. Salustra took a glass from the server, smiling at Raven.

"Thank you for asking me to attend tonight."

"My pleasure. Now be quiet. I want to look at these freaks without being bothered by a bunch of chatter." Raven leaned back, crossing her legs and gazed at her engagement ring. A red flame danced in the center of the diamond, producing a sudden calm that smoothed her anger. "If you want a slave, Salustra, I'll buy one for you. You're a good friend and I shouldn't be bitchy with you."

Salustra nodded. Cinder glanced over at Raven and stuck out her bottom lip and batted her eyes. Cerberus saw what the queen was doing and looked alarmed.

"I'll buy you both a human," Raven said, smiling wide enough to reveal her fangs.

Cinder clapped her hands. "Oh goodie!"

A tap on her shoulder turned Raven's head. Bechtel was frowning at her. She narrowed her eyes and he looked away. The band faded, as an announcer dressed as a ringmaster took the stage. He made his introductions while vampire guards hauled out a dirty pack of zombies on chains.

Zombies and cyborgs demanded a better price than Raven would have guessed, while the lone werewolf required a moderate fee. The humans looked well-fed. Cinder selected a tall, blonde, German specimen. Salustra chose a female shipped from Hawaii who demonstrated her mastery of flaming lances in the arena. Cerberus declined. Bechtel purchased both humans at Raven's nod.

"Acquire him," said Raven when Loki was presented. "No matter the cost, I want him."

Bechtel waited until the last second to bid. The auctioneer was ready to slam his gavel when the captain raised his hand. The bid was at two-million in jewels or two-hundred humans, buyer's discretion. Pointing at Bechtel, the auctioneer banged the gavel three times, giving no chance for anyone else to lift their hand. The bid closed.

"He is yours, Duchess," said Bechtel.

"Of course he is. Now go and fetch him. I want Loki to ride home with us in the limo. He's been to Italy. I want to hear about Europe's Death Games."

Chained and sedated, Loki sat next to Raven on the drive back to the Citadel, unable to speak or move on his own. He was no longer a skinny boy with pimples. Loki had filled out and added a jagged scar to his left cheek since she last saw him. Two humans huddled together on the floor of the limo, with the werepuma and werewolf.

Raven stared out the frost-covered window until they pulled up in front of Miramont Castle. Cinder and Cerberus climbed out with Stephan and their new human fighter. House guards hurried to escort the new arrivals. When they were on the move again, Raven allowed Salustra to sit next to her.

"A pity Loki had to be sedated," said Salustra. "Didn't he used to be one of your friends, Raven? Wasn't he a Viking? That was your old patrol team, yes?"

"Yes," Raven said, nodding. "I don't like his scar. Were superhumans not impervious to wounds?"

"I could be wrong, but the scar comes from a werewolf. Not the kind we have here. The Old Ones live in the dark forests of Europe. They are nothing like Stephen. Old Ones don't keep their human personalities and only turn during a full moon."

"I still want one. Bechtel, you will contact Lord D'Aquilla and tell him I want an Old One as a wedding gift. I'm sure he'll send one."

The captain bristled. "It's enough that I purchased Loki for you. The Kaiser won't be happy about your indulgence. Unlike my predecessor, I do not intend to be demoted due to pandering to the whims of a girl."

"What is to be Pallaton's fate?" she asked, unable to resist.

"Pallaton was demoted to a lieutenant. I'm told he will recover, but he suffered serious injuries."

At Salustra's soft gasp, both Raven and Bechtel turned toward her. She was trying not to cry, but Raven knew she was upset.

"It's the loss of an eye," the captain said. "He has another one. Be content the Kaiser spared his life. Pallaton failed to capture Highbrow. I'm sure he will try to redeem himself."

The limo arrived at the Citadel. Shadowguard were out in number, gathered around several vehicles parked in the courtyard. Pallaton wore an eye-patch and stood on the steps of the mansion, flanked by vampires escorting a line of disheveled humans.

Bechtel flew out before the limo stopped, appearing beside Pallaton, while Raven and Salustra climbed out with Luna and the Hawaiian woman. Guards dragged Loki as the two vampires talked for a moment. Bechtel continued inside with the humans, leaving Pallaton to the activity in the courtyard.

"Are those the bounty hunters?" asked Raven, flustered. They had waited days for their arrival from Texas. Rumors informed her they were militia, but they looked like a gang of ruffians and hardened killers. The heavy odor lingering from the unwashed humans was too overwhelming to follow.

Salustra took her slave's leash from a guard. "I'm sure they are. This is why your engagement party was postponed. Thank you again, Raven. I'll see my slave to her new quarters. Aleka isn't anything like Dragon, but she should be amusing to watch. Of course, I'll split my winnings with you. We girls need to be able to afford our own comforts without having to rely on the men."

Raven boiled as she watched Salustra walk down the sidewalk with her slave.

The Kaiser preferred the company of bounty hunters to her? It was an insult. Furious, she tore off her engagement ring and tossed it across the courtyard, breaking her finger. It vanished in the snow.

"Oh, no. What have I done?" Raven looked for someone to help her and found Pallaton standing at her side. Her mind cleared, the world was no longer fuzzy and her emotions overwhelmed her. "I lost my ring!"

"Forget it," said Pallaton. "You're better off without it."

"What a horrible thing to say. The Kaiser will be furious."

Pallaton extended his fangs and peered at her with one glowing, yellow eye offset by his eyepatch. He was upset with her.

A moment ago Raven didn't care what anyone thought, least of all Pallaton. Without the ring her emotions emerged, leaving her confused and frightened. A tear slid over the crest of her cheek. Pallaton lifted a finger to wipe it away.

The moment he touched her, a flood of feelings for the former captain returned. Raven threw her arms around his neck. He moved with such speed she didn't realize he was carrying her until they appeared behind the mansion in a gazebo surrounded by pine trees.

She was delighted. "I thought you were dead. I'm so happy to see you."

"The ring is cursed," said Pallaton, holding her close. "I should have left this place with you when you asked me to."

Raven silenced him with a passionate kiss. "Tell me what happened, love. Why didn't you capture Highbrow? How did you fail?"

"Because you released Star. She killed my men within minutes. Tandor is the one who blinded me. I escaped with my life." Pallaton rested his head on top of hers, squeezing her tight. "Bechtel has replaced me, but he'll do no better."

"Then let's run away, tonight."

"Throw all your cares aside? What about Luna and Loki?"

"Salustra can take care of them. Please, Pallaton. If we don't leave now, he'll put the ring back on my hand, and I will be forever lost."

"I want to, but there's no safe place we can go. The Kaiser will send Bechtel to hunt us. If we are to be together, then I must destroy the Kaiser. His death is our only way."

"His true name is Balan," said Raven. "I'm sure I read that name in a book on demonology. Bechtel removed the books from my room, or I could go upstairs and look him up. You must use this information to kill him."

"I'll think of something."

Pallaton kissed her one last time and sped away from the gazebo. It started to snow. Wrapping her cloak around her body, Raven stood up and headed back toward the mansion. As she rounded the corner, she found Captain Bechtel waiting for her on the landing. Several guards carrying flashlights and spear-guns with coiled ropes stood with him. Given their choice in weapons, Raven realized Pallaton's replacement was cruel.

"Where have you been?" he asked, in a deep, distant voice. "We were coming to find you."

"It's none of your concern," said Raven.

Emotions welled inside of her when Bechtel held out his hand holding the ring in his palm. He grabbed her arm, bruising her flesh as he forced the engagement ring on her finger. The moment it was on, Raven felt her worries and concerns flee. The darkness became a veil of deep, midnight blue, and the snow converted to a vivid pearl. She became furious for being handled so rough by a subordinate. Raven wrenched her arm free and slapped Bechtel hard.

"Don't touch me again, animal, I'll have you killed," Raven snarled. "If I want to go for a walk, I will. Those humans stink like pigs. I wasn't about to enter the mansion after them and sully my clothes with their foul odor." She adjusted her ring and held it up to her face. "So beautiful. I'm glad you found it. However, if the Kaiser ever puts humans before me again, I'll throw it away. I won't be second best."

"Don't dream of it, duchess. Follow me, I will return you to his care. He's busy at the moment, so you may go to your room and see to your clothing. You smell more of cologne than pig."

Raven reached out and clawed Bechtel's face, leaving four scratch marks across his cheek. He stepped back, shocked by her actions.

"I hate you," she growled. "You'll be sorry for speaking to me in that manner. The Kaiser will not be pleased to hear how you treated me."

Bechtel bowed low. "Nor will he be pleased you were with Lieutenant Pallaton. I'm sure you don't want the Kaiser to know about that." He lifted a hand to his face, cheek already healed. "Good night. Enjoy your new slave."

Raven entered the mansion and marched straight to her room. Luna sat on a pillow in front of her bed, licking her paws. She threw her arms around the furry creature, and held her close. The therianthrope licked Raven's face. Her tongue was rough and scratched Raven's skin, but she allowed the cat to lick the scent of cologne off her face. Then she lifted her hand to gaze at the red flame dancing in her ring.

"You're a good girl, Luna."

She kissed the werepuma on the head. "I promise I won't let anything happen to you, as long as you are obedient and always stay in your pretty cat body. I love you best this way. So keep me happy and I'll make sure you're well fed. Would you like a venison steak, my good girl?"

The werepuma dropped her head, tears rolling from her eyes. Luna shook her head, trying to communicate her sadness. Raven mistook it for a cat's hunger, unable to see the broken heart of the woman within.

Chapter Twelve

Midmorning found Highbrow in the Dark Angels' R.V., which now served as Rose's lab. Trailers belonging to the deceased were turned into the new hospital. One R.V. was used for minor surgery, another for those with pneumonia or bronchitis, and a third for newer cases of the flu. Only twenty children under the age of twelve remained in camp, and each one was sick. If things kept going this way, Highbrow would have to commission the mess hall as an infirmary, and let people cook their own food in their R.V.s. Campfires were now forbidden, and time spent outside was kept at a minimum. He worried another attack was imminent.

Rose was taking Star's blood, while Marie, an older female vampire, worked in the back room administering diagnostic tests. Highbrow stood while he watched Rose finish up with Star. The petite chameleon sat at the kitchen table with one hand holding up her head and the opposite arm stretched across the tabletop. Her shirt sleeve was pushed up, exposing a bulging vein in the crease of her elbow. A needle jutted from her vein as dark maroon liquid filled the final vial. Star squirmed and tried not to watch, causing Rose to smile.

"I didn't realize you were squeamish, Star. You wouldn't make a good vampire." She removed the needle and placed a bandage over the puncture. "I'm done with you, young lady."

Star shivered with relief. "Good. Maybe now I can go see Thor. A hike is just what I need."

"Not today," said Highbrow. "I know you want to head to Cadence's camp, Star, but I need you here. You're the official guard-dog until I get more muscle in here. I'm about to make the rounds, if you would like to join me."

Star wrinkled her nose. "Everyone is always telling me what to do. Go here. Do this. Sit in the corner. Eat your mush. Give more blood. I'm getting sick and tired of not getting to do what I want. And I want to see Thor."

"We appreciate your help, Star," Rose intervened, handing the vial to Maria who capped it with a rubber top and placed it on a tray. "While I will not start injecting everyone with your blood to see if they grow wings, I might be able to modify it to use as a cure for the flu."

Highbrow became unsettled when the two female vampires moved so fast he could no longer see them. He hurried outside with Star and found Odin with the Bull Dogs. Trudging to the nearest R.V., Highbrow opened the door and looked inside. Several children were bundled together in one bed or on floor pallets. Coughs, sniffling, and crying were intermittent. Nomad sat in a chair holding a little girl in his arms.

"I wouldn't come in, son. We all have the flu. You don't want it."

Star pushed Highbrow aside and entered. "Well, I can't catch the flu, so I might as well help. You look like you need to rest. Take a break, I'll hold her. Sorry, Highbrow, but you'll have to make the rounds without me."

Highbrow closed the door and took a deep breath of fresh air. The Bull Dogs remained outside, bundled in coats, gloves, and stocking caps. He left with Odin.

"At this rate," Highbrow began, "we're not going to have anyone on patrol or guarding the gate. Tandor better send help soon. How are you holding up, private?"

Odin shouldered his rifle. "I'm not sick, but I'm a little depressed. Lieutenant Sterling has a handful of soldiers at the front gate, and there's a few up at Moon Tower. I don't understand why antibiotics aren't doing the job. The drugs aren't that old, but no one is getting any better. It's getting worse."

Micah came around the corner of an R.V. and beckoned Highbrow. The vampire still carried an air of gloom about Ginger's death, but he looked well rested. "What's all this moaning and groaning? I've been up and down the road several times and the camp is in good shape."

"For now," said Highbrow. "I keep wondering if I should send you into town to the vampire nightclub and dig up some local gossip."

"I might swing by tonight," said Micah. "But I heard that D'Aquilla is here from Italy with three of your people. Loki, Monkey, and Skye are here. We could get everyone out of the Citadel at the same time, or so we hope. Man, its bright today, and just when I was getting used to the gray clouds."

The sunlight would not hurt the Dark Angel, but he put on sun-glasses and zipped up his leather coat as a precaution. A long sword hung at his side and a pearl-handled revolver rose from the holster strapped to his waist. Odin gazed with longing at the revolver. The vampire noticed him staring and held it out to him as the trio walked to the waterfall.

"Where did you get the Smith & Wesson?" asked Odin. "This is cool. It must have cost a fortune."

"EBay," said Micah, grinning at the younger soldier. "Before the Scourge I used to be a gun collector. I also owned a flower shop in Santa Fe." He re-holstered the gun. "Man, I haven't thought about the past in ages. I used to teach on witchcraft at the local university."

"Is it just me or is it freezing today?" asked Highbrow. "I'm wearing two sweaters under my coat and a thick pair of wool socks. My toes feel like icicles." He pulled back as Micah reached for his forehead. "I'm not sick."

"Yes, you are. I can smell it. You have the flu, Highbrow."

The captain shrugged. "Tell me something I don't know."

"Rose mentioned you were worried about the Kaiser using black magic on the camp and it might be the reason everyone is getting sick. Magic is real. One of my students once lost her brother in a car accident and asked if I'd arrange a séance so she could communicate with him. I agreed and contacted the coven."

Highbrow crossed his arms and raised an eyebrow at the vampire. "Is this going somewhere?"

"Though I'm not a medium, I've been able to contact the dead many times. On this occasion something went wrong, because it wasn't her brother we contacted, but something else. Something dark. A few days passed and she didn't show up at class. When I looked into it, I found out she committed suicide. That's when I started to notice a dark shadow following me around at the shop and university. I've seen a similar shadow at this camp, but I didn't say anything because of everything else that's been going on."

Highbrow felt his skin crawl. "I've seen it too. Several times. I thought it was my imagination running wild. Is it what you summoned?"

"You know, I've thought about that possibility. The same shadow was in Denver. It's one of the reasons I joined the Dark Angels and came here. I hoped it wouldn't follow, but when the Kaiser showed up with the Shadowguard, I started to think it wasn't a coincidence. I think the shadow belongs to the Kaiser. If that doesn't scare the crap out of you, it does me."

Highbrow glanced over at Odin. "I don't want anyone to hear about this until you've had time to look into this more. I need to know what it is, and how we can get rid of it."

"I'm doing that very thing," said Micah. "After being turned by Salustra I believed I'd lost my magic, but it's grown stronger since coming here. I don't want to scare you anymore, but what I summoned back then was a demon. Which one, I don't know, yet. Ginger saw it, and it was here during the battle. I saw it hover over Ginger's dead body before it vanished into the trees."

Hearing the pain in Micah's voice touched Highbrow. "I'm sorry. We've all lost people we love," he said. "I have to ask more of you. I need to know how to defeat the Kaiser and anything working for him. If you feel Salustra can shed light on this, then I want you to contact her and find out what she knows. Whatever can be used against the Kaiser and this demon is top priority."

"To control a demon, you need to know its true name, and if it manifests into physical form you will need a holy relic to kill it. With any luck, the shadow can't take solid form or we'll have a much bigger problem."

"You don't think we're safe here, do you?"

Micah wiped a stray lock of white hair from his eyes. "Pallaton's visit was a wake-up call, captain. We must vacate Seven Falls and move these people to Cadence's camp, or start digging graves now. Even there, I'm not sure we'll be safe."

After making rounds, Highbrow and Odin returned to the barracks and jumped in the Jeep. As the vehicle rounded the Pillars of Hercules, Highbrow spotted a dark shadow gliding across the canyon wall. He broke into a sweat and turned back to watch the road. Odin parked outside the former tourist cabin.

"I heard you and Micah talking, sir," said Odin, opening the vehicle door. "Demons have scared me since I learned about them in Bible school. I still wear a crucifix that my mother gave me at my first communion. Never took it off."

Highbrow slammed the door behind him. "The Kaiser isn't the devil, Private. I'm sure of that. But he is evil and twisted. Just keep saying your prayers and you'll be alright."

Once inside the control room, Highbrow took off his coat, swiped a bottle of water, and sat down in front of the shortwave radio. Odin turned the small space heater to high and stood at the window mesmerized by the sun as it vanished behind the mountains. Static greeted Highbrow, no matter what channel he tuned into. He picked up the telephone, but it was dead.

He slammed the phone back in its cradle, startling Odin and Star. The chameleon had entered the room without a sound.

"I know what you're going to say, captain, but Tandor should have arrived at the other camp and sent someone back by now. I'm going to their camp, and I'll find out what is going on. But I need to know where I'm going."

"It's not safe for you to leave," said Highbrow. "The moment you do, the Shadowguard will attack. I need you here, Star. I'll send Micah."

Star faced Highbrow. "This isn't a request. Micah and the Dark Angels are here to protect the camp. I'm going and I'll send some people back to help."

Packing the entire camp and leaving at that precise moment was not possible, even though Highbrow wanted to go. He knew he could not keep Star at camp any longer and did not bother giving an order she would not follow. She missed Thor. She was worried. He had to let her go.

"I can't tell you where their camp is," said Highbrow, "but they might be at NORAD." He picked up a map from his desk, opened it, and pointed at the location. "It's not far for someone with your speed. If I'm right, tell Cadence I need reinforcements. If you return with Thor and Phoenix, I'd feel a lot better. Of course, if I'm wrong about NORAD, then you'd best get back here fast.

Star was there one second, and the next she was gone. Highbrow took a sip of water, set the bottle down, and flopped onto his cot.

"Have you ever been in love, Odin?"

The younger soldier's cheeks burned. "No, sir."

"Love is the only thing that can make you feel miserable and happy at the same time. It makes you do stupid things, and sometimes it's the only thing that matters. I hope I sent Star to the right place." Highbrow grew quiet and heard Christmas music playing in the barracks.

"*White Christmas.* Is this the only album we have? I feel like that song has been on repeat. Would you please go find some new music?"

Odin hurried out of the room laughing. Highbrow checked in with two guards posted at the door, and went back to his cot. He wanted to rest his eyes for a few minutes before he was back on duty. As his eyes closed, he heard a deep growl outside his window. The captain grabbed his pistol and turned toward the window. Something scratched at the pane. He stood and peeked through the blinds.

A black werepuma stared back at him. She was leaning on the windowsill with her paws and her nose pressed against the glass. The right paw was bloody and missing three toes. He threw open the window, and stepped back.

"Barbarella!"

The big cat leapt in the room, and shook her fur, sending wet snow and ice flying across the room in every direction. Highbrow shut the window and turned toward his guest. Barbarella stood in human form, wrapped with the blanket from his bed. She stole his water bottle, finished it, and tossed it aside.

"How did you get here?" asked Highbrow. "I thought you were still at the Citadel."

"Logan helped me," she said, curling up on his cot. "He found me in the lab. After you defeated Pallaton, he lost his fighters. I was handed over to the Kaiser's doctors. They would have killed me if Logan hadn't arrived. I didn't know where else to go, so I came straight here."

"Star escaped from the Citadel as well," said Highbrow. "You just missed her. She's going to Cadence's new camp."

Highbrow looked around his room. He had cases of ammo, cans of beans, and extra blankets. It was all he had to offer.

"Are you hungry? I'll send Odin to find you something to eat. You're about my size, Barb. You can wear my clothes."

"All I want to do is sleep," she said, "I hope you don't mind, but can we talk later? I need to sleep."

Highbrow nodded. "Sure, sure. Later is fine. Just rest."

Highbrow stepped out of his room to give her room. He notified the guards and met Odin in the hallway, who was successful in finding some new music. Odin blushed when he heard Barbarella had arrived.

"You're fond of Barbarella? I'm sure she wouldn't mind if you checked in on her."

Odin perked up, grinning from ear to ear.

Highbrow smiled in return. "You sly fox. I had no clue you had a crush on Barbarella. She's been through a lot and needs to rest, but you should come back later and spend some time with her. I'm sure she'd like that, private." He patted Odin on the back.

"I wouldn't know what to say. I don't even know if she likes me."

"Then we'll find some mistletoe and you can give her a Christmas kiss." Highbrow snickered. "She may bite you, but then again, she might kiss you back. You never know. The ones that play hard to get are the most fun to chase. Better get your running shoes on, because you sure picked one that runs fast."

Odin beamed as he and Highbrow walked into the snowy night.

Chapter Thirteen

Rain poured on the small church. Blaze used her lighter on several candles, lighting the grainy altar with a warm glow. Cadence scrutinized the humble interior. There were no modern conveniences. No electricity, no heater, and no phones. Many of the hand-crafted wood pews were overturned and broken. Wind and rain intruded through holes in the wall. Cadence attempted to block the larger holes with benches, and was able to secure the entrance with some of the broken wood. Hay and debris littered the floor, and rats were not strangers here.

A thread of moonlight appeared on the altar, capturing their attention. Mary, the baby Jesus, Joseph, and the winged archangel, Michael, completed the scene depicted in stained glass watching over the altar.

"There's a full moon tonight," said Blaze.

The distant cry of a wolf snapped them from their inactivity. Cadence closed shutters as Blaze formed a barricade around the altar with the remaining pews. When they finished, Blaze cleaned her gun. Cadence scrounged through a bundle of rags behind the altar and returned with an armful of odorous, tattered clothes. She dumped them beside Blaze and pulled out a faded, green tunic and a frayed tan cloak. These she put aside for Blaze. Cadence chose a large dress made of burlap.

"I'm not wearing this," said Blaze, lifting up the tunic. "It stinks."

"It was probably worn by a dead person. We need to look the part if we're going to pass as villagers. Put those on over your own. A priest may show up here and I don't want a lot of hassle."

Blaze stood up disgusted, and put them on. She sat back down, threw the rest of the rags to the floor, and picked up her rifle. A scurry through a pile of nearby rubble caught Cadence's attention. She lifted her gun, resisting the urge to shoot. A rat. She spotted a Bible in the rubble. Cadence picked it up and sat with Blaze. The Bible was damp and the blue ink inside was mostly smudged. The date written on the inside cover was legible, however.

"It's dated 1345," said Cadence, in awe. "That can't be right? I can't remember why, but the date is familiar."

"Lots of graves. Lots of rats," said Blaze. She'd been talking a while but Cadence wasn't listening. "Sound familiar?"

"The Black Plague? Yeah, that makes sense. But that's not why I re-member that date." Cadence set the Bible aside and took out Mallory's journal. "I think I read something about 1345 in here. I need more light. Get me a candle, will you?"

"My watch doesn't work," said Blaze. She held up her wrist. "Why doesn't my watch work? If you want a candle, go read by the altar, my lady. I need to take inventory."

Cadence moved to the altar, while Blaze rummaged through her pockets. She had two pistols, a knife, a flashlight, and a pack of cheese crackers. Opening the crackers, she shoveled one in her mouth and pointed her gun to threaten an approaching rat.

"It's stale, but it's better than nothing," said Blaze. She froze as they heard another wolf howl, much closer this time. "Did you hear that?"

"I'm hurrying."

Flipping through the journal, Cadence scanned the pages until she came to the parts mixed with Latin and English. She started reading out loud.

"Mallory was from Lester and served as a surgeon to King Henry, the third. He came to Pevensey Caster in 1342, by invitation of his brother, Sir Thomas, to investigate several disappearances and animal deaths. The castle was built on top of an old Roman fort called Anderida, where a monolith, called the Roman Stone, was found."

Another howl brought Blaze to the altar. She placed two pistols beside the Bible, and clutched the carbine. "Read about the monolith later. Does Mallory say anything about werewolves? A wolf pack is closing in on us. They don't sound normal."

"The werewolves in this age are called Old Ones. They're man-eaters, turning at full moons with no conscious or rational thought. They can only be killed with silver." Her voice caught in her throat as she turned the page and studied the illustration of a rustic wooden spear with an iron tip. "The 'Spear of Destiny' is the only known weapon that can kill a Prince of Hell. It can be found in Anderida, guarded by legions of the damned." She paused. "Don't you get it, Blaze? We're here to find a Roman spear. It will kill the Kaiser. Mallory knew about it."

"Okay," said Blaze. "Sounds great. None of this will make any difference if we're eaten, so put those books away. They're coming."

Cadence pulled the jeweled dagger from her boot. The blade was silver. She placed it on the altar and stuffed the journal into a coat pocket. When she turned to pick up the Bible, it was no longer there. With no time to look for it, she prepared for the attack.

A chorus of growls and snarls encircled the church. Cadence held a knife and pistol, one in each hand. Frantic scratching terrorized the door. Several creatures answered another deep howl and a large body slammed against the church door. The door and its blockade were smashed into pieces.

Part-man, part-wolf entered, walking on its hind legs. Its wolfish head framed an elongated muzzle and slanted, yellow eyes. With a savage snarl, the werewolf and its pack charged, saliva flying from their massive jaws.

Blaze launched a grenade and pulled Cadence to the ground. The explosion erupted into a shower of splintered wood and bloody anatomy over their heads. Both stood and opened fire as three more werewolves rushed through the door, moving with fury toward the altar.

Cadence riddled a black werewolf with bullets. Unwavered, the beast jumped onto the altar, knocked over a candle, and caught its own tail on fire. Howling with pain, the Old One leapt from the raised platform and ran out the door as two of its companions rounded the altar to attack Blaze. She kept firing until one knocked her aside with its paws. The second beast raced toward Cadence. As the creature extended to its full height Cadence plunged her silver knife deep into its heart. The werewolf let out a scream and toppled to its side. In an instant, she dislodged the blade and rushed to help Blaze.

The werewolf attacking Blaze was missing half its head and bleeding from numerous bullets wounds. It extended its neck and opened its jaws wide to rip into Blaze. Cadence pierced the creature, sinking the knife deep. Chameleon and beast fell to the ground beside Blaze.

An entire pack of glowing eyes appeared in the doorway. As the wolf-pack pushed through the door, even more crashed through the church windows. The teenagers lunged into the stained glass window, trying to shield their faces. After a rough tumble, they took off running across the field.

They ran toward the castle faster than the pursuing werewolves. Pale, ghostly figures soon joined the chase, however.

"I thought you said no zombies!" cried Blaze.

Cadence shook her head. "I don't think those are zombies."

Reaching the hill out of sight, the two scrambled up the side of a tower. Guards on the battlements poured boiling pitch on an invading horde. The tumult of battle mixed with otherworldly sounds of monsters. The castle was under attack. Fiery arrows arched in the sky and dropped to their marks. The line of werewolves and ghouls erupted in fire, while dense lines of monsters were crushed and set ablaze as catapults launched thick fireballs over the walls into their centers.

The guards didn't notice Cadence and Blaze as they crossed the courtyard and took cover behind a cart. Twenty leather-clad guards made a clamor as they came rushing down a cobblestone path. Nearby, a company of mounted knights, in colorful regalia, gathered beside yeomen wielding longbows and staffs.

"Sir Thomas," said a loud, male voice, "we cannot open the gate and send out forces unless you want those demons to get inside."

A rotund knight in bronze armor and a servant walking two mastiffs on thick chains passed by the cart where Blaze and Cadence were hiding. The dogs caught a new scent and pulled toward the wagon, alerting the men. The large knight let out a cry of alarm and drew his sword as he walked around the wagon. His eyes and his sword were lowered toward the young women.

"Stand fast, Sir Wallace," shouted a knight in silver. "It is merely two servants you have frightened to death. Come here, girls. Why are you not in the kitchen?"

The knight was broad-shouldered and draped in a red tunic bearing the crest of a unicorn. As he approached, Cadence was unsure if she should run or hold her ground. She still held the jeweled dagger and noticed the knight was staring at it with recognition. Cadence threw the dagger at his feet.

"Sir, they are thieves in the night," said Sir Wallace. "That's your brother's knife. I would recognize it anywhere, for it matches the one you wear." He picked up the knife, examined it, and handed it to his noble companion. "But I don't know these servant girls, and I know every female in this castle quite well."

"I am Sir Thomas Mallory, captain of Lord Montagu's guards, and brother to Sir Richard Mallory," said the knight in silver. "Do not be afraid. We will not harm you. Are you from the village? How long have you been here stealing our food, and how did you come by my brother's dagger?"

"We're not thieves," said Blaze, angered. "Sir Richard gave us that dagger!"

The dogs growled and tested the slack in their chains. Blaze stood keeping her weapon covered and her hood low to hide her purple hair.

Stepping in front of Blaze, Cadence spread out her hands as she addressed the knight. "What my servant says is true. Richard Mallory left it in my care. He also presented me with his medallion to show you, lest you doubt we come in good faith." She reached in her dress and pulled out the Celtic cross on its long, gold chain.

A gasp swept through all that were watching. Sir Wallace's one good eye opened wider. Sir Thomas motioned his men back. He approached Cadence and took the medallion from her hand, scrutinizing and releasing it.

"Sir Thomas, your brother said you are an honorable man," Cadence continued. "We had nowhere else to go. He led us to believe you offer sanctuary to those in need, and we are in need."

The howling reached its zenith outside the wall. Sir Thomas whispered to a squire and sent him to the warriors waiting at the gates. Instead of opening the gate and riding out, the company divided and joined the guards on the battlements.

"Send a man to fetch Sir Lachlan," said Thomas. "I believe these may be the companions he spoke of. We'll know soon enough if they are friends or foes."

A squire enlisted the servant with the dogs and they both left to find Sir Lachlan.

"Sir Lachlan?" Blaze nudged Cadence. "Your Lachlan. That means Whisper is here, too. We're in luck. Tell him about the silver."

"You have more treasure?" Sir Thomas eyed Cadence. "What does your servant speak of?"

"Your brother discovered if you use silver against the Old Ones, and don't remove it from their bodies, they will die. Werewolves can regenerate, so fire wounds them, but they heal from their injuries. Even if you think you've killed them, they will rise again."

"Fire can kill the wraiths," said Sir Thomas. "These ghouls rise each night from their graves and have troubled these lands for many months. They work with the Old Ones, trying to reach where we hide. If my brother sent you, then you know of what I speak."

Sir Wallace laughed. "With that silver dagger, the little lass saved herself from being eaten by big, bad wolves. She doesn't know that I bite twice as hard."

"Your lechery is well known to me, old friend," said Sir Thomas. He gave Cadence a meaningful look. "Go to the blacksmith, Sir Wallace, and order the old fool to make me a silver tipped arrow. I will see if silver kills the Old Ones. Be quick about it. I wish my brother had shared this with me."

Leaving two squires with Sir Thomas, the large knight hurried off with another squire to do their captain's bidding. Sir Thomas looked at her thoughtfully.

"I don't think your brother knew at the time he was here, Sir Thomas," said Cadence. "It was in his journal, written after he left Pevensey Castle. He also mentioned a Roman spear; the one used to pierce Christ. I believe it's important."

"Longinus was the Roman's name. I know where this spear can be found, my lady. Those creatures beyond the walls guard the Roman fort Anderida, and the holy spear. Men have attempted and failed to retrieve it, including my brother William."

Cadence glanced at Blaze, struggling to contain her excitement. So much more made sense and she again felt as if a higher power was looking over her.

"Come with me, ladies," said Thomas. He led the way past a fountain and into an enclosed garden where nothing grew. Overhead torches from the battlements provided the only light. The squires remained at watch beside the wooden door, while Thomas led them to a bench and motioned for them to sit. "It's far safer to talk here. Fear not. Sir Lachlan is my friend. We have shared many stories. I know how he came to be here, and that others were to follow. Would you be Lady Cadence?"

"Cadence Sinclair. My friend is called Blaze."

"Some find my interest in genealogy ridiculous, but I speak truth when I say my knowledge of Latin and the origins of words far exceed any man here. The name Sinclair is Latin. 'Clarus' means 'pure' or 'illustrious.' It might interest you to know that the Sinclair Clan fought beside William the Conqueror against King Harold, before settling in the land of Roslin in Scotland."

Cadence knew nothing of her heritage. Now stuck eight-hundred years in the past, she encountered someone who knew of her distant relatives. "What does the name Mallory mean?" she asked.

"It means 'unfortunate man,' which I am in many ways." Sir Thomas turned toward the gate. "Ah, my squire returns with your friends."

The vampire, Lachlan, looking handsome in a coat of armor and a light-green tunic, strode into the garden ahead of two squires. One was the messenger and the other was a familiar figure. It was Whisper. Both were at ease in the castle, giving Cadence the impression they had been there for some time.

"Did I not say that my lady was fair, Sir Thomas? Her companion is a gypsy, so take care you do not incite her wrath. 'Blaze' is a name chosen to fit her temperament." Lachlan laughed with gusto as he winked at a fuming Blaze. "Have you missed me, Lady Cadence?"

"Lachlan!" Without regard, Cadence ran to Lachlan and threw her arms around his neck. She planted a kiss on his scruffy cheek. When she stepped back, the Irishman's eyes were dancing. "I have been worried sick about you and, um, Squire Clay. Are you okay?"

"We are both fine," said Lachlan, reaching out to touch her face. "Had I known we would end up here, I would have left a note. You understand. But I've the luck of the Irish. Sir Thomas proves to be a good man, and friend. We are safe here."

Blaze and Whisper walked off to a corner holding hands, and talking in soft voices. Cadence reached through a slit in her dress and into her coat pocket. She pulled out the journal and handed it to Lachlan.

He flipped through it and glanced at Thomas, handing it to him. Sir Thomas' eyes lit up.

"I never believed I would see my brother's journal again. I would recognize his hand writing anywhere. Richard kept his secrets inside this journal. He came here three years ago to study the Roman Stone and vanished through it with his friend. I never gave up searching for him and hoped one day he would return. This can mean one thing. My brother is dead."

"It's true," said Cadence. "I'm sorry."

Sir Thomas sat down on the bench, overcome with grief. "I suspected as much when you showed me his medallion. I would like to know how he died. Were you with him, Lady Cadence?"

"No, but I buried him. Your brother found another monolith and brought it to my people to study. I fear Richard may have also brought the Black Plague to our world. Everyone in the mountain fort where I found him fell ill and died, only to rise again as the living dead. We were told the disease came from a place called Afghanistan, but it was a lie. Your brother died before he became one of them. I believe Richard was trying to help my people and yours, but he ran out of time."

Cadence avoided giving too many details. His brother's suicide was not something Thomas needed to hear, nor that he was cremated and buried in a common grave.

"You were brought here for a reason, Lady Cadence," said Sir Thomas. "I do not know of the Kaiser that Sir Lachlan spoke of, but there are twelve monoliths scattered throughout the world. He may have stepped through one and entered your time."

"Why is yours called the Roman Stone?" asked Cadence.

"At one time, a Roman fort encircled the castle and village. The second fort I mentioned was built not far from here. It was an outpost. If this place had another name, there are no records of it. The Romans guarded the stone and the spear and kept them in separate locations. For centuries both have been forgotten. The stone was found on its side in the graveyard, and when righted, the cloaked figures appeared and carried out their vile ceremonies before it. After Lord Montagu ordered the Roman Stone brought inside the castle, servants started vanishing. He wrote to the royal court and requested my brother and his colleague, Dr. Jarvis Leopold, to come here. It didn't take long for them to discover the Roman Stone had mystical properties. Leopold claimed the ancient gods used it to travel to other dimensions. They also believed the spear had great power, but despite their efforts it hasn't been retrieved."

"I know who Leopold is," said Cadence. "He wasn't with your brother when I found him. Leopold abandoned Richard and now works for the Kaiser, our enemy. If this man was once good, he is no longer."

"Too much has transpired to be mere coincidence," said Lachlan. "We fight a common foe, Sir Thomas. There is someone here, like the Kaiser, who is controlling them. It would be someone with great charisma and strength of purpose to be able to influence these monsters to do his bidding. You mention the Roman outpost is guarded. Who commands these creatures?"

"It would be a vampire lord," said Cadence. "One who rules all of the others."

"For a long time, I have suspected who is behind the attacks," said Sir Thomas, in a grave voice. "His is called Lord Darkmoore and he was once a great knight. He was the first man killed by a wraith and buried in the village graveyard. After two nights past I saw him again, standing outside the castle gates with an army of demons."

He shifted, looking uncomfortable, and Cadence wondered what else he knew.

"I thought the wraiths to be mindless creatures," the knight continued, looking at the ground, "yet Lord Darkmoore is intelligent. He resides at the Roman outpost with his minions. But I dare not go there, not even in the daylight. The Old Ones stand guard in human form protecting the Spear of Destiny. The men are as fierce as the wolves."

Lachlan glanced at Cadence. "I know the spear you're both talking about," he said. "I assume Richard wrote about it in his journal, and I also know what you're thinking, Cadence, but you heard Thomas. We know nothing about Lord Darkmoore and going to the outpost will be dangerous."

Cadence nodded and sat next to Thomas, sensing he was troubled by what they discussed. "First things first. None of this matters if we can't get back home. May we see the Roman Stone? I need to make sure it's the same type of monolith we went through."

"Lord Montagu forbids any to come near it," said Thomas, gazing up at a lit window in the castle keep. "The priests are the only ones allowed near the Roman Stone. They came from Rome following my brother's disappearance, intent on labeling him and Leopold as dark sorcerers. Since then, they say a demonic force threatens this castle. The pope denies this and will not send help. Nor will the king. I dare not arouse their suspicions. I do not trust them. Let me think on this and I will find a way to take you to the stone, unseen."

Whisper approached and bowed. "Sir Thomas, might I be allowed to take Blaze to the battlements? She wants to watch me fire the silver arrow at a werewolf. I assume I'm to be given this task?"

"Go on, Squire Clay. You are the finest archer here, and I would have no other but you loose the first silver arrow," said Sir Thomas. "Find Sir Wallace, and after you pierce a wolf's black heart, come tell me the outcome." He smiled as the couple left the garden, hand in hand. "Squire Clay never misses. Why Sir Lachlan has not already knighted his squire is a mystery. If your sweetheart does not do so, I will knight Clay myself, and ask him to stay. We need more fighters like him."

"Oh, Lachlan's not my...," Cadence fell silent when she heard Lachlan laugh. "My sweetheart has an odd sense of humor, Sir Thomas. You must be an understanding man to overlook an Irishman's shortcomings. I am the commander in my world, and I assure you, Squire

Clay ranks high on the list with my best warriors, which includes Sir Lachlan."

"A woman warrior like the Viking shield maidens of old." Sir Thomas took her hand and lifted her from the bench. "There is time before Lord Montagu rises for you to change into more suitable apparel, my lady. Conversation during meals is lacking with so few of us left. I am sure his Lordship will take heart to find a fair maiden gracing our dining hall."

"How long have you been here, Lachlan?" asked Cadence, as they walked through the garden gate. She held onto his arm, taking comfort in his presence.

"Sir Lachlan has been here a fortnight," said Thomas, answering for him. "We must be cautious. Word has surely reached Lord Montagu of you and Blaze. Tell him your coach was attacked on the road, and by God's grace, you found this castle and seek his protection. Let that be your story, my lady, and nothing else. If we are fortunate, the priests will not join us this night."

Entering a side door from the garden into the keep, Thomas led them through a long hallway into a large, organized kitchen. The servants were preparing a meal, cutting vegetables and tossing them into a giant kettle over a roaring fire, and garnishing a roasted boar on a silver platter. A formidable older woman in a white apron and cap was giving instructions to the servants, and stopped to present herself before Sir Thomas.

"What is this? A wet kitten?" asked the woman.

"Mrs. Fulbright," said Mallory, "this is a special guest. Take Lady Cadence and make her presentable. A dress of Lord Montagu's late wife should fit her. Let no one see you with her until Lady Cadence is ready. Nor do I want any gossip among the servants. Lady Cadence is from Clan Sinclair and has brought word from my brother, but that is for you to know, Mrs. Fulbright, and no one else."

"You can put your faith in me, sir. I know just what to do." Mrs.

Fulbright took Cadence by the arm and led her through the kitchen. "Don't be frightened, dear girl. We've seen many strange things since Sir Richard left and I do not question Sir Thomas. He's the only reason the night creatures haven't found their way inside this castle. If he wants you to look the part of a lady, then that is what he shall have."

Through a secret passage, Cadence emerged in a small chamber with many chests and trundles filled with clothing. Mrs. Fulbright was patient and waited as Cadence removed her wet clothes, choosing a dark green gown hemmed with gold and gold slippers to compliment. The older woman was curious about the blue jeans and military boots, but asked no questions.

Cadence placed her clothes inside a trunk and covered them with another layer of clothing. She washed up in a basin before the woman had her sit for grooming. Her hair was brushed and braided into coils, then pinned on top of her head. Mrs. Fulbright led Cadence to stand before a full-length mirror, and she was amazed at her own transformation.

"Thank you," said Cadence.

"You're wearing Sir Richard's necklace. His brothers each have matching necklaces," said Mrs. Fulbright. "We never speak about Sir William. He died a few months ago and Sir Thomas has never recovered from his loss. Poor man. It was bad enough when Sir Richard left in such haste, giving no explanation. It broke poor Thomas's heart. I've been in the service of the Mallory family my entire life. First to their father, and then his three boys. This castle is cursed, my lady. You must not stay long. No, you must leave as soon as possible or suffer the same fate as so many others."

Mrs. Fulbright escorted Cadence through a corridor and a draped doorway. They entered a spacious hall with a vaulted ceiling and a blazing fireplace. Tapestries hung from the stone walls, weapon displays and suits of armor stood in the corners of the room. Two hairy hounds lay before the fireplace, gnawing on bones, while servants cleared plates from the tables. A young maid in a dirty frock tossed fresh straw onto the ground, glancing at Cadence. Mrs. Fulbright approached Sir Thomas, who was standing with Lachlan near the fireplace.

"You look magnificent," said Lachlan, bowing low. "My eyes have never beheld such a vision, my lady. Green suits you. So does this castle. When I picture us together, I always think of being in Ireland at the McNeill's castle. Shame we don't have time to visit my ancestors."

It was like a dream and Cadence expected to wake up back in her bed at NORAD. The main hall was a scene straight from a movie, and the smell of rotting hay, dirty dogs, and unwashed bodies was hard to duplicate. It was real. Lachlan slid his arm around her, holding her close. His embrace was real, too. Cadence wanted to tell Lachlan everything she kept locked inside. One look into his hazel eyes told her he felt the same.

"I don't think I can stand this close to you," said Cadence, feeling a rush of heat. "Yes, you can," Lachlan said. "Let me enjoy the moment a bit longer, Cadence Sinclair. It may not come again and I will remember you like this, always."

Sir Thomas came over to join them, holding a goblet of wine. Mrs. Fulbright was fluttering about nearby, ordering the servants here and there. A young man in a yellow tunic approached and placed a tray with a pitcher of wine and two goblets on the table. Lachlan filled both glasses and handed one to Cadence.

"This is the first time I've dared feel any hope for our future," said Sir Thomas. "God works in mysterious ways." He tapped his goblet against theirs.

Realizing how thirsty she was, Cadence took a gulp of red wine. It wasn't the taste she'd expected and tried not to gag. The wine was unfermented and tasted more of the vinegar than grapes. She set her glass down and took a seat on the long bench. Lachlan either pretended to be drinking or could actually hold it. Servants arrived and placed a large gold tray containing fresh baked bread, butter, several cheeses, and a roasted suckling pig on the table before them.

Sir Thomas provided Cadence with Richard's dagger. Slicing into a block of cheese, she took a bite and discovered it was goat cheese, and found it tasty. Lachlan joined her on the bench, carving slices of meat and filling her plate. He grinned when she ate with her fingers and washed it down with the bitter wine.

A commotion caused Cadence to turn toward the fireplace. Lord Montagu entered through a side door, draped in a long blue robe trimmed with white fur, and assisted by two attendants wearing matching yellow tunics. The elder noble was not in the best of health and walked with a limp. Once seated, an attendant covered his lord with a blanket and positioned his feet upon a stool. A dog trotted over, circled at the feet of Montagu and sniffed his shoes.

Sir Thomas set his goblet on the table and approached Lord Montagu, bending to whisper in his ear. The old man craned his neck to peer at Cadence.

"Come here, girl," said Lord Montagu, in a feeble voice. "Sir Thomas and Sir Lachlan can talk death and doom over wine while we have a nice, long chat." He cackled as Cadence approached and kicked over a footstool. "Be seated, young lady, as I would have words with you."

Seeing another chair in front of the fire, Cadence ignored the dirty footstool and sat across from Lord Montagu. He looked to be well over ninety years of age, which did not seem possible for anyone living in the Middle Ages.

"William the Bastard bestowed this castle to my family for services rendered. We have held it ever since."

Lord Montagu broke into a wracking cough, gripping the sides of his chair, and quivered head to toe. The attendant hurried to fuss over the old man.

"Are you my wife?" Montagu asked the attendant, irritated.

"Enough of this, Percival. I am not dying. Not yet, in any case. Go fetch us wine. Bring the good stuff."

"I'm not sure that wine is what you need, my lord. Perhaps mead would be better, with a dash of honey, for your cough?" asked Percival. A servant in his twenties, he was gaunt, pale, with yellow hair and rather large ears. The second attendant held less favorable appearance and stood at the side door, reviewing Cadence.

"We both shall have wine, not honeyed mead," said Lord Montagu, wrinkling his face in disgust. "Why are you standing there, Percy? Why is a goblet of wine not in my hand? Make haste, you bag-of-bones, before I toss you outside the castle walls!"

Percival sent the second manservant dashing off to do his lord's bidding and remained at Montagu's side. He stared at Cadence with obvious dislike.

"Sir Thomas tells me your coach fell into disrepair," the old man croaked. "Yet, Lord Darkmoore is at the gates. I can't understand how two little girls could get through enemy lines to seek sanctuary in my castle. Oh, I have ears, lady. I know a little more than you, and that is saying quite a lot. Tell me, girl, what do you know of the creatures stalking this place? Are they vampires? Werewolves? Demons? The priests argue that all come from Hell, for those simple minds see anything unexplainable to be demonic in origin." He had a look in his eyes that made Cadence feel like he was hiding something from her. "But we understand differently. You are here because of the Spear of Destiny, aren't you?"

Montagu had ruled his castle for decades and Cadence imagined he had not always been meek or mild, nor tolerated uninvited guests bearing strange stories. Someone had been spying on them, and had advised the old man. Lying now seemed foolish.

"We are here to help you," said Cadence. "We come as friends."

"Yes, that is what I thought." Montagu's dark eyes locked with her own. "The priests won't approve of you being here. They are from

Rome and I do not trust Romans, though I shall not send them away either. If you are here to help us, then you and your friends will leave in the morning to find Lord Darkmoore and kill him. In the Roman outpost you will find the spear you seek. I cannot say what power the Spear of Destiny holds, but it must be great or Lord Darkmoore would not protect it. I want it." A smile appeared on his wrinkled face. "If you refuse, then you will all be burned at the stake for witchcraft while Sir Lachlan and his squire watch, and then they will die."

"Oh, we'll go," said Cadence. "That's why we're here, my lord."

Moments later inside Lachlan's quarter's, Cadence kicked off her slippers, not at all pleased with Lord Montagu or his threat. She escaped her dress, and tossed it aside before diving under the animal pelts covering Lachlan's bed. Blaze and Whisper were across the hall. She imagined they had a similar fire providing light, but little warmth. Lachlan tossed a few logs on the fire, waiting until it caught fire before turning toward the bed.

"I'm not looking forward to tomorrow," said Cadence. "So much depends on us finding the spear and getting back home. I believe it's the only weapon that can kill the Kaiser."

"Destiny. We're meant to be here, and you are meant to be with me this night. I've waited for this moment a long time."

The firelight gave Lachlan's red hair a copper sheen, revealing no blemishes on his muscular body. Cadence's heart sped up as a whimsical smile spread across his handsome face. He climbed into bed beside her and pulled her into his embrace, showing no fear of her toxicity to vampires with a deep, passionate kiss. As the logs crackled and sparked, Cadence clung to Lachlan. Lord Darkmoore, burning witches, and the sacred Roman spear slipped from her thoughts.

Chapter Fourteen

*L*ogan watched from his bedroom window as a line of vehicles drove away. He counted over forty human bounty hunters climb into the trucks. The men all carried big guns, chewed tobacco, and looked geared up for a hunting excursion. "Rednecks from hell," Logan mumbled.

Bechtel warned Logan the Kaiser had hired humans to track Cadence. He also reminded Logan it was Friday night. The Kaiser would announce his engagement at dinner later tonight, and the explosives had to be rigged to detonate at midnight. His job was complete.

"Bye-bye, you sons-of-bitches," Logan growled.

Taking a handful of snow from the windowsill, he iced his glass of scotch. Logan felt like a waiter in his white tuxedo and tie framing his black shirt, although tonight he would take no orders. He sipped his scotch and thought about how Leopold had thanked him for causing the 'breakthrough' in their research. Logan set his drink aside and straightened his tux, whistling *Grandma Got Run Over by A Reindeer* as he strolled into the dining hall. He was late.

Already seated the vampires paid no attention when Logan slipped into his chair at the head table. A floorshow imported from Italy was in progress. Circus performers pranced around the room in colorful costumes. Jugglers, sword-swallowers, fire-eaters, and Tarot fortune-tellers spun their hypnotic brands of magic and entertainment. The Kaiser sat on his throne with Raven beside him. Salustra sat with them while Dragon stood behind her, not as a fighter, but as a servant instead.

Star was not present. Logan had heard the rumors.

He expected a speech from the Kaiser, but figured he had missed it when the first course was served. Logan glanced at his bowl of soup and stirred, unsure if it was blood or tomato. To his surprise a piece of paper floated to the surface. A message written in black ink read, *Limo outside.*

Logan scooped the paper onto his spoon and swallowed it. He glanced at Bechtel, but the new captain showed no response. Like Salustra, Bechtel refused to look at him. The paper stuck in Logan's throat and he gagged. He chugged a glass of water as a firm hand pounded him on the back.

"Thanks," said Logan, seeing it was Bechtel. "It's tomato soup. Glad you didn't switch bowls on me."

"Why would I do that?" asked Bechtel. His black eyes were emotionless. "I am now Captain of the Shadowguard. Pallaton failed to capture Highbrow. You should congratulate me, Agent Logan. Much has changed since we last talked."

"Duly noted," said Logan, resting his spoon. "Guess that means you're taking this promotion seriously. I have a new bodyguard."

"So I heard," said Bechtel.

Logan wanted to stab the vampire in the ear with his spoon. Bechtel was not the same Dark Angel, and Logan felt the new captain was intending to cause a problem. He wondered about the timed bomb in the lab and whether Bechtel had discovered it. The vampire was wearing a new diamond ring. On closer inspection, a tiny red flame danced in its center.

Logan was more than a little disappointed. His gut told him he had lost another friend and gained a new enemy. He leaned back, pretended to enjoy the entertainment, and waited for a reaction from the vampire. Instead, Bechtel turned and smiled as Dr. Leopold made a surprise entrance. The tall, bald freak appeared wearing his lab coat and green gloves. He hurried to the Kaiser's side and whispered into his ear.

Leopold's appearance caused a stir among the guests. The doctor never left his lab, nor did the Kaiser ever leave a party. Bechtel grew interested when the dwarf sprang up from his seat, kissed Raven's hand, and exited with the doctor. Logan stiffened as the dark shadow glided away from the Kaiser's chair and followed.

"I wonder what that was about," Logan said, scrutinizing Bechtel's reaction. The captain acted worried. "Shouldn't you check it out?"

"Yes, I should," said Bechtel, eyes glued to the door. He followed the Kaiser and the doctor out.

Logan felt the corners of his mouth turn upward. The one thing he was good at was reading people. There was no doubt in his mind that Bechtel switched sides in the war.

A servant cleared his bowl and silverware. Logan refused wine, fearing it might be drugged. Three more courses were served exclusive to vampires. Several performers swaggered over and stood before Logan. A juggler dressed as a Harlequin and two tumblers in bat costumes danced in front of him. One of the bats was familiar, causing Logan to lean in for a closer look. It was a boy in his teens.

"Enjoying yourself?" asked the bat. He gripped the table and flipped into a headstand. The crowd applauded. He spun around, now facing Logan. "I wouldn't drink anything they serve you. It's drugged."

"I gathered that."

The bat winked, somersaulted off the table, and grabbed the bat girl's hand. The two danced between the tables, spinning and twisting the audience into a frenzy.

Three minutes later, the building shook. A low rumble resounded through the walls. Fire alarms blared as sprinklers inside the dining hall came to life. Screams and shouts followed, as vampires knocked over glasses and chairs, and one another, in their haste to leave. In the confusion, Logan left the dining room through the main doors and slipped toward the front entrance. It was too easy.

On his way out, someone placed a trench coat around Logan's shoulders and a supportive arm around his waist. Rushed outside into the blizzard, snow and wind stung his eyes. The ground was treacherous and Logan would have fallen if his helper's arm had not kept him on his feet. Logan was tossed into the backseat of a limousine parked at the corner. A group of people dove inside with him, slamming the doors and sealing them inside the warm cab.

"Good evening."

Dragon's voice startled Logan. The two dressed up like bats from the party pulled their masks off and gave Logan a smug look. He recognized them both. Dodger and Xena.

"Well, I'll be damned," said Logan, his mouth hanging open. "And you! Weren't you Cinder's prisoner?" he asked the limo driver.

"Someone let me out," Rafe said, catching Logan's eyes in the rearview. "Found car keys on the carpet, went outside, and found this limo waiting for me. There was a note on the dashboard with instructions to be at the Kaiser's mansion at 12:05 a.m. It was signed by Rose, so I did as she asked. It appears she brought you on board as well."

"No thanks to Bechtel," said Logan. "He was promoted to captain over Pallaton, but I can't say whether he helped pull off our escape or not. He didn't act too friendly tonight. Then again, my bomb did go boom. Someone has to be blamed." The heater clicked on and warm air blew. "Much better. Thank you, Rafe."

"You're freezing," Xena said, handing Logan a blanket. "Get out of your tux and wrap up, scavenger. We're going to Cadence's camp, and Rose is meeting us there. She'll be ticked if you come down with the flu."

Dodger leaned forward and shook Dragon's hand. From the folds of his cloak, the younger chameleon produced Dragon's two famous swords, Hèbi and Lóng. "Salustra handed them to me on the way out.

She said Pallaton arranged for our escape. Bechtel isn't a Dark Angel. He's the Kaiser's spy."

Xena nodded. "They found your bomb, but Pallaton had a backup plan. Barbarella snuck a bomb into the lab. Thanks for freeing her, Logan. You put your neck on the line to help us."

"Damn!" said Logan, feeling better now he was dry. "Then you all know bounty hunters were sent to look for Cadence. Watch the road, Rafe. The bounty hunters headed out right before the party started and there will be spotters on the main roads."

"They'll go straight to Seven Falls," Dragon said, in a throaty voice. "Pallaton went to warn Highbrow. We're going to Cadence's camp. She's missing, along with Blaze, Whisper, and Lachlan. We need your help again, Agent Logan."

Logan stared out the window as Rafe turned off the highway and onto a mountain road. A short drive brought them through the whirling snow to NORAD. The car drove past the gate and into a long, well-lit tunnel. A small group of people holding flashlights stood at the end. As they drew closer, Logan recognized Tandor, Thor, Star, Freeborn, Smack, and Lotus.

Dragon was first out of the limo and ran straight to the group. Everyone hugged him, asking questions all at once. When he saw Freeborn, Dragon slid his embrace around her with a kiss. Smack pushed through everyone and jumped into Dodger's arms. He caught the freckle-faced girl and spun her around, laughing.

"It's not a lynch mob," said Rafe, standing by Logan's door. "Get out and face the music. They don't like me any more than they like you."

Logan climbed out of the vehicle. Rafe stepped back as someone spun Logan around and connected his face with their fist. Logan sprawled backward against the car and held his face.

"Hello, Thor," Logan murmured.

The blonde chameleon cracked his knuckles. "I heard you were coming and I wanted to be the first to greet you. That was for setting my team up at Midnight Falls. Two Vikings died because of you, and Raven remains a prisoner. Why the hell didn't you bring her with you?"

"I'm lucky to have made it out. Raven isn't the same girl you remember. She's the Kaiser's mistress, pal. I didn't think it a good idea to drag her along with us when she'll just run back to him. And I couldn't free your other friends, but I do know Raven purchased Loki. Monkey and Skye are back from Italy too."

"Why didn't the Dark Angels free them, too?" asked Thor.

Logan shrugged. "Why don't you ask them?"

"Both of you stop it," said Star, giving both men a disapproving look. "Getting even a few of our friends back is nothing less than a miracle. We'll figure out a way to save everyone in time." She noticed Rafe sulking. "Everyone is welcome. Now, if you two are done bickering, let's go inside. We have a lot to talk about."

The control room was far smaller than Logan had expected. It was crammed with too many people crowded into computer cubicles or sitting in front of screens.

"Now that we're all here," said Picasso, "let's get straight to business. Yesterday, Cadence and Blaze vanished through a monolith found at the fourth reservoir. Lachlan and Whisper disappeared earlier. We know the stone was brought here from South Dakota. There are twelve of these bad boys called the Babylonian Stones spread out around the world. The one we have here is called the Cheyenne Stone."

"They have monoliths like this on the Easter Islands," said Logan. "Stonehenge has similar sized stones as well. The Druids conducted their rituals there, even into modern times. No one knows what the stones do."

Picasso nodded. "From what we've read, Native Americans considered the Cheyenne Stone a gift from the gods and sacrificed animals to ensure plentiful crops and good hunting. Captain Richard Mallory was the expert on ancient and medieval cultures. He spearheaded the research here on the Cheyenne Stone and had teams searching for the other stones around the world.

"We aren't sure why, but from what the team tells me, the monolith pulled Cadence and the others through an opening. I think you will understand if I just show you Mallory's work. Tandor found the security tapes that showed Mallory and his team with the monolith over the last few years."

"Bring up the video, Picasso," said Tandor. He regarded Logan through narrowed eyes. "We want your help to determine how this monolith works, Logan, so we can mount a rescue team and bring back our friends."

Six flat screens displayed different angles of the cavern. Lights illuminated the perimeter and soldiers guarded the monolith around the clock. Scientists under Mallory's direction ran many tests on the stone. They were taking photographs and brought in machines to calculate its age and electromagnetic readings until one day in late September when something extraordinary happened.

Mallory left the cavern. Cameras tipped over as the ground shook. A green light poured from its center as the stone cracked open. Soldiers fell to their knees, covering their ears just before the screen went black.

"What happened?" Logan asked.

Picasso held his finger up. "Just wait."

The image returned, cameras running. The soldiers were all dead and a figure in a black cloak picked through them with curiosity. A few moments later, the cloaked man wandered off camera.

"After the incident," said Tandor, "Captain Mallory and five hand-picked Marines were allowed at the fourth lake. The electromagnetic readings at the time were off the charts, and they didn't just interfere with the equipment here. We've experienced an electrical blackout at the survivors' camp, as well as violent behavior. The Citadel is too far to feel the effects. So far, it seems only humans and animals are susceptible."

"We're lucky all of us here are something other than human," Star said. "And none of us would have thought that a year ago."

Logan mumbled, "Am I chopped liver then?"

"We found a way around it by covering the stone with a magnetic net," said Picasso. "The cloaked figure wasn't the only thing to come from the monolith. In a storage room, we found hundreds of ceramic molds of footprints taken from around the lake, but they're not human. Each track has five digits giving the impression of humanoids, but with claws instead of toes."

"You said there's audio?" asked Logan.

"Not really," said Picasso. "The cloaked figures first emerged a year ago. When Mallory isn't present, the tapes are distorted or just fade to black. Something about Mallory allowed the equipment to record, but the team never discovered why. If the audio is played, all you hear is a strange humming, which we now know comes from the stone."

The tapes continued blacking out when Mallory was absent. The cloaked figures were caught on tape a few times, but they never stayed on screen for long. This continued for a year.

"He stopped coming to the lake around the fourteenth of September. That's when the inhabitants here were exposed to the H1N1z virus and attempted to flee."

Logan poured himself a cup of coffee. It was strong and provided the jolt needed to stay awake.

"Cadence picked Mallory's room to stay in," said Thor. "She found his journal and told me she'd been dreaming about a monolith in England. She had the journal with her when she left, so we can't be sure what Mallory knew about the Cheyenne Stone. His computer still works, but we can't break his password to get in."

Tandor looked guilty. "I've been too busy here to do it myself."

"Take me there when we're done and I'll hack into it," Logan said. "I want to see what happened after Mallory stopped coming to the monolith."

The cameras continued recording long after NORAD fell to the zombie virus. When the generators kicked on, the cameras switched to infrared, making it easier to see the large, black stone. Animals gathered again in October, starting with small mice, and then larger animals appeared on their own, ending with a brown bear.

Where the animals came from was a mystery. There had to be a tunnel at the lake. Not one animal drank from the lake, but each died within a few minutes of entering the cavern. When they died, the stone would glow and the cameras stopped. Picasso sped forward to a tape showing Whisper and Lachlan in the cavern. They hid from a brown bear as it sniffed the water. It wasn't long until the bear toppled over, and the cameras cut out. When the video came up again, Whisper and Lachlan were gone.

"Do you have any idea who the cloaked figures are?" asked Thor.

"I've been all over the world and I've seen a lot of strange things, but nothing like this," said Logan. "The monolith is fashioned from obsidian. Most monoliths don't have carvings or symbols, unless they are Neolithic. If these markings are Babylonian, I'll need time to translate them. Monoliths are said to be doorways to other dimensions, used by ancient gods to go from one place to another."

"Can you read the markings?" asked Dragon, pointing at the screen. "Maybe they say how to open the monolith?"

Logan set aside his cup and leaned forward, scanning the carvings on the screen. "I'm rusty, but I think it says, 'All who enter…shall be led down the same path.' They have a library here. Someone needs to find a book on ancient ruins. If there isn't one, then I'll see what I can find on Mallory's computer."

Smack and Dodger got up and announced they were going to the library. At least someone was trying to help, Logan thought.

"Rose mentioned Dr. Leopold claimed that he brought the Black Plague here," Star said. She went over to sit on a desk. "Do you think he's the cloaked figure that keeps coming and going from the monolith?"

"Leopold claims he's immortal. He said he served under Hitler, so he must have been here this entire time trying to create immortal vampires. I'm just guessing, but I think he needed a sample of the original plague, so he used the portal to return to the fourteenth century to collect a sample and bring it forward in time. I believe that figure is Leopold and the people coming back with him are the vescali. If that's the case, then Leopold is the one who brought the vescali into the future. It also explains why he's been trying so hard to increase the strength and longevity of his own species."

"I've never heard of the vescali," said Star.

"I have," said Tandor. "They appear in ancient Japanese stories. They drink the blood of children, and then vanish. I always thought they were a myth."

Logan continued. "They are a race of demons that were said to have died out centuries ago. From what I gather, the vescali have been working for the Kaiser for a long time. With a network of these stones, an immortal could travel from place to place and return to their original location in the same period. Think of it as a revolving door. We've seen Leopold go back and forth bringing more vescali with him. What the Kaiser doesn't know is Leopold never had any intention of making vampires immortal. He wants his own species to be stronger, and he has with Cadence's blood."

Dragon let out a snort. "The Kaiser is a vampyr, different from a vampire. He's immortal. There were other plagues, like the Spanish Flu epidemic at the turn of the century, so why bother going back in time? The virus is already here."

"Because the virus is always mutating," said Logan. "It sounds like the Black Plague is what the Kaiser needs to create vampires. It wasn't until Leopold came through the portal and contacted the Kaiser that they perfected it. Only those lunatics merged the H1N1 virus with the fourteenth century virus to create immortal vampires. Since the virus can't be controlled, it also created zombies, therianthropes and superhumans. The Kaiser and Leopold don't care if they wipe out the human race to obtain what they want."

"Well, you seem to know everything, Agent Logan," Rafe said. "I guess your time in the Death Lab paid off. It's a shame you didn't kill Leopold when you had the chance."

Dragon crossed his arms, looking pissed. "The Kaiser knew the monolith was here all the time, yet he never tried to take over NORAD. Leopold could have infected the soldiers here, but instead he just kept bringing the vescali into the future."

"I knew it was a government conspiracy," said Phoenix. "If the government hadn't found the Cheyenne Stone, the Kaiser wouldn't be in power and the vescali wouldn't be here."

A door to a side room opened and Micah stepped in. By the group's reaction, Logan realized only the Dark Angels knew Micah was present.

"I've heard everything I need," said Micah, zipping up his coat. "I'm going back to Seven Falls to inform Captain Highbrow what we've learned. Rose should have arrived by now. She must have run into trouble coming here. Care to go with me, Tandor?"

"Is it a good idea for Tandor to go?" asked Rafe, smirking. "Pallaton is at the camp. He went to warn Highbrow about the bounty hunters. Knowing Rose, she stuck around to talk to Pallaton. If it matters, I heard from Jean-Luc that Pallaton's been replaced by Bechtel as the new Captain of the Shadowguard. The worm moved quick through the ranks and got in good with the Kaiser. Trust me. Bechtel is far worse than Pallaton."

Logan was not surprised, he never trusted Bechtel in the first place. No one realized how close the Shadowguard came to setting them up. Pallaton had saved their lives, but he wasn't getting any credit and neither was Jean-Luc.

Tandor bristled. "If Pallaton is going to the camp, then I'm going with you. I also think Dragon should tag along. He's the best fighter and we may need him."

"I'll go," said Dragon looking at Tandor, "but you should stay here and help Picasso. We don't want any trouble." He placed his hand on Freeborn's shoulder when she started to protest. "I know I just arrived, but I need to convince Highbrow to bring the camp here."

"Just be careful," Freeborn said, kissing him.

Dragon put on a coat, strapped his swords to his back, and left the control room with Micah.

"Shouldn't you be sorting out this puzzle, Logan?" Rafe asked. "What are you waiting for? Thor, take the good agent to Cadence's room and get to work. Let's solve this riddle and bring Cadence back where she belongs."

Thor took Star by the hand and went out the door. "Let's go, Logan."

Logan dropped his blanket, slipped into his coat and joined them in the hallway. Logan followed the young couple up two flights, through a mall-like area, and to Mallory's sparse quarters. His living space had minimal furniture, along with a computer and several shelves filled with books. It was the pictures of English castles covering one wall that interested Logan the most.

Logan studied the photos. "Was Mallory British? The Romans ruled Britannia. It was the furthest outpost in their empire. The Roman Stone could be the one Cadence came out of and one of these castles may be where it's hidden."

"Computer's on," Star said, moving away from the desk. She joined Logan, examining the castles. "Thor, what did Cadence tell you about her dreams?"

"Something about a graveyard, a monolith, and a castle. I found a drawing of the monolith in Mallory's journal, but it's not like the one we have. The markings are different. Maybe they're different on all the stones."

Logan sat at the computer and rolled out the keyboard. His fingers whizzed across keys as he searched until he located a coded file. The password was easy to skirt around.

"We're in people!" Logan wanted a pat on the back, but it wasn't coming. Popping his fingers, he started typing and brought up a list of hidden files on Mallory's hard drive. He scanned them, whistling when he opened one that looked interesting. He gave a triumphant hoot when he found one titled *English Monoliths*. "How quaint."

Logan read the report, memorizing paragraphs as he went. Star and Thor stood behind him scanning faster than he could read, but he refused to move aside for amateurs. "Well, this is interesting," said Logan. "Mallory was born around 1301 A.D. in London, and arrived at Pevensey Castle in the summer of 1342 to study a monolith called the Roman Stone. Tandor should have hacked into this computer when he arrived and you would have had the answers you needed."

Star sat on the bed. "1342?"

"Mallory claims the Babylonians created twelve monoliths," Logan continued, "but the Romans found them and scattered the stones throughout their empire. Under Emperor Vespasian's orders, the Roman Stone was brought to Britannia. The Ninth Legion guarded it, but they vanished without a trace along with the monolith. William the Conqueror unearthed the monolith in the ruins of a fort, named it the Roman Stone, and built Pevensey Castle to stand guard over it. Two hundred years later, Mallory arrived at the castle with Dr. Jarvis Leopold to unravel the monolith's secrets."

Logan leaned back, as things started to make sense.

"They found a way to open it and arrived in Colorado in 2003. The Cheyenne Stone was already at NORAD. Leopold disappeared, but Mallory came here to find a way back home."

Star cuddled up to Thor as he sat down next to her.

"Someone must have been helping Mallory," said the Viking, "or he never would have been able to infiltrate NORAD. He needed a high-level security clearance. That person could still be at another base. Phoenix could be right. This may be a government conspiracy. Does Mallory know if they found the remaining monoliths?"

"Hold on, tough guy. There are lots of files stored on this computer. I know you two can read faster than I can, but let me do my job. Okay?" He opened a new file and laughed. "Mallory translated the ruin's symbols. In short, a blood sacrifice is required to open the portal and only immortals can use it to pass through. Fortunately, you chameleons are immortal. At least some of you are. You can use the portal to go after Cadence."

"It's close to six in the morning and some of us chameleons are tired," said Star, hiding a yawn behind her hand. "You should send a team to the fourth lake and find those tunnels, Thor. There's got to be one that animals and the vescali use. We should close them off until we're ready to use the Cheyenne Stone."

Thor kissed the top of her head. "Go on. I'll join you later." When she left, he turned to Logan. "I wonder if Mallory warned our government about a possible epidemic. Does he say anything about it? If he figured out how the monolith works, he could have changed the course of history and been a hero instead of a catalyst."

"Big word for a big guy. I didn't realize you were smart," Logan said, not disguising his sarcasm. "Mallory was smart, but he didn't know Leopold was vescali. Leopold is the only reason that portal opened. The vescali are immortal, but somehow they died off during the Black Plague. Even if Mallory realized the stone was opening and Leopold was using it, our soldiers couldn't have used it since they're mortal. Mallory couldn't use the monolith to return home either."

"What does Mallory say about Pevensey Castle?"

Logan pushed his chair back. "Richard had two brothers at Pevensey. William was the eldest, and Thomas, the youngest. Both served Lord Montagu, whose family received the castle from William the Conqueror for their help at the Battle of Hastings. The brothers should still be there. If Cadence finds the Roman Stone at the castle, she should be able to come back home."

"Not if the vescali are guarding it. A team should go after her."

"Which reminds me, I have something for you." Logan reached into his pocket and withdrew a vial of purple liquid. "Leopold claims this is a cure to the H1N1z virus. He's had it this whole time, though never had any intention of using it. Sorry I didn't think of it before Dragon and Micah left."

Thor pocketed the vial. "We have medical equipment here. I'll give it to Tandor. We can always catch a zombie to try it out on."

Logan yawned. There was a small coffee maker on the desk, complete with a can of coffee. He used the bathroom sink for water and brewed a pot to stay awake. "Do you have a team at the monolith, Captain Thor? Not to be an alarmist, but Dragon had the right idea. No vescali should be allowed through the stone, and you have enough chameleons here to make sure they won't."

"A team is there now," said Thor, standing up and stretching his arms wide. "I want everything that's stored on that computer, Logan. I need what Mallory knew about the monolith, about Leopold, and anything else helpful before I send a team in after Cadence."

Thor went to the bathroom. Logan opened another file as the coffee brewed and found detailed drawings of a medieval breed of werewolves. There were notes on the Old Ones, as well as vampiric wraiths.

"Cadence has more than vescali to worry about," said Logan. "So does your rescue team. They better take Holy Water, wooden stakes, and silver bullets. Pevensey Castle is crawling with vamps and werewolves. And not the friendly kind."

Thor stepped out of the bathroom. "Good to know."

Logan frowned. "You could have sprayed before coming out."

"I wanted you to remember me after I'm gone."

Rising to shut the bathroom door, Logan returned to the computer and continued reading Mallory's reports. The odds for Cadence returning were not good. Even if Thor sent a rescue team after her, Logan expected none of them to return.

As he scanned Mallory's files, he came across one that struck him

165

as odd. The captain had written about the Roman fort called Anderida located near Pevensey Castle and the Spear of Destiny guarded within. In bold fonts, Mallory wrote 'the spear is the only weapon that can be used to kill vampyrs.'

Logan caught his breathe. The spear that had pierced Christ's body existed. The spear was real, and it was beneath the Roman outpost. If Cadence was as clever as he believed, she would get her hands on the spear. Though it was tempting to volunteer for the rescue mission, the stakes were too high and survival rate low.

Those were odds he didn't like.

Chapter Fifteen

A flurry fell on the roof of the Crystal Palace as Raven knelt before the altar. Her groom was shorter still. A priest in a black frock presided over the ceremony. Everyone wore black, including the best man and matron-of-honor, Bechtel and Salustra. Luna was on a leash held by Salustra, her snow-white fur contrasting with the black figures. Lord Salvatore D'Aquilla sat on the front row along with the American vampire lords. The Shadowguard lined the sides of the chamber, silent as statues.

Raven heard the Kaiser say 'I do' in a loud, commanding voice. Raven muttered the words when it came her turn to speak, but she was ready when her husband turned to kiss her. The Kaiser's eyes gleamed bright yellow, matching her own. Raven tasted blood in the kiss. Drawing back, she noticed a drop of blood on the Kaiser's lips. Fangs extended, he licked it away before taking her by the hands. He lifted her up, turned to the crowd and declared, "Behold, my beautiful bride!"

Applause shook the palace. Vampires beheld the newlyweds with glowing eyes and protruding teeth. Vampire lords were quick to congratulate them, as did vampires closest to their path. Raven paid little attention as they strode along a sidewalk flanked by torch-bearing Shadowguard. Escorted to a white limo, the couple waited for Salustra to bring Luna. Bechtel climbed in armed with an automatic rifle, and they were ready to depart.

"This calls for a celebration," said the Kaiser, smiling wide.

Bechtel popped a bottle of champagne. As soon as he and Salustra had served everyone a glass of the delightful bubbly, they toasted and drank.

"Salvatore offered you his villa in Rome. Of course, Italy is best in spring. Will you accept his offer or postpone your honeymoon?" asked Salustra, pulling her cape around her shoulders.

"Perhaps we'll fly there in April." The Kaiser's voice was tired. "The lab must be rebuilt and Leopold requires new assistants. Trotsky was the sole survivor of the explosion." He patted Raven on the hand. "But I have a surprise for my dear wife. Queen Cinder has prepared a reception for us at Miramont Castle. We will stay the night in the bridal suite and return home tomorrow evening. I am looking forward to this night."

Raven drained her glass and gestured to Bechtel for a refill. "I'd love to visit Egypt. I want to see the pyramids."

Raven stroked Luna's head and smiled when she purred in response. "Of course you will go with us, dear Luna." The puma's mouth spread wide, revealing her fangs. "Won't she, darling? Do reassure Luna, Balan. I know you won't mind."

The Kaiser began to twitch and convulse. Raven screamed as her husband shook from his seat, and fell to the floor. Bechtel threw himself onto his master in an attempt to restrict the thrashing. Raven's screams grew louder. Salustra removed her shoe and lodged the heel between the Kaiser's teeth, holding his tongue down. As the chaos ensued, the back window of the limo cracked and the champagne glasses shattered.

Salustra's eyes grew wide. "It's a seizure."

Raven was silent. Luna still growled, the fur on her back standing on end. Bechtel put his arm across the Kaiser's chest, pressing hard.

"All great leaders suffer from it. It's nothing to be afraid of. It will pass," Salustra kept the heel between his teeth and cringed when the Kaiser crushed it. She attempted to jam her other shoe in his drooling, snapping mouth, but it was no use.

"You've seen this before," said Bechtel, grunting from the effort.

"Not in the Kaiser. But I know the disease. My brother suffered from it his entire life. There's a medicine to help. Let's get him up on the seat and cover him."

Raven embraced Luna, not daring to touch the Kaiser. His eyes had rolled back and he was snarling. The werepuma pushed her aside, placed her paws on the Kaiser's shoulders and helped Bechtel restrain him.

"We should go home," said Raven. "Let's not go to the party. My husband needs rest, that's all."

Salustra shook her head. "That's not what he'll want. This is the Kaiser's moment of triumph. He's searched his lifetime for someone like you, Raven. To send him home would enrage him. Move aside, Luna. He's growing calm. Help me, Bechtel. We must lift him into the seat. Raven, come here and sit next to him. It will help if you hold him."

Reluctant, Raven positioned herself to hold him as Salustra and Bechtel lifted the Kaiser beside her. He stopped thrashing, his head was hanging and his clothes were wet with drool. Salustra tidied the Kaiser as Bechtel found a blanket to cover him. Luna moved to the far side of the limo and watched the Kaiser, exhaling a soft growl.

"This isn't right. If this is a seizure, how do you explain this?" Bechtel asked, holding up the broken bottle of champagne.

Salustra paled.

"You said something caused this," Bechtel accused. "What did you say to him, Raven? This is your fault. Both of you are scheming against him."

"Don't be stupid. Raven said nothing. It broke in the ruckus. However, my shoes are ruined now and I must go to the party in my bare feet. Go sit, Bechtel. Your bad breath is enough to cause anyone to convulse."

Left alone with her husband, Raven smoothed the Kaiser's hair from his brow. She wondered what she said to upset him. Confused and frightened, she wrapped her fingers around his and pressed his head against her shoulder. He began to stir.

"What happened?" asked the Kaiser. He wiped his hand across his mouth and shuddered head to toe. "My head aches and there's pain in my spine. Perhaps I'm getting too old for weddings; the price for marrying someone so young."

"Better, darling?"

The Kaiser nodded and sat up straight. "You asked if Luna could travel with us, and the answer is yes. Whatever you wish for the asking, Raven. Ask for the moon and I'll give it to you. This time I've found my true soul mate. Of all my wives, only you can make me feel this way."

"Don't speak of other women. I will not share you with any other." Raven pushed his graying hair back from his forehead. "You are mine. No one else matters but me."

The Kaiser beamed. "Protective and jealous. I chose wisely."

At Miramont Castle, a crowd greeted the couple as they climbed out of the limo together. Shadowguard dotted the porch like decorations, pushed aside as guests hurried through the front door.

"It will be a night to remember," said the Kaiser, as he led Raven inside. Queen Cinder and Lord Cerberus waited. The Kaiser removed his overcoat and tossed it at Cerberus. "I hope you prepared everything as specified, Cerberus. You know how I am about details."

"Everything is ready, my lord." The boyish vampire handed the coat to a servant and bowed to kiss Raven's hand. "My lady, welcome back to our home. Your friends await in the parlor. Tonight's banquet will far outshine your previous experience."

Raven took it all in. The decorations, loud voices, music, and the odor of cinnamon and vanilla swirled in her senses. Friends kissed her cheek, and Raven's eyes found the pretty, wrapped gifts that covered the expanse of a table and trailed across the floor. Raven joined her husband on a red velvet couch near the fireplace. She was grateful when Salustra appeared with Luna. The werepuma was without her leash and trotted to Stephen, the werewolf. The two touched noses.

"Luna likes Stephen," said Raven. "I said I didn't want any more pets, but I want a werewolf puppy as a playmate for Luna. She gets lonesome and needs a companion."

"We will see," said the Kaiser, tolerant of her request. He gazed toward the entryway as D'Aquilla entered the room, dressed in gray and accompanied by two alluring women. "I must greet our guests, my dear. I won't be long." He kissed her cheek and walked over to welcome the Italian as more vampires entered.

D'Aquilla spotted Raven seated alone and joined her. He kissed her hand and recited something in Italian. Raven's fangs extended.

"Congratulations, my dear. I have a gift just for you." He reached into his pocket and produced a slender, velvet box and opened it exposing a breathtaking ruby bracelet. "This once belonged to the infamous seductress and murderess, Lucrezia Borgia."

Bedazzled, Raven held out her left arm and watched as D'Aquilla placed it around her wrist. Once fastened, the Italian kissed the back of her wrist and slid his fingers the length of her arm, causing her to tremble.

"It's lovely," she said, breathless.

"Had I met you first, I would have made you my wife and given you a castle of your own. Colorado Springs is no place for someone as enchanting as you."

She caught a whiff of D'Aquilla's cologne and leaned closer, smiling. "I want a castle of my own. Tell me of the Old Ones. Are they as vicious as the legends say? If only one fought in the Death Games, it would be so exciting."

"Stephan is tame compared to that ancient breed," said D'Aquilla, as he crossed his legs and leaned against her. "Old Ones age slower and many have been alive for a thousand years, but you can always tell them apart from younger werewolves." He smiled, revealing bleached-white teeth. "I think it's something about their gray hair."

Raven reached to pet Luna's head aware that D'Aquilla watched. "I purchased your fighter, Loki, because I knew him once. My real interest is the story of his battle against an Old One. Is it true? Did you really pit an Old One against Loki?"

The vampire lord nodded as he stopped a server and reached for two glasses of champagne. He handed a glass to Raven. D'Aquilla was the most handsome man present, and from Salustra's glances, Raven knew they were intimate in the past.

"That's when the problem started," D'Aquilla said. "Loki defeated one of the most vicious Old Ones that had ever fought in the European Death Games. The werewolf's name was Titan, and he came from the Black Forest. It was an exciting fight between the pair. Had it not been for Loki's superior speed, Titan would have defeated him. The scar on Loki's face is a reminder that the Old Ones are the most dangerous creatures on the planet. You can find them in the ancient forests of Europe and often in abandoned cities."

"I'd like to visit Italy one day and watch the games."

D'Aquilla laughed and let his fingers glide across Raven's neck. "You are unaware of the bleak conditions in the Old World. Zombies rule the land. Most of my days are spent at my castle on Lake Garda, which you would enjoy."

"Stop filling her head," said Salustra, scolding. The dark-haired woman squeezed between D'Aquilla and Raven. She sat on their laps before they separated and made room. "Be careful, Raven. This man is a cobra, and he bites. He's also an impossible flirt, so take nothing he says to heart."

"I always say what I mean." D'Aquilla reached into Salustra's lap and lifted up a shrunken head with stringy, black hair. "Is this a Christmas ornament, my dear?"

Salustra laughed. "It's a gift from Queen Cinder. The child thinks every woman needs an Amazonian shrunken head. You are more than welcome to hang it on the tree."

Raven took the shrunken head from D'Aquilla and examined it. Two large rubies filled the eye sockets. She walked to the lobby, and instead of placing it on the Christmas tree, she dropped it in her evening bag. The rubies were exquisite, and she wanted them for herself.

Dinner was announced. Raven found her nametag at the far end of the table. Queen Cinder and Salustra sat on either side. The Kaiser sat at the opposite end and was flanked by Lord Cerberus and Big Mike, a vampire lord from Wyoming donning a cowboy hat. D'Aquilla and the other vampire lords sat spaced between women on both sides of the table. The atmosphere was festive, yet Raven found little taste in the courses. Luna and Stephen curled up near Raven's chair, both content with their beef soup and bone.

"It's unfortunate the lab was destroyed, Madam Monique," said D'Aquilla, addressing a woman with flowing red hair seated next to Jean-Luc. "But it's my understanding the culprit was caught and dealt with. I doubt anyone planted a bomb under this table, but if you care to look, I'll join you."

"You make fun, Salvatore, but it was sabotage," said Madam Monique. Diamonds sparkled on her neck and ears. "Just go to the Graveyard club for all the exciting gossip. I heard Rose and the Dark Angels are to blame. Wasn't Rose a close friend of yours, Jean-Luc?"

Jean-Luc forced a smile. "I wouldn't say that. Nor would I credit Rose with planning the prisoners' escape. It had to be Rafe."

"Is our society nothing more than rogue juveniles and malcontents?" Madam Monique asked, licking her spoon. "I think they should be captured and executed."

Raven listened with intent to D'Aquilla, Madam Monique, and Jean-Luc. Their conversation was far more interesting than Salustra and Cinder chatting about tribes in the Amazon. Everyone was eager to blame Pallaton for failing to capture Highbrow, and Rose or Rafe for masterminding the escape of Dragon and the other fighters. She sensed Jean-Luc was nervous. He reeked of fear, dabbing his forehead with a napkin, each time dotting it with more blood.

"What's important is that the Christmas games aren't cancelled," said D'Aquilla. "Aries of Athens is my finest fighter. Without Dragon to fight in the arena, the only ones who stand a fighting chance against him are Loki, now owned by Raven, or two of my own. Monkey is a bloody-thirsty superhuman and must be kept sedated when she's not in the arena. Skye is my vicious little werepuma. I should like to show them to you before Friday's fight if you care to see them, Madam."

"You own a Chameleon?" asked Monique. "I came all the way here from New York to see Dragon fight. However, if you're willing to have your own fighters face each other, then I'm sure Friday night will be quite the exciting event. Though, I'd love to see this Cadence in the arena."

Jean-Luc lowered his champagne glass. "Our host has hired bounty hunters to track Cadence. Human bounty hunters."

"Shall we make a wager?" asked Madam Monique. "Something light and unpretentious." The vampire lords looked at her. "I wager fifty humans that by Christmas Eve the Kaiser will have captured Cadence."

"I'd prefer to have your broach, my dear. It belonged to Queen Elizabeth I, did it not?" D'Aquilla pointed at a large diamond that Monique was wearing. She gave a subtle nod. "In return, I will wager my private jet that Cadence will not be found. What can bounty hunters do that Pallaton could not? They'll have no better results, I can assure you. They are human."

A horrible scream came from the kitchen and the sounds of a scuffle ensued. Lord Cerberus moved with invisible speed, tipping over his chair as he swept through the room. Cerberus returned a few seconds later dragging a girl by the hair. The child was only ten years old, her little hands covered with blood as she was forced to her knees at the Kaiser's chair.

"If you will not freely sacrifice your blood for the feast, Dolly, then it shall be taken by force," said Cerberus. Producing a small knife, he slit the girl's throat from ear to ear and caught her spouting blood in a goblet. Relying on his speed, the vampire filled several glasses before tossing the girl to a female guest who fed upon her. Goblets were handed to the Kaiser, D'Aquilla, Cinder, Salustra, and to Raven.

"A diet of chocolate made her blood rich and savory," said Cerberus, a note of pride in his voice. "I apologize there isn't more to offer everyone else."

Raven stared at the bloody goblet. A drop of blood spilled over the goblet's rim and she watched as a stain spread across the white tablecloth.

"A toast to the bride and groom," said D'Aquilla, in a loud voice. "Long may they enjoy love's passions and each other's fidelity."

Goblets of blood or champagne were raised. The Kaiser, Cinder, and Salustra drank the child's blood, but D'Aquilla passed his goblet of blood to Madam Monique and lifted a glass of champagne instead. Raven felt everyone turn and stare at her. She regarded the guests and her husband with a cold gaze. She made no effort to pick up the goblet, but instead passed hers to Jean-Luc.

"It's delicious," said Jean-Luc.

"You look nervous, Jean-Luc. Why?" Raven stared at the gray-haired vampire. "Is it because some people claim you are a Dark Angel? Someone helped Rafe escape. Cinder and Cerberus wouldn't help him, but I think you did. Are you a traitor, Jean-Luc?"

"What's this?" asked the Kaiser, surprised. "Jean-Luc, explain yourself. Why does Raven think you are a Dark Angel? Did you help Rafe escape from the castle? Is this true? Speak up!"

Raven stood. "When I was here last, Jean-Luc made it clear he's a

Dark Angel. He's been lying to you, my love. I know when people are lying. I want this traitor executed."

Jean-Luc moved so fast he upset the goblet, dark blood staining the tablecloth. "I will not sit here and be accused of something I did not do. Rafe was here under the protection of Cinder and Cerberus, yet I am singled out. I may have been a Dark Angel once, but I swore loyalty to the Kaiser."

"You are nervous, Jean-Luc," said D'Aquilla, smirking. He pointed at small droplets of blood sliding down the man's face. "If you are innocent, why are you sweating?"

"Why, indeed?" asked the Kaiser, his voice sounding deep and powerful. He stood and glided over to Jean-Luc. His shadow rose with him, making him appear taller than usual. He clasped Jean-Luc's arm and forced the weaker vampire into a chair. "It's time I learn who is loyal and who is not. We will start with Jean-Luc."

"But I didn't do it," cried out Jean-Luc. He pointed at Salustra. "She did it! Salustra is the one who told me to release Rafe. She made arrangements to free Dragon and the other slaves with the help of Bechtel! It was their plan, not mine. I was just following orders."

Watching close, Raven noticed Salustra neither trembled, nor grew nervous at the accusation. Captain Bechtel took a sip from his champagne, smirking. The Kaiser smiled at Raven, and with sudden, vicious speed, he plucked Jean-Luc from his chair and sank his fangs deep into the vampire's throat. A groan escaped Jean-Luc as the Kaiser extracted every drop of blood before tossing the body to the floor, bones shattering on the tile.

"You should all see who I am in my true form," said the Kaiser

Stepping over Jean-Luc's remnants, the vampyr walked to Raven. With each step, he grew taller until he towered over six feet. Commanding a muscular frame with handsome features, he leaned down and kissed Raven's forehead.

"What magic is this?" asked a stunned Raven.

"By choosing the form of a man much smaller than anyone else, I was testing you all. Most of you respected me out of fear. Some saw profit in it. A few of you believed I was weak." He stepped back from Raven and spread out his arms, bristling with authority. "Is this shape more befitting your lord and master?"

"You have others?" asked D'Aquilla, worried. He put his hand on Madam Monique's arm, keeping her from leaving her chair. Most of the vampires appeared nervous and frightened.

The Kaiser lowered his arms, turning his gaze upon him. "Maybe I do. The rest of you are made in my image, but none of you are as strong or powerful. It's true. A spy destroyed my lab. Logan was no doubt responsible, but I shall find out who helped him. You will either serve me or suffer the same fate as Jean-Luc. I will have your oaths, now." His words reverberated through the room, shaking the silverware and filling their ears.

Bechtel stepped forward. Shadowguard appeared in the room and took position behind each of the vampire lords' chairs. The Turk, the large and powerful ruler of New York City, also rose from his chair. Others followed. Mr. Rafferty, the west coast lord, along with Big Mike, the cowboy hat-wearing controller of the northern states.

"If you want us to swear our allegiance, Kaiser," said Big Mike, "I would be the first to kiss you and your bride. I must admit, though, I prefer Raven."

"I signed a contract to serve you and you alone," D'Aquilla said, rising from his chair. He tossed aside his napkin. "Shall I sign one that assures you my soul upon my death? If that is what you want, then it is yours."

Mr. Rafferty used the tablecloth to dab his forehead. It came away wet with blood. "When you gave me Los Angeles I swore an oath of faithful service to you, my lord. I will do whatever you ask."

Raven had never seen her husband this angry before and it set her heart racing. He was the fiercest man in the room. She had no doubt he could have killed every guest in a moment.

"I never questioned your loyalty, Salvatore. When I make you an immortal, you will then swear your soul. As for the rest of you who are Makers, I need you. Be at ease Mr. Rafferty, before you bleed from every orifice. Everyone here is a friend. If I suspected otherwise, you would be dead." The room hung on those words, comprehending the threat in his voice.

"I am loyal only to you, my lord and master," said Bechtel, in a firm voice. "I have done my best to uncover the Dark Angel spies at the Citadel. Jean-Luc is but one of them. As for Salustra and Pallaton, I could not find proof they are involved. I am certain Rose orchestrated the prisoners' escape with Logan's help, and I'll find out who her contacts are among the Shadowguard. I swear it."

The Kaiser inclined his head and the captain stepped back. Taking Raven by the hand, the vampyr brushed past the captain toward the stairs. Bechtel cried out as the shadow slipped from the wall and enveloped him, before traveling up the stairs ahead of the couple. A smile appeared on Raven's face as the terrified captain pushed through the Shadowguard and exited the front door.

"I want Bechtel replaced," said Raven. "He's not loyal to you. I'm sure of it."

The door to the bridal chamber opened on its own, revealing a canopied bed and a roaring fire in the expansive fireplace. The shadow entered and caused the firelight to fade. Raven led her husband in, comforted by her new protector.

Chapter Sixteen

*H*ighbrow woke from a dead sleep. Something cold and sharp pressed against his neck. His eyes adjusting, he brought into focus a gray-bearded man crouched over his cot, holding a knife to his exposed carotid. Sparse moonlight revealed they were not alone. He was not sure how many, camouflage and guns blending in the gloom. Two men stood guard at the door, and another watched the window.

"Your bodyguard didn't put up much of a fight." The bearded man glanced over where Private Odin's still form lay on the floor. "The kid ain't dead, but he'll have one helluva headache when he wakes up. Where's the girl?"

"I don't know," said Highbrow. "Cadence left weeks ago and hasn't been back."

The leader pricked Highbrow's throat with his knife. His breath reeked of booze, onions, and tobacco. Highbrow grabbed the man's wrist, pulling the knife back. A dribble of blood slid down his neck.

"That's no answer. Tell us where she's at, boy, and I may leave you with your skin. I'm handy with a knife. Don't bother shouting for your guards. There aren't any left to help you, cap'n. Where's she gone?"

"Kill me and you'll never find her," said Highbrow, trying to sound braver than he was.

The leader drew back and slugged Highbrow. The strike broke Highbrow's nose and cut open his lip. A few more blows left Highbrow dazed and in considerable pain.

"You ready to cooperate?"

Highbrow grabbed his nose and shifted the cartilage back in place. He wiped it and spat out a mouthful of blood. Someone must have noticed the bounty hunters entering the camp. He expected soldiers to arrive any moment. He had to stall.

"What is the Kaiser paying you? I'll double it."

"Vamps pay with weapons, booze, and women. They allow us to go where we want, when we want, and that's something you can't offer. Dawn's breaking. I'll give you one minute before I slice your throat. Where's the girl?"

Highbrow caught his breath as he felt a thump on the underside of the bed. No one else noticed as Barbarella stirred. "You can't trust the Kaiser. The Shadowguard never keep their word. I hope you were paid in advance. Even if you give them what they want, they'll kill you. That's what they do. Kill humans."

"What a crock of shit. The soldier boy's not going to tell us a damn thing," said a man with pockmarks on his face and a red scarf wrapped around his neck. "I say we blow the barricade sky high, let the zombies in, and get the hell out of here. These dumb kids'll never know what hit 'em. We can double-back and look for the girl in Manitou Springs."

"Shut it," said the leader. "I'm not spending the next few days scouring the countryside. This is an in-and-out job." He pulled back his arm, ready to hit Highbrow again. "Where is your commander, Captain Highbrow? Last chance."

"We had a fight," said Highbrow. "Cadence is infected and dangerous. She took off with my best fighters a few weeks ago and hasn't been heard from since. The radio is out, so is the phone. The only way Cadence can contact us is to come here. She's not welcome and knows it. If she's not at Pike's Peak, she'll pick a place close to the Citadel that is well-defended. She can't be far, but your guess is as good as mine."

"Wrong answer," said the leader.

"Wait!"

Highbrow scrambled, intending to reason with the leader, but found himself struck in the face once again. A well-placed kick sent Highbrow flopping back onto the cot. As he struggled to rise a second time, the man in the red scarf drew his hunting knife and lunged. A brief scuffle left the blade lodged between Highbrow's ribs. Searing pain reduced Highbrow to an unresisting lump the moment his attacker pulled the knife free. He pressed a hand to the wound, knowing he had but minutes to live and shouted for help.

"Barbarella! Kill!"

From beneath the cot rose a low, fierce growl. The bounty hunters were fear-stricken as the enormous werepuma appeared from under the bed and attacked the bounty hunters. One blow from her black paw ripped the red-scarfed man's head from his shoulders. She turned her attention to the leader and sank her teeth into his neck. Both men collapsed, dead before they hit the ground. Shouts, screams, and gunfire erupted from the other hunters, rupturing the walls and shattering the windows. Highbrow navigated himself to the floor trying to avoid the terrified men, and crawled toward Odin. He managed to grab the unconscious private's leg and pull him behind the desk. Blood showered them both.

The door crashed open. A bounty hunter turned to flee, and impaled himself on Dragon's katana. The longhaired chameleon struck down a second man. Dead bounty hunters and two soldiers lay outside the door. Panic spread as Dragon and his swords vanished from sight, reappearing and killing them where they stood. Barbarella pulled a bounty hunter from the window and shook him like a rag doll. The hunter fired a few more rounds before slamming to the floor.

Dragon flipped on the lights. He bled from several gunshot wounds to his chest, but remained steady on his feet. Barbarella lay on top of the grisly remains of a bounty hunter, just inches from Highbrow. In the fray, her claws had gashed Highbrow's leg, though he felt no pain. As he inched forward trying to reach Barbarella, Dragon knelt beside the werepuma. He lifted her massive head, but the werepuma did not respond.

"Micah is outside with Sterling and your soldiers. I don't think any bounty hunters escaped." Dragon tore a black scarf from his neck and pressed it against the hole in Highbrow's side. "This is bad. I'm sorry we didn't get here sooner."

"I don't have long to live," said Highbrow, unable to hold back his emotions. "Take over for me, Dragon. You have to move the camp to Cadence's hiding place. Tell her I'm sorry and that I love her."

"Tell her yourself."

Dragon harnessed his sword and ripped open Highbrow's pant leg, examining the deep puncture marks. He dabbed his fingers in a bleeding cut on his own forehead and touched the hole in Highbrow's ribs and the wounds on his leg. Dragon found another scarf on the floor and wrapped the bite mark. Lifting Highbrow into a chair, Dragon turned to check on Odin. The young man was starting to come around.

"What happened?" asked Odin. "My head feels like a cracked egg."

"Bounty hunters," Dragon said, pulling Odin to his feet. He helped the soldier onto Highbrow's cot. "You're lucky to be alive. It's just a bump."

Micah appeared in the doorway. "Is everyone alright?"

The white-haired vampire held a bloodied sword and a pistol, but was unscathed. He took one look at Highbrow and Barbarella, and then glanced out the door. Pallaton and Rose appeared, both damp with snow, blood, and zombie sludge. Rose dropped her backpack and knelt beside the werepuma.

"We're too late," said Rose, as she examined the body. When she raised her hands, they were slick with blood. "There are so many gunshot wounds it's a wonder she could keep fighting. I'm sorry, Highbrow, but there's nothing I can do for her."

"It's my fault she's dead," said Odin. He sat beside her as she transformed into human form. Rose covered her with a blanket. "I never got a chance to tell her, Doc. She was the bravest girl I ever met."

"I'm sorry, Odin," said Rose, in a gentle voice. "Her death isn't your fault. Nor is it Highbrow's. She died trying to save you. That was a brave thing to do."

Odin nodded, his eyes streaming. He lowered his head, lips pulled taught and unable to speak.

"Why is he here?" Highbrow struggled to ask, jabbing a finger in Pallaton's direction. His grief was bordering on anger. "How dare you show your face. Can't you see what you've done? Do you know how many lives you've taken already?"

The former Shadowguard captain looked menacing with an eye patch. Pallaton's left eye focused in sharp on Highbrow.

"My purpose in coming was to help Rose and the Dark Angels. I came to warn them about the bounty hunters," said Pallaton, "but found Rose pinned down on the highway in a skirmish between the hunter's scouts and zombies. Micah and Dragon showed up and convinced me to come with them to camp. Perhaps I shouldn't have bothered. None of this has any meaning now that Raven has married the Kaiser."

Rose stood between them. "Enough of this. I know what he's done in the past, but he's a Dark Angel. Barbarella's death was not his fault. I won't let any harm come to him." She glanced at Pallaton. "Are you staying? You can't go back to the Citadel."

"The Kaiser will kill you if you return," said Micah. "Forget Raven. She's lost to you. I'll smooth things over with Tandor and Picasso. They'll understand you were trying your best to protect this camp. We don't blame you for these attacks."

"I damn well do!" Highbrow winced as his ribs flared with pain. "You're not welcome in my camp, Pallaton. I don't care what Rose or Micah say. Because of you, three of my patrols are dead."

"Because of me Rose is alive. I know you don't trust me, Captain, and I don't blame you. If you allow me, I intend to return to the Citadel and help free the rest of your people and Raven."

Before Highbrow could protest, Pallaton had vanished. Micah and Dragon cleared out the bodies. Rose reached in her backpack and gave two aspirins to Odin. He threw them back without water and gagged.

"You'll be fine, young man," said Rose. She laid a blanket over him. "How are you holding up, captain?"

Highbrow shrugged. He brushed at a tickle on his face, and became concerned. He felt a single, thick whisker protruding from his cheek. "What's on my face?"

The vampire doctor looked startled. Highbrow pulled a whisker out of his face and stared at it. Rose peeled the scarf from his stomach. She probed the wound and lifted his shirt. Pink scar tissue had replaced the hole in his stomach. The doctor unwrapped the other scarf, running her fingers along the bite marks. Both wounds had healed.

"This is odd, Highbrow. How did you survive a stab wound, unless…." Rose met Highbrow's concerned gaze. "You're infected. Dragon and Barbarella. It's the only explanation for your recovery. Your wounds have already healed."

"Highbrow is a chameleon?" Odin asked through his tears. "And a werepuma?"

Rose took the whisker out of Highbrow's hand and looked over it. "It's a cat whisker," she said. "I don't think Barbarella bit you on accident. She knew you were dying and did what she could to save your life."

In the distance, Highbrow heard the doors to the barracks open. His ears twitched as he picked up a conversation between Dragon and Sterling. He scanned a further distance and could hear groups of children outside talking all at once. Trying to sift through the voices, he focused on Dragon and heard him say the bounty hunters were dead. Nomad found their cars parked down the road. After Lt. Sterling alerted the camp, the officer sent the Dark Angels to the ridge to scout for

Shadowguard. Highbrow closed his eyes and ran his fingers across the new scar tissue.

"I'm no longer human, Rose." Highbrow glanced over to see the vampire comforting his bodyguard. She smiled, sympathetic. Highbrow snapped to his feet. "I need fresh air. It reeks of death in here. Stay with Odin a while, please? I've got to sort things out in my head."

"I understand," Rose said. "But it isn't the end of the world."

Unable to listen anymore, Highbrow snatched his coat and stumbled out. Slain bodies were being loaded onto a truck, and Barbarella was carried out with respect.

The Bull Dogs, Blue Devils, Panthers, Razorbacks, Valkyries, and a few remaining Amazons stood near the trucks. These were the last of the teen patrols. Highbrow gazed up as the morning sun streamed through the frost-covered tree limbs, noting how everything smelled different and appeared much brighter. His senses were sharper. Cadence must have felt lost when she changed too. He wondered if his teams would still follow him when they learned the truth.

Aware of the sound of boots crunching through snow, Highbrow watched Nomad walk toward him.

"Barbarella was a remarkable young lady," said Nomad. "She was the reason more ladies didn't die or get infected when that puma attacked her team. Always selfless. I sometimes thought she'd become one of your best officers."

"Instead, I'm burying her," said Highbrow. "Barbarella loved the trails near Midnight Falls. Will you help me bury her there?"

"Of course," said Nomad, looking back at the teen patrols. "I'm sure they will want to join you. I doubt they would stay away even if you ordered them to. Funerals, grief, bring people closer together."

Highbrow nodded. "Anyone who wants to is welcome. I'd appreciate you asking the teams, Nomad. They respect and admire you. I'm not sure they feel the same about me. Some may blame me for Barbarella's death."

The scruffy biker walked to the crowd of teenagers and shared the opportunity with them. At once the teams loaded into a nearby passenger vehicle. Nomad joined them and climbed behind the wheel. Dragon and Odin delivered Barbarella to the vehicle and handed her body to the teams. With care, they positioned her in their midst.

Midnight Falls was nothing more than a creek with a small, flowing waterfall that iced over in winter. Highbrow selected an area near an oak tree to bury Barbarella. The patrol teams worked together to dig a deep grave, lining it with pine boughs. The Amazons wrapped Barbarella in blankets and lowered her in the ground. Odin stood nearby, flanked by the Bull Dogs. Once they covered the grave, everyone gathered around. The Panthers watched the funeral from Moon Tower. Nomad sunk a cross fashioned from two crowbars at the head of the grave, and joined the circle.

Highbrow removed his beret. "Barbarella was brave and strong, willing to put others first no matter the cost. She died trying to protect me. I know the last few days have been difficult for everyone and we've lost many friends and loved ones. Humans, vampires, and werepumas alike. It doesn't matter who we were before we came here, but it matters who we have become. We are a team, but we were also part of Barbarella's pride and she cared for us." He glanced at Rose, who gave him a tender smile.

Highbrow was reminded of just how many had been lost, and filled with emotion. He recited the 23rd Psalm, weeping.

The others joined him, reciting the Psalm. Their voices touched him, and he felt a sense of calm. But as they spoke the words, 'Even though I walk through the valley of the shadow of death, I fear no evil,' Highbrow scanned the trees for an ominous, dark shadow. He spotted Micah and the Dark Angels standing among the teams. Following the prayer, Highbrow tore the Fighting Tigers' patch off his sleeve and dropped it against the cross. Each teenager did the same, except Odin, who removed his crucifix and hung it over the upright iron pole.

The sense of calm soon turned to anxiousness. Highbrow knew they needed to leave Seven Falls.

He did fear evil and it was just miles away, occupying the Citadel.

Chapter Seventeen

*A*t the break of dawn, they rode for the Roman fort as Sir Thomas, Sir Wallace, Lord Montagu, and the entire assembly of castle guards watched from the battlements. Four strange priests had blessed the team invoking an air of impending doom rather than victory. Each wore silver-coated hauberks, and white tunics bearing a red cross. Cadence felt like a crusader, except she had not ridden a horse in ages. The saddle was too narrow and the stirrups were short.

Blaze, unused to riding horses, moaned in misery as they trotted over a well-worn Roman road. Lachlan and Whisper, in comparison, rode like experts.

As they passed a nearby graveyard, Cadence listened to birds singing in the surrounding forest. Their gleeful songs were deceptive, as she noticed armored men following them. They stayed hidden among the trees, unnoticeable to human eyes.

"Whisper," said Cadence. "Are you sure this is the right way?"

Whisper remained calm. "It's twenty miles to the outpost. I see the dog soldiers in the tree line, too. We stay on this road until we come to the fort. They won't attack us out here in broad daylight, but will wait until we're inside."

"I don't like horses." Blaze complained, agitated. "They're too slow. It'll be noon before we arrive."

Lachlan rode beside Cadence, appearing noble and poised. A silver shield engraved with the figure of a hawk hung on the side of his saddle. His Irish galloglass was strapped to the horse's saddle and he wore a long-sword on his side. It was no wonder Sir Thomas found great value in Lachlan's friendship and skill as a fighter. The dog soldiers would not find Lachlan an easy opponent. It was ironic. The monolith had sucked in the three teammates Cadence would have chosen to retrieve the Spear of Destiny. She could not help but feel optimistic.

"We don't have to go on this mission," said Lachlan, light-hearted. "This isn't our fight, Cadence, nor are we obliged to fight Lord Montagu's war. Whisper has maps in his saddle bag, along with a few days of rations."

"Run away? At a time like this?" Cadence shook her head. "Not my style."

The big, red-haired vampire laughed. "And that's but one of the reasons I love you, Cadence Sinclair. You're fearless in battle, yet you never know when I'm teasing you. I wouldn't want you any other way."

A dole of white doves flew out of the forest, and somewhere in the distance church bells rang. Cadence looked over at Lachlan and caught him staring. She had no doubt he loved her. Lachlan made a handsome knight with his square jaw, freckled nose, red hair, and dark green eyes. But she loved him because he was kind and tender.

"I care about you," she said. "More than I've ever cared about anyone."

"I'm honored," Lachlan replied, chuckling. "When we get home, I intend to see you more often. I like sharing a pillow with you. Who knows? You might realize that you can love a vampire, and I hope that vampire is me."

"Trust me. You're the only vampire I'm interested in, Lachlan." Cadence's cheeks burned as she remembered their night together. "If you don't stop staring at me, I will not be able to focus. I need my game face on, so cut it out."

"Whatever my lady desires," Lachlan said, bowing in his saddle.

Cadence could not help but laugh. Lachlan joined in, stopping when Whisper passed them and took the lead, leaving Blaze to bring up the rear.

"We must be close," said Cadence. "Be careful when things heat up, Lachlan. You're reckless and foolhardy at the best of times. Please try to act more like Whisper. Being cautious and deadly is needed here, not Irish heroics."

"I'm a knight," replied Lachlan. He looked straight ahead, trying to hide the smile on his face. "I'll do no less than any other knight would for his lady. My life is yours. I will do what it takes to protect you and see you home, and that's a promise I intend to keep."

The team grew quiet as they approached a small, abandoned village. Homes stood exposed to the elements. There were no graves or graveyard, or any sign of what might have happened to the villagers. A mile further they reached a section of land where no trees grew and the high, green grass swayed in the light wind. The ruins of a Roman fort sat on a cliff beside the sea. There was a stone wall surrounding a few remaining buildings. Broken pillars and statues of Roman gods lay on the ground, impressive even in decay.

Swords drawn, they rode through the gate and entered the outpost. Armored guards appeared from every doorway. More marched around corners wielding spiked maces and spears. Black fur capes draped their armor and some had the jaws of large animals attached to their helmets. Shouts revealed the mounted cavalry through the gates, circling Cadence and her team. Archers appeared on the high above them all. The largest of all the guards stepped forward, swinging his axe. His face was scarred and visible beneath an ancient Roman helmet.

"We're outnumbered, but we have speed on our side. I'll kill their commander. Deal with these dog soldiers," said Cadence wheeling her horse around. She pointed her sword at the leader. "Stand aside or die!"

"You are not welcome here," he said, snarling. "We will kill you and eat your flesh. After that, we'll join our brothers at Pevensey and devour Lord Montagu and his knights."

"We can handle this, Cadence," said Lachlan, bringing up his shield. "Fight your way into the main building. We'll join you soon. Get moving."

A trumpet blared and the commander signaled his troops forward. Cadence charged the big brute. Archers brought down Cadence's horse. She sailed over its head and was already running when she hit the ground. Her sword clashed against his axe with such might that the leader staggered, a stunned expression twisting his face further. Cadence swung again and tore through the commander's heart. As he fell, she removed his head with yet another offense of her blade. The dog soldiers looked at their dead leader and fled.

The door was unguarded. Cadence entered the building and found the ceiling had collapsed and vegetation was growing wild. Vines covered the walls and filled every crack in the stones. The sea-facing wall had crumbled, revealing a blue ocean. Mature trees grew in the center of the square room, surrounding a hole in the ground that on closer inspection unveiled a staircase leading into darkness. As she advanced toward the stairs, a wraith leapt from behind a broken altar. It wailed in fear as it scrambled through the undergrowth and vanished to the far side of the room.

Two guards emerged from the stairs, glaring at Cadence. They lifted their rusty, chipped swords as she launched into the air and landed behind them. With a spin, Cadence split the nearest guard in half and caught the second man in the shoulder, producing an arterial gush. His arm detached, he howled in pain before she struck his neck. The guard's head flipped backward, hanging by loose flesh. He slammed hard to the ground, motionless.

"The Old Ones are fleeing," shouted Lachlan, as he entered the room. He rushed to Cadence's side, scanning the empty space. "There are many more below. We should wait for Whisper and Blaze."

Cadence shook her head. "How sharp are your vampire senses? Is Darkmoore below us? Are you able to detect him or his guards?"

"They're below. So is Darkmoore." Lachlan held his shield aside and peered into the darkness. His eyes turned bright violet and his fangs slid out as he sniffed the air. "There's a lot of them, too. Best let me lead."

"Gallantry isn't necessary," said Cadence, noting a gash in his cheek that drenched his tunic with blood. "Let me go first. I can't be injured or killed."

Lachlan laughed. "If you want the glory, babe, help yourself. I'll be right behind you every step of the way."

Cadence walked down the stairs with caution, giving her eyes time to adjust to the dark. Lachlan followed close. He pointed out several shallow graves and a row of clay, wine jars. Whisper and Blaze appeared behind them, both splattered with the remains of their battles. They fell into step behind Cadence and Lachlan as the ground shifted. Vampires sprang from the ground, shrieking. They attacked with eyes glowing and fangs dripping.

Together they fought the weak vampires, learning that silver swords worked as well as wooden stakes. The wraiths streaked across the room trying to outflank them, but her team was faster and equipped for what they faced. They stabbed and hacked their way through the ghoulish creatures, until they reached another staircase. This one led to a dank, wet cavern.

Torches gave ample light showing stone, Roman coffins lining a wall. Chests sat piled together while gold coins, human, and animal remains dotted the dirty floor. Whisper threw off the stone lid to a coffin and impaled its occupant. As he and Blaze approached the next coffin, they heard a growl from the back of the cave. A large werewolf crept forward on its hind legs. Countless gray beasts, each towering well over seven feet tall, stood behind it. The remaining coffin lids crashed open. Armor-clad wraiths crawled out and joined the werewolves.

"It's time to get mad," shouted Blaze, "and bring out the big guns!"

Blaze threw her sword, landing it clean through a wolf's skull.

She pulled the M4 carbine from her shoulder and unloaded the silver rounds fashioned by Sir Wallace, before launching a grenade at a pack entering from another door. Werewolves and wraiths alike dropped like flies around them. Whisper kept his sword available and watched her back. Lachlan raised his galloglass and attacked an advancing group of ghouls.

Cadence surged forward, cutting through the monsters until she was far ahead of the rest of the team and facing a large, stone coffin. The creatures moved around her, striking ineffective blows while she cut, sliced, and decapitated them. Behind her, Cadence could hear shouts from Whisper, Blaze and Lachlan, mixed with the furious howls and eerie cries of werewolves and wraiths. Most of the Old Ones attacked her team, trusting the ghouls to protect the stone coffin. Lachlan appeared, swinging his massive broadsword and scattering the monsters.

"Go for Darkmoore," Lachlan called out. "He has to be inside the coffin."

Lachlan was attacked from behind and pushed into a group of wraiths, vanishing from view. Cadence kicked the large coffin over, its occupant tumbling to the ground. A knight with a pallid face and yellow fangs stood and faced her. Wisps of hair hung in strands from his sallow scalp. A Celtic cross that looked similar to her own adorned his neck, except the corners folded inward.

"You're Lord Darkmoore?" said Cadence. "I thought you'd look… better."

The vampire lord glared at her with blood-red eyes, extended his talons, and opened his mouth to scream. A rush of beasts came at Cadence from all sides. She swung her sword as jaws flashed and teeth tore at her arms. She was pushed from behind into the coffin, losing her sword. As she struggled to rise, the Old Ones stepped back and waiting for their leader.

Darkmoore kicked her sword out of reach. "Did my brother send you?" he asked in a rasping voice. "You're not like the others who came here to steal the spear. But like them, you shall die and I will feast on your blood."

"I came to kill you."

She rose to her feet, watching the Old Ones close. In an instant, Cadence drew her silver-loaded pistol from its holster and laid waste to three of the monstrosities before the rest turned tail and ran. Darkmoore yowled with the fury of hell as Cadence landed a round in his shoulder. The vampire lord vanished into another tunnel. Lachlan gave chase, followed by the remaining wraiths.

"Wait for us, Cadence!" shouted Whisper.

Blaze tightened her grip. "More coming in! Stand your ground."

A horde of ghouls covered the walls and ceiling of the cave, blocking the tunnel. A wraith dropped from the ceiling biting at Cadence's neck. More fell like spiders from the darkness above, scattering around Cadence, clawing at her armor, screaming when they burst into flames. But it was Lachlan's screams that terrified her.

Her thoughts raged with killing and reaching Lachlan. With inhuman speed, she flew through the cave, carving up ghouls and dismembering the remaining werewolves. She butchered her enemies until there nothing remained. The only thought in her mind now was reaching Lachlan.

Whisper and Blaze were close on her heels, as she entered a larger section of the cave. A crystal coffin glowing a strange shade of pink was the centerpiece of the room. It was transparent, through which Cadence could see a body holding a spear.

Not far from the coffin, Cadence spotted Lachlan face down in the dirt. A ghoul crouched on her lover's back, chewing his fingers. She shot the wraith in the head. Her heart was slamming in her chest as she hurried to kneel beside Lachlan. Cadence turned the Irishman over and felt her heart skip a beat. She slumped forward, fighting back a wave of tears. Laughter came from behind the crystal coffin. Cadence stood to her feet, turned, and glared at Lord Darkmoore.

"Whisper, see to Lachlan," said Cadence. Her voice was cold. "Blaze, guard the entrance."

Consumed with thoughts of revenge, Cadence advanced toward the crystal coffin. Darkmoore stood behind it, holding a sword in his clawed hand.

"Is this what you've come for?" Darkmoore hissed. "Did my brother Thomas tell you who is contained inside this coffin, or did he fail to mention that?" He pointed at the transparent crystal lid, his red eyes never leaving Cadence's face. Paying no heed to who was in the coffin, she continued forward. "This is Apollo, the last remaining Roman god. He was present at Golgotha and took the spear from the Roman guard Longinus. With it, he led what Roman gods remained against a demon prince. Their army fell to defeat and his immortal family killed. He was captured and brought here. For centuries the vescali have guarded Apollo, but they are leaving these lands, and I am now in charge of guarding this place."

Cadence glanced at the body in the coffin. She saw golden hair and a pale face. "This can't be Apollo. The ancient gods were myth and legend. This is just a man. He's no god and you're not invincible, you little worm."

"Alas, Apollo failed. When he was close to death, Prince Balan enclosed him in this coffin with the spear. The Romans found far more than they expected when they built this outpost. The vescali killed the Romans and those in the fort. When William the Bastard came here and built his castle, the vescali were waiting until the plague struck and the dead rose from their graves to consume them. The vescali used the Roman Stone to travel to a far-away land, leaving me to guard Apollo and the spear."

Cadence took a leap of faith. "Prince Balan was a demon? Did you ever meet him?" She smiled when Darkmoore nodded, suspecting Balan was the Kaiser. "I suppose for your service he promised to make you immortal. That's what Balan and the vescali trash told you, isn't it?

Before they came to my land and in my time to destroy everything I loved."

"Why tell you more? You will kill me regardless of what I say."

"I'm not interested in you. Only the spear," Cadence said, a glint of danger in her green eyes. She stabbed her sword into the ground and reached out to grab the lid.

"No mortal can touch the coffin," shouted Darkmoore. "Touch it and you will die, as your friend did. His death is not of my doing. Like an Irishman, he was brash and foolhardy to the end."

"Let's kill this freak and get the hell out of here." The anger in Whisper's voice was palpable.

Darkmoore's ravaged eyes darted toward Whisper, and then back to Cadence. "Who are you? Why would Montagu send a few men and women when so many have failed?" He laughed. "It's true then. You came out of the portal that took Richard. Has my brother returned?"

"Your brother is dead."

Darkmoore smiled, revealing his yellowed fangs. "Then prove your greatness. Open the coffin and take the spear. I will not stop you."

Gazing at the coffin, Cadence saw a strong-featured man wearing a white toga, holding a wooden spear in his hands. He did not look dead, but sleeping. His skin was flawless, as if made of marble with a faint blush of pink high on his cheekbones. She held her hand above the lid. The vampire knight approached the coffin, and grinned with malevolence.

"Kill him," shouted Blaze. She ran to Cadence. "He killed Lachlan. This monster deserves nothing less."

The vampire gazed at Blaze, a proud creature.

"No. Darkmoore should be rewarded for bringing us to the spear. Drink my blood," said Cadence. "It will give you the immortality that your Prince Balan denied you. Go on. Bite me, Darkmoore, and find out why Richard sent me."

Cadence held out her hand, offering it to Darkmoore. He stared at her, confused. A moment later, he sped forward, seized her hand and sank into it. A shiver shot through Cadence as his yellow teeth pierced her flesh. One taste of her blood sent Darkmoore into convulsions. He fell to the ground, writhing in pain. He was dead seconds later.

"Disgusting," said Cadence, as she wiped her hand across her tunic.

Whisper approached Cadence, carrying Lachlan's sword. "I know you cared about Lachlan," he said. "He was an honorable man."

Cadence nodded. Her heart ached. "Lachlan was that and much more."

"Come on you two. Let's open it," said Blaze. "Take the spear, Cadence, and let's go."

Placing her hands flat on the crystal coffin, Cadence felt a surge of a warm energy prickle through her palms and arms. She gave a shove, and the lid moved an inch. Whisper and Blaze joined her and together they opened it. The lid fell unbroken to the ground and they watched the man inside. The scent of vanilla rose from the coffin. Apollo wore gold bracelets, and his necklace held a medallion engraved with two horses pulling a chariot. A gold circlet adorned his head, and blonde hair filled the sides of the coffin, curling around the spear like ivy.

"Is he alive?" asked Blaze. "Touch him. See if he's breathing."

Cadence leaned over and cupped Apollo's cheeks. His flesh was pliant and cool to the touch. She placed a hand on his chest and felt a faint heartbeat. His strong hands grasped the ordinary-looking spear. Flecks of dried red blood covered the iron tip. If this was the Spear of Destiny, its supernatural properties provided her with the means of killing Prince Balan.

"Well, he's not dead," said Cadence. "Being in an induced-coma for centuries is the worst imprisonment I can think of, but he is sleeping." She ran her finger across the puncture marks on her hand before they finished healing. Cadence rubbed her blood across his lips and his gum line. "You need to wake up. We need you, Apollo. You've slept long enough and the world is suffering. Wake up." She gave him a slap.

Whisper leaned over the coffin and gave Cadence a quizzical look.

"Apollo is infected with the virus," said Cadence. "My blood will either wake him or he'll stay this way forever. Perhaps we should take him with us?"

"No. Leave him."

"It's hard to imagine he's like us," said Blaze, hefting her gun against her hip. "Every god or goddess was just like us. They had the virus and turned into superhumans."

Whisper stood straight. "Take the spear, Cadence. Hurry!"

Holding her breath, Cadence reached for the spear. His grip was firm. She tugged the spear upwards, pulling it from his grasp. She half-expected his hands to crack and crumble into dust. It surprised her that the spear was so light, and fragile as a splinter of wood. She held it out for her friends to examine.

"So much fuss over an ordinary spear," said Blaze. "I thought it might be made out of gold or something."

"It's Christ's blood on the tip that makes it a potent weapon. Set fire to the rafters and let's get out of here," said Cadence. She took Lachlan's weapon, leaving her own sword behind, and slid the spear into the scabbard at her side.

Whisper and Blaze set the wooden beams aflame, after which they set the dead bodies throughout the cave on fire. The werewolves' fur sizzled and popped, and the wraiths withered like bad fruit on a vine.

Cadence knelt beside Lachlan. The Irish vampire showed no sign of injuries and looked peaceful in death. She brushed his red hair away from his eyes, closed them, and leaned in to kiss Lachlan one last time.

"It isn't fair. We had so little time together," said Cadence, letting her tears flow. "Forgive me for leaving you here on English soil, Lachlan. I will never forget you. Never, my love."

It was late afternoon when Cadence and her two friends emerged from the caves. Clouds filled the sky and rain mingled with the stench of death. Blood drenched the ground, but there were no bodies to be found. Whisper gazed over a cliff and whistled. Cadence and Blaze hurried over to see countless bodies of the Old Ones thrashed upon the rocks.

"We must run," said Cadence. "The Old Ones will be waiting for us on the road."

"What's the rush?" said Blaze. "The monolith isn't going anywhere."

"You heard them earlier. Pevensey Castle is under attack. We need to help Lord Montagu and Sir Thomas if we don't want the stone to fall into the wrong hands."

Whisper took off running without saying a single word, racing for the trees. Cadence and Blaze glanced at one another, and ran after him.

The dog soldiers followed.

Chapter Eighteen

L ogan walked the entire fourth lake, bundled up against the cavern's chill. He had a printout of Mallory's translation of the Babylonian script on the monolith. He knew with certainty he was looking at a portal through time.

After a long discussion with the Dark Angels, they agreed to set up explosives where the vescali had dug the tunnel leading to the Citadel. They constructed a net lined with magnets and covered the stone to contain the electromagnetic energy. They left the front unveiled and positioned high-watt lights around it. Logan carried a camera, filming their expedition in case of any new activity in the cavern.

Dodger and Smack stood behind a barricade of sandbags and watched for any activity in or around the stone monument. Phoenix and Moon Dog walked with Logan who relayed the information he was collecting to the Dark Angels in the control room. Thor led a second team setting explosives in the tunnel.

"I can feel a breeze on my face," said Phoenix. "The tunnel the animals were using is close. Come on, Moon Dog. Use that nose of yours to find it."

The werewolf trotted forward with his nose to the ground and let out a woof. He raised his head as Sheena raced toward them. As she approached, the werepuma morphed into human form. Logan didn't mind. He found her attractive.

"Smile," said Logan grinning as he pointed the camera at Sheena.

The Dark Angels had to be enjoying the images. "What's got your tail on fire? Run into something scary?"

She laughed, cheeks dimpling. "If an intricate labyrinth of tunnels is scary, then yeah, that's what we found," she said. "One leads to the Citadel. Some are dead ends, but a few lead further into the mountain. Thor thinks the vescali have their own underground bunker, but he didn't want us exploring. He sent me back to tell you not to advance beyond this position."

"I think we've found the tunnel to the outside," said Phoenix. She stood with Moon Dog who was sniffing the cave wall. Logan hoped Moon Dog was not simply trying to find a place to urinate.

"Why don't you morph back and help Moon Dog find the exit?" asked Logan. He lowered the camera. "A werepuma's nose is as good as a werewolf's, plus yours is cuter."

Chuckling, Sheena walked over to Moon Dog. "What do you smell? Bat crap?" She winked at Logan.

Moon Dog transformed into his human form. His bare backside pointing straight up in the air was not a pretty sight. Logan had not expected to spend his morning with two naked people at the lake. Perhaps it might have been fun in another setting.

"Rotting flesh," said Moon Dog. He whipped back his long, black hair and looked up at Phoenix. "There's fresh air coming out of a crack here. I also smell foam padding and paint." He tapped the wall with his fingers. "Fake. Thought so."

Logan placed his hand over his pistol as Moon Dog pulled away a large section of the cave wall. He tossed the foam piece aside and revealed the entrance to a tunnel. Light was visible from the far end where fresh air was escaping.

"Good work," Logan said, kneeling beside Moon Dog. He was grateful that Moon Dog turned back into a wolf. Lifting his camera, he took a shot down the tunnel and heard Picasso talking in his ear. The audio chip in his left ear came in clear.

"Send Sheena through the tunnel," said Picasso. "She's small, but strong. Have her blow up the outside entrance. Freeborn and Star are waiting out front. She's to go with them to escort the survivors back here."

Logan relayed the message to his team. He held out a bag containing a small mound of gray clay. "This is powerful stuff. I assume you've used plastic explosives before? Just set the bag at the entrance and position yourself far enough away to get a clear shot. Let's hope the mountain won't come down on your head."

"I know what I'm doing," said Sheena. "Good grief. I was a Head Hunter once. Don't worry about me. I can handle myself."

Phoenix handed Sheena her side arm. The young woman took the bag and gun and climbed inside the tunnel. Moon Dog replaced the foam in the wall. They followed the side of the lake and stopped to look back as a loud explosion rumbled through the cavern. Ripples danced across the black lake. Smoke and red flames burst out of the small tunnel sending blazing foam along with a shower of rocks into the water.

Logan tapped his earphone. "Are you getting this, Picasso?"

"Affirmative," said Picasso. "Thor's isn't responding. His headpiece must not be working, so tell me when he comes back."

A loud splay of water turned everyone toward the lake. The hairs on the nape of Logan's neck rose as he spotted something big moving under the surface. He aimed his camera at the water. The heat signature showed a large mass that was bright red, fringed with yellow in the dark, cold water. It was coming straight toward the shoreline, fast.

"I've got movement. Something is in the lake!"

Moon Dog and Phoenix stood only ten yards from Logan, staring at the lake. A large serpent lifted its scaled green head out of the water. Logan dropped the camera and reached for his weapon as the creature smacked the water with its tail. It stretched out its neck and lunged for the werewolf, jaws snapping. In one continuous movement, Phoenix pushed Moon Dog aside and swung upward with her sword. She opened a large gash across the monster's head.

Logan fired into the gaping jaws of the beast. Dodger and Smack appeared on the far side of the lake, targeting the serpent's head. The beast swung toward the two teens, as Phoenix jumped and landed on its back. She plunged her sword deep into its neck. Its screech echoed through the chamber as it flailed backward trying to reach Phoenix. She held on, moving out of danger each time it snapped for her legs. Thor, Xena, and Rafe came out of the tunnel and joined the battle. They stood near Logan, filling the cavern with the deafening sound of gunfire.

"What's going on?" shouted Picasso.

"Something creepy and angry just came out of the water," Logan replied. He retrieved the infrared camera and turned it on the creature. However, the chameleons were the real entertainment as they worked together to destroy the monster.

They moved so fast the creature could not keep up with them, nor could Logan. Its thrashing tail sent waves of water slopping out of the lake, while its head hit the ceiling hard, sending rocks tumbling through the air. Phoenix released her sword and leapt to the shore. The group exhausted their ammo, bringing it down. With a final screech, the water serpent vanished beneath the murky water.

"Did you even fire your gun?" Rafe shouldered his M16. "Or did you just film the action, Agent Logan? Because it didn't look like you did a whole lot."

"I did as much as you," said Logan, annoyed.

Thor stuck a cigar between his teeth, lit it and exhaled a cloud of smoke. "You were both useless, if you want to know the truth. From now on, leave the serious fighting to us. Get back to work, Logan. As for you, vampire, why don't you go into the kitchen and make us lunch? I'm starving. Get yourself some bear blood while you're there, and take Picasso and Tandor some."

"Are you serious? You can't order me about, you Neanderthal." Rafe brushed a hand across the sleeve of his coat. "I'm a Maker. Not a cook."

Rafe stomped off. He gave Logan a push as he walked by, sending him staggering toward the water. "This is your fault, Agent Logan. How could something this big go unnoticed? If you'd done your job and read all of Mallory's reports, I'm sure he must have mentioned something about a giant serpent in the lake."

"Mallory mentioned nothing about the damn thing, so get off my back."

"Maybe you just told no one, hoping it would kill us. I think we should have left you at the Citadel. You're pathetic."

"Hate isn't good for the soul," Logan called out after the vampire. He waited for Thor to catch up. "You rigged the tunnel leading to the Citadel? What about the other tunnels?"

"I know what I'm doing, Logan," said Thor, defensive.

Logan turned the audio up on the camera so Picasso and Tandor could hear the conversation loud and clear. "We could use the tunnel and attack the Citadel tomorrow night. You still have friends imprisoned there."

"Thanks for the insight," said Thor, spouting out smoke. He patted Logan on the shoulder. "Keep those ideas coming, Agent Logan. I might like one of them. Then again, I doubt it."

Logan fell silent. There was no winning with this guy.

They walked by the monolith toward the barricade where the rest of the team waited. As they did, the stone emitted a loud hum. Logan stumbled as the ground beneath his feet shuddered with violence. Thor dragged him to the barricade. Xena, Dodger, Moon Dog, and Phoenix were already behind it. Logan set the camera, aiming it toward the monolith as it opened wide and released a bright, green light.

"This is what we've been waiting for," said an excited Picasso. "Be ready, Logan. Something's coming out."

Logan crouched and peered over the sandbags as five cloaked figures emerged from the center. They shielded their eyes from the lights shining in their faces. Thor let out a shout and his team stood, weapons ready. The figures threw off their cloaks and morphed into their true demon forms. These were vescali. Like Trotsky, they were tall, thin, and had small bat-like wings that flapped swiftly as they rose off the ground. One demon flew across the lake toward the tunnel, leaving the other four to attack.

Moon Dog rushed after the departing demon. Logan stood up and fired at the lead demon as it flew toward him. The rest of the team shot down its companions, but the leader broke through. Logan fell backward and lifted his arms as the demon slammed into him. He grabbed the demon's head to keep it from biting into his face.

Phoenix hit the demon in the back of its head with the hilt of her sword. The creature went limp, and Logan scrambled to his feet.

"Don't move," said Thor, placing his foot on the demon's stomach. Its wings were riddled with holes and it bled from a shoulder wound. Thor pointed his gun at the demon's head. "Come over and talk to this thing, Logan."

"As if I'm an expert," said Logan. "It speaks English."

The demon looked at Logan. His expression revealed hope, until Moon Dog returned carrying a vescali leg in his jaws.

"Where did you come from, pal?" asked Logan, eyeing the demon. "See, if you cooperate, these guys may not kill you. Start talking. What do you know about the monolith?"

Thor tossed a cloak at the demon. He stood back as the demon returned to the form of a man.

"I am Tamal," said the vescali. The demon's voice pitched high. Logan imagined glass shattering if the demon's voice reached one more octave. "My slain companions were priests. We were guards of the Roman Stone at Pevensey Castle until the battle broke out. We fled through the stone."

"Do you work for Dr. Leopold?" Thor kept aim at the demon's head. It was an effective way to pry answers from the terrified demon.

"Dr. Leopold is our master. Yes, that is true. We've used the portal for some time now. Few of us remain."

Logan leaned forward. "What my associate is trying to say, Tamal, is a few of our friends went through the portal. We want to know if you ran into anyone from our time period. Four went through. Two women. Two men."

"I met two strangers who arrived at Pevensey Castle a fortnight ago, Sir Lachlan and Squire Clay. Sir Thomas told us they were old friends. But when the woman with purple hair and the tall one arrived, we knew they came from the portal."

Logan lifted his lip in a snarl. "And? What happened to them?"

"Lord Montagu charged them with killing Lord Darkmoore. I blessed your friends and watched as they rode away. I do not know what has happened since."

"Ask him about the monolith," said Thor, impatient.

Not caring to argue or to point out the demon spoke perfect English, Logan continued. "Tell us about the stone. How does it work? How do you open and close it?"

"Only immortals can use the stones. The portal allows us to travel to parallel moments in time, chosen by the Great One whom we all serve."

"Great One? You must mean the Kaiser," said Logan, "but I somehow doubt that's his true name. Enlighten me, Tamal. What's the Great One's true name?"

Tamal seized, shaking his head.

Thor pulled the trigger, just missing Tamal's leg. The loud report echoed through the cave and caused the demon to panic. "The name," said Thor. His voice was calm, threatening.

"P-p-prince Balan," Tamal sputtered. "A great demon lord, the only one of his kind. He has gone by many names through the centuries. Is it revenge you seek? We can help. We are tired of being his servants."

Thor squinted, tilting his head.

Tamal continued. "We do not serve him by choice. He's held us captive, ever since the defeat of the old gods. Let us join forces and free both of our people! Together, we can—"

Thor picked the vescali up by his cloak. "How do I know if I can trust you?"

The creature blanched, shrill voice catching in his throat. "I-I-I could help retrieve your friends," he offered.

The Viking eyeballed Logan, nodding. "I like that idea. If what you say is true, you will lead us back to Pevensey and help rescue our friends. Do that, and I'll help free the vescali from Balan."

Tamal bowed before Thor, trembling with excitement. He then turned and walked toward the monolith.

"A blood sacrifice is required, yet…" The demon sniffed the air and turned toward the lake. "I smell fresh blood. A vargan has been slain." He let out a heavy sigh. "This was a Babylonian lake worm, as ancient as the vescali, left here by Leopold to guard the portal. It was the last of its kind."

"Who cares," said Phoenix. "We needed a blood sacrifice."

"It is so," said Tamal. "But still, I mourn its death."

"You're enjoying this a little too much," said Logan, as Thor puffed out his chest.

Thor's eyes filled with amusement. "I think I have found something that suits your skills, Agent Logan. Redemption can be yours if you return with Tamal, Cadence, and the others. A man such as yourself shouldn't have any problem being stealthy and clever."

Rafe returned carrying a tray stacked with sandwiches. He placed the tray on the sand bags, took one look at the demon and laughed.

"Ah, the third member of the team has arrived." Thor's smile broadened as he waved the Dark Angel over. "Forget lunch, Rafe. I have a job for you and Logan."

"Where did you get this nut bag?" said Rafe, glaring at the demon. He glanced at the monolith. Seeing the light spilling from a crack in the stone, his eyes glowed and his fangs extended. "It's open! What are we waiting for? Let's go find Cadence!"

"Tell Rose I'll be back," said Logan. "I guess that's it. Just let her know that I care and I'll do what I can to save Cadence." Smack was the only one in the group that gave an encouraging nod.

Logan threw on one of the black cloaks. As Rafe pulled the odorous garment over his head, he snorted and gave the demon a dirty look. Dodger handed them both weapons and Logan placed his into a pocket in the robe before tying it closed.

"Priests do not carry weapons," said Tamal.

"This one does," Rafe said. He hid an automatic rifle under his cloak and stuffed a pistol in the waist of his jeans. "So, where does the portal lead? Where will we find Cadence?"

"England, in the year 1345. During the Black Plague," said Thor, all business. "You three are priests. Blend in with the locals, get Cadence, and bring her home. Should be no problem for a vampire, a demon, and a scavenger."

"Thanks for nothing," Logan said, pulling the hood up. With Rafe at his side, they followed Tamal to the center of the stone. "This better not be a one way trip to Hell. I'm not ready to go yet."

The demon smiled and scurried into the light, leaving Logan feeling he was embarking on a suicide mission. Rafe ran after the demon and vanished, while Logan resisted the tug of the monolith.

Thor pointed at the stone. "That's the way to the other side, Agent Logan. We'll be waiting here with Rose, when you get back."

Logan closed his eyes and stepped forward, feeling an invisible hand pull him into the stone. He fell into darkness.

Chapter Nineteen

Christmas Eve found Raven with her husband and a few of close friends watching the Death Games in a private box. Dressed in fur, Raven rested her feet on Luna's back. She held the Kaiser's arm as fighters marched into the arena. Salustra, the vampire lords, and their escorts sat with them, drinking champagne. Vampires bundled up for winter, more for style than for warmth, filled the stadium. The announcer sat in the press box, wearing a red business suit with a peppermint-print tie. His voice dripped like honey through the speakers.

"Merry Christmas! I know all of you have been naughty this year, but Santa Claus is now a vampire and he doesn't mind. Those with winning tickets will receive a special prize this Christmas. Don't think we forgot the rest of you. Under every chair is a gift, compliments of the Kaiser and his new bride!"

The crowd erupted with applause and cheers as vampires opened presents containing six-packs of Glorious Night, the new synthetic blood manufactured by Mr. Rafferty in Los Angeles. Guests in the press box were drinking Venetian Pleasure, imported from Italy by D'Aquilla. Raven and her companions, however, sipped on Dom Pérignon or drank from human slaves offering their necks and arms for a taste.

"I am pleased to present Loki," said the announcer. "Loki is new to the Colorado Death Games. He hails from the Roman Prime Time

Games, where he has killed forty-four fighters to take the title of Best Newcomer. Let's hear it for Loki!"

A bright blue light hit Loki standing on a center platform in the arena. The teenager wore a gold helmet and snug, green-scale body armor. Keeping with the comic book version of his namesake, he carried a gold trident and net, turning this way and that as the crowd chanted his name. Cameras flashed as T.V. crews closed in on his face, showing live footage on the screens.

"Happy holidays," said D'Aquilla, lifting Salustra's hand and slipping a diamond bracelet around her wrist. She kissed his cheek and leaned over to Raven to display her gift. "A small token of my esteem. This once belonged to Elizabeth Taylor. In fact, her entire collection has been delivered to your room."

"What did you get me?" asked Raven, smiling. "A pony?"

"A jet, so you may visit me in the spring." D'Aquilla laughed when the Kaiser glanced over his wife's head. "I hope you don't mind? The plane is waiting for you, under guard. The runways were in need of repair, and since I fly here so often, my gift to you, Kaiser, is a functional airport. Bechtel recommended putting one of your Shadowguard above security there. What about Pallaton?"

"Pallaton is in charge of security at the arena," Raven said, watching her fighter wave to the crowd. "I'd rather Bechtel go to the airport. That way I don't have to look at his ugly face anymore."

"Thank you, Salvatore," said the Kaiser. "Raven and I spent half the night wondering what to give you for Christmas. I think what you find waiting in your jet will more than fulfill your every fantasy."

"A dozen gorgeous women I selected myself," Raven said, not able to resist. "Did you bring Salustra's present, darling? I can't wait for her to see it."

The Kaiser reached into his pocket and handed the velvet box to Raven, who placed it on top of the leopard-fur blanket covering Salustra's legs. She opened the box, gasped, and held up a white pearl necklace.

Raven grinned. "It belonged to the Star of the East, Umm Kulthum, and was given to her by Sheikh Zâyed bin Sultân Âl Nahyân. A friend in Cairo found it inside her tomb and sent it here for you, dearest."

"I am touched," Salustra said. She kissed Raven on the cheek, and let out a shout when Aries of Athens appeared on the platform. "Aries has arrived. Now we'll see how good a fighter Loki is. I hope he wins, Raven."

The cyborg zombie threw off a golden robe, lifted his mechanical arms, and turned to flaunt his massive body. Aries wore a gold loin-cloth and gold-laced boots. Because he was a zombie, big, black spots stained his flesh. Curly blonde hair accentuated an unnatural square jawline. Trainers led Aries and Loki off the field.

The stadium lights lowered and heavy metal boomed from the speakers and announced the 'zombie round.' Over sixty zombies emerged from the tunnels. A group of young vampires zigzagged across the field, dragging cow carcasses. The zombies followed the blood trails and sauntered for the corpses as the vampires leapt out of the arena. A platform rose from the center of the field, bringing into view a cage filled with terrified humans. The Class-E fighters were dressed as Spartans. The sides of the cages sank into the platform, leaving the humans huddling together on the field.

Three of the fighters showed initiative. They jumped from the platform as a team, attacking the zombies who were busy feasting on cow flesh. When the main group of humans refused to branch out and attack, the platform lowered. They scrambled off the platform and turned to face the zombies, looking pathetic. When the platform rose again, bodies of mutilated cows littered it. The smell of fresh blood brought the zombies shambling toward the platform, sparking fear in the fighters who fled to an end-zone.

"I love this part," said Raven, taking hold of the Kaiser's hand. "Only a few humans realize they have to fight to survive. It will be a slaughter!"

"Dr. Heston outfitted these zombies with computer chips he controls, and has injected them with steroids designed to increase their hunger. We'll release zombie cyborgs after the fighters are thinned out and the best remain."

"I wish Dragon was here." Salustra sounded heartbroken.

Raven reached out and took hold of her friend's hand. "Oh, it's alright. This is the second time Dragon was scheduled to fight Aries of Athens, and both times we've been disappointed."

"Dragon may yet be caught." The Kaiser retained his handsome appearance, though his smile was cruel. "Captain Bechtel is leading a strike team against the survivors' camp. This time we'll take the camp. I've sent in the Black Hawks. Nothing will remain by morning."

"Darling, don't spoil the festivities with talk of war. It's so boring," Raven said, wiping away a tear from her friend's face. "You and I, Salustra, will drink champagne and cheer for the winners. Tonight I intend to have fun."

Raven took two glasses of champagne from a slave girl. The girl stepped on Luna's tail and the werepuma jumped, snarling, upsetting the entire tray from her hands. Glasses toppled, and Salustra squealed. She stood, wiping champagne off her leopard-skin coat, which hung open. Her slinky dress was wet from her breasts to her navel. The slave girl gathered up the glass and left.

"My dress is ruined," Salustra said, angry. "I must go to the bathroom to clean this up before it stains. I won't be long." She stood and held her coat together.

"The fight is just getting exciting," said D'Aquilla, letting out a yell when zombies engulfed another human. "The cyborgs are about to be released. I'll get you another dress, Salustra. Sit!"

Salustra turned to Raven and the Kaiser. "Give me a few minutes to refresh myself and I'll return. Poor Luna. You little darling, you'll cut your paws on the glass. Take my seat."

Luna jumped into the vampire's seat, purring in gratitude, as Salustra hurried away. Concerned for her friend, Raven glanced over her shoulder and watched Salustra glide toward the exit. D'Aquilla and the Kaiser turned back to watch the games. The crowd cheered as the cyborgs entered the field. The remaining humans congregated in the center of the field, forming a circle and joining their shields together to block the zombies. Fighters stood in rotation, jabbing at attackers, and kneeling again. The cyborgs marched for the circle of humans and fired with flamethrowers. The crowd went wild.

"I will check on Salustra," said Raven, giving her husband a peck on the cheek. "It's my fault her dress is ruined. Look after Luna. Blood excites her and I don't want her jumping into the arena."

The Kaiser nodded. He turned and spotted his shadow gliding along the aisle, motioning for it to follow Raven. She hurried down the ramp and entered a section roped off for the Kaiser's favorite guests. Vampires were playing carnival games. They threw daggers at humans tied to spinning wheels, and sat in a shooting gallery firing at moving targets dressed to resemble jungle animals. Others gathered at an open bar to drink overpriced champagne and blood-mixed drinks.

Raven found the bathroom empty at first. Unsure where Salustra had gone, she bent and looked under the stalls. Not seeing any legs or shoes, she turned to leave when she heard a soft voice speaking.

"Tonight. It's tonight," came from a stall on the end.

Raven held still and listened. It was Salustra's voice. A few women entered the bathroom, spotted a shadow blocking their reflection in the mirrors, and hurried out.

"Yes, I'm sure," said Salustra. "Black Hawks. It's confirmed. Get out now."

Seething with fury at her friend's betrayal, Raven removed a small revolver strapped to her leg and turned toward the stall, pointing the gun at the door. Salustra stepped out, startled to find Raven and the Kaiser's shadow waiting.

"Who were you talking to?" asked Raven, her eyes glowing yellow. Her tongue slid across her lowered fangs. "Was it Highbrow or Rose? It was Rose. You're the one who arranged for Dragon and Logan to escape. No doubt you blew up the lab too. All this time I believed you were loyal to the Kaiser. You are not my friend. You're a traitor!"

"Darling, you're mistaken." Salustra held up her hands. "I wasn't talking to anyone. Lower your gun. We are friends. Best friends."

"I heard you. We're going back to our seats and I'm informing my husband you've alerted Rose. Don't try anything clever. You may be older and stronger, but the rounds in my pistol are dipped in Loki's blood. One bullet and you're dead, friend. I suggest you get moving before I use it."

Salustra stared at the gun. "You wouldn't."

Raven stepped back and blocked the doorway. The shadow expelled a deep groan and moved toward Salustra. As the blackness engulfed Salustra, the Maker screamed, emerging pale and gaunt. Salustra's eyes glowed violet and her fangs cut into her bottom lip. Panicked, she rushed Raven. Salustra was able to push past her, and fled.

"Stop her!" shouted Raven.

The demonic shadow swept in pursuit of Salustra, with Raven not far behind. Vampires cleared the way as the shadow flew through the crowd. Raven spotted a woman in a red dress ahead of them, moving through the press of the crowd. Raven took aim, fired, and struck a vampire playing carnival games, inciting panic. Vampires scattered in all directions as the shadow moved over their heads, giving Raven a clear path to follow.

Joined by the Shadowguard, Raven chased Salustra into the stadium. The vampire Maker moved with blinding speed, doubling back into the stadium. Raven ran headlong into a group of spectators. The audience let out a cheer as she broke through the group. She spotted

Salustra on the field. A pink spotlight found Salustra and followed her every move as she darted through zombies and cyborgs trying to reach the far side of the arena.

"It seems we have a new fighter tonight," said the announcer, so excited his voice reached a new octave. "That's Salustra! But wait, another fighter has joined her. It's Raven, the Kaiser's new wife!"

As Raven leapt over the barrier wall and onto the field, a new cage emerged and caught her by surprise. She slammed into the cage and several cyborg zombies reached out for her. One latched onto her shoulder and pulled Raven against the cage. She seized the zombie's hair and crushed its head between the bars, shattering metal and bone. The cyborg body fell twitching inside the cage.

The arena cheered as the doors to the cage fell open and two remaining flame-throwing cyborgs marched toward Raven. A wave of flame missed her as she ran to where zombies trapped Salustra at the opposite end of the field. Shadowguard advanced through the arena with their red lasers dotting Salustra's face. In the same moment, over two-hundred zombies entered the field from four different tunnels. Salustra turned and ran toward the Shadowguard who were now busy firing at the zombies surrounding them. The cyborgs followed Salustra, gaining ground as the Shadowguard blocked her path. She turned back, unsure which way to run, as a cyborg ripped her dress from her body. The crowd became a lustful frenzy as Salustra stood exposed in nothing except her lingerie. She ran.

"This isn't something you see every day," said the announcer. "I've just been told three Class-A fighters are being released into the arena. Loki, Monkey, and Skye! Place your bets folks!"

Loki, followed by Monkey in a black bodysuit holding two katanas, emerged along with a werepuma at her side. Another crowd of zombies followed the three chameleons, moving faster than normal. The trio ran toward a group of five remaining human fighters trying to bring down a cyborg swinging a chainsaw. Instead of eliminating the

Class-E fighters, they stood with them against the approaching zombie horde.

Raven kicked off her heels, zigzagging through the bloodshed and zombies. Something white leapt onto the field, and Raven spotted Luna running toward her. She tucked her gun inside her bra and in one fluid move, picked up a discarded sword and shield. With Luna at her side, they cleared several zombies in their path as they raced toward Salustra. The zombies were too thick to cut through.

"Is this a surprise or what?" shouted the announcer. Raven and Luna appeared on the jumbotrons, battling the zombies. "Why don't the owners make it a little more exciting and release a few more Class-A fighters? We want our local heroes, Cricket and Red Hawk!"

"Cricket! Red Hawk!" the crowd responded, pounding the seats with their fists.

Thunderous applause filled the air as Cricket and Red Hawk appeared. Cricket was small and fast, having no trouble picking off zombies, while the werewolf knocked over the walking corpses like bowling pins. They soon reached the center of the field and joined the human survivors with Loki, Skye, and Monkey. At that moment, the zombie horde finished the Shadowguard and headed straight for them.

Raven lost sight of Salustra among the zombies. She kept close to Luna and targeted a gathering of zombies. They slipped past the ragtag horde and ran into Loki. He saluted Raven with his gold trident and stepped forward, allowing her and the werepuma to move around him. His threw his net over an incoming cyborg's head and thrust his trident through the mechanical torso, short-circuiting its system. Loki turned to Raven and bowed.

"I didn't expect to see you here," said Loki. "What are you doing?"

"Trying to find Salustra. She's here somewhere."

A growl from Luna turned Raven's attention to a familiar face attached to a cyborg zombie body. Seeing its swords for arms, her mind flooded with memories of the Captain. He was fighting Lieutenant

Habit and Nightshadow of the Freedom Army. The three had once been leaders at their camp on Pike's Peak. Luna and Loki fought around Raven.

Hundreds of images overwhelmed Raven, beginning with her first day at Pike's Peak as a scared Arizona refugee fighting her way to the front of the check-in line. Her memory reminded her of a raven that had landed on the registration table. Nightshadow saw the bird, then looked at her. She was known as Raven from that day forward. She remembered meeting Thor and joining the Vikings, fighting against zombies, and the day she first saw Luna and fell in love.

Raven met Nightshadow's hope-filled eyes and hesitated as Luna ripped through a zombie that came too close, splattering her fur with goo. Lt. Habit turned and spotted Raven. For a moment, she knew she was fighting for the wrong side. A surge of zombies separated Raven from her former allies. Luna grabbed Raven by the end of her dress, pulling her away as the horde surrounded Lt. Habit. His screams faded as Raven and Luna broke through the press of filthy zombies and moved into an open area.

"Raven, help!"

It was Salustra. She was on her own fighting a group of zombies. Luna and Raven attacked the zombies from behind, clearing a path to Salustra. The Maker had several bite marks and was missing an arm. Salustra collapsed to the ground, sobbing and begging for help. As Raven moved toward her, a black shadow swept past and surrounded Salustra. Luna held back the zombies as Raven dropped her shield and sword, reaching for her pistol. Salustra withered in the gloom of the shadow. Raven took pity on her and shot her through the heart, and then the head.

The foul shadow lifted from Salustra's dead body and vanished into the stands. Raven felt an overwhelming wave of guilt. Killing her best friend was the last thing she wanted to do. She dropped her gun and reached for her wedding ring to pull it off while she still had the strength, but it had fallen off somewhere on the field. She fought back tears of grief and regret. Luna yowled in excitement As Loki ran by holding a small red werewolf, followed by Cricket, racing toward the end of the field. The two superhumans leapt upward, clearing the stadium, and vanished.

"That was incredible. Did you just see that? Loki, Cricket and Red Hawk have escaped," shouted the announcer, aglow with the bloodlust.

Blinking back tears, Raven turned and gasped to see the number of dead bodies littering the field. Shadowguard surrounded Skye and Monkey as more vampire soldiers arrived, shooting the remaining zombies and whatever still twitched.

Raven looked up in the stands and spotted the Kaiser's glowing eyes as he stood under the pavilion beside D'Aquilla. He waved at her. She looked at Luna.

"I'm no longer under Balan's thrall. We can go too, Luna. But how? Where do we go? We won't be able to jump out of the stadium like Loki and Cricket."

"May I have your attention?" Pallaton's voice boomed over the speakers. "Would the guards in the arena please escort Raven to the north tunnel. This evening's events are canceled. Please leave the stadium at once. There has been a bomb threat. Please locate the exit nearest you and depart in an orderly fashion."

Sirens blared. The crowd panicked, pushing and shoving to escape. A tide of bodies poured over walls and through the tunnels. Raven and Luna started for the wall intending to flee with the crowd, but were surrounded by guards in trench coats. A few wandering zombies distracted the Shadowguard, and they left Raven and Luna unguarded. The two descended the ramp and entered the north tunnel's chaos as vampire fans attempted to escape from the stadium.

A familiar, eye-patched face appeared at Raven's side. He wore black, but no trench coat. In his hands was a folded Death Games blanket used by the fans when it snowed. Before she could speak, the disgraced captain threw the blanket over Raven's head, holding her arms tight as he guided her through the crowd. The sounds of screaming, along with Luna's angry snarls and Pallaton's words of encouragement kept Raven moving despite the terror she felt. He led her back into the arena. Freedom had been so close.

"I'm not taking you back to him," said Pallaton. His strong arm wrapped around Raven, guiding her through the mob. "You can see under the blanket. Just watch your step, try not to trip. Luna is right here with you."

Raven glanced at her bloody feet, careful as she took each step. People pressed from behind and in front. Now and then, she spotted Luna's white paws gliding along beside her own feet. The last step brought the stench of the level below the stadium under her blanket. The voices of fighters could be heard begging for release, as they were hauled back to their holding cells.

"What's going on?" asked Raven, trying not to shout under the blanket.

Pallaton pulled her head to his shoulder. "Highbrow is moving to Cadence's camp. Bechtel will find an empty camp at Seven Falls. I was told to get the rest of your friends out of the Citadel. Loki knew the plan, too, but he wasn't able to get Skye or Monkey out with him. The Shadowguard took them to a secure location."

Raven trembled. "And the bomb?"

"The stadium is rigged to blow by me," said Pallaton. "Now that the cursed ring is off your finger, you're realizing just how powerful the Kaiser is. I'm sorry I wasn't able to get it off before Salustra blew her cover. She's a Dark Angel, like me, and soon you will join us."

"Why do you care? I was horrible to you, to Salustra, to everyone. I deserve to die," cried Raven. "Take Luna and go to Cadence's camp. Save yourselves and leave me."

Pallaton pulled the blanket from her face. He glanced over their shoulders, making sure no one watched. Luna stood guard and glanced back to hear the answer, ears pricked forward. They were at the end of a hallway. A stream of well-dressed vampires filed into the bomb shelter behind them, helped by the Shadowguard. Pallaton wiped away a tear from her cheek and offered a tender smile.

"I will not leave you," said Pallaton. "I'm going to save us, including Luna."

Pallaton took her by the hand and led her beyond the hall, around a corner, and down a flight of stairs. He opened a maintenance door and allowed Luna to trot in first, then pulled Raven into a dark room filled with pipes running across the ceiling. He locked the door behind them.

"Trust me?" asked Pallaton.

"With my life. You are the two people I love most in this world," said Raven. "This time we are running away together."

They hurried through the room and came to another door leading to a service tunnel beneath the stadium. Pallaton again secured the door behind them. The lights were dim and the scent of gasoline mixed with waste were overpowering. Luna objected with a snarl as they walked. Rats scurried away from the direction they were taking, moving fast. Something frightened them at the end of the tunnel. The werepuma sensed danger and crouched low putting her nose to the ground, twitching her long tail in agitation. Raven and Pallaton followed behind her, unable to see far ahead. Midway, a deep blackness enveloped what little light was in the tunnel.

"Do we have to escape through the sewers?" Raven's bare feet squished things that oozed between her toes. The smell was horrible.

Pallaton drew his gun. "I've been planning this a long time. No one uses this tunnel. It leads to Colorado Springs. I have a car waiting."

"But where will we go from there?"

"You're not going anywhere," said a deep, angry voice.

The darkness moved aside onto the wall next to the tall, muscular form of the Kaiser. Eight of his own private guards stood behind him. Luna growled as the Kaiser's eyes glowed bright. Raven had trouble seeing, but it appeared the Kaiser's nose, ears, and fingers were growing longer. The Kaiser held out his hand. In it glittered her ring, with a red flame dancing in its center.

"You dropped your wedding ring in the arena, my dear."

Raven shivered and squeezed Pallaton's hand. Luna hissed and bared her fangs, snarling as the Kaiser continued to grow larger.

"How clever of you," said Pallaton. "I'm sure one of my men ratted me out. Only a few knew about this sewer system."

"Oh, they didn't tell me plans." The Kaiser gestured to the shadow on the wall. Under a dim light, the darkness revealed its expansive wings and horns. "You have blinders on, my friend. Rose Standish has filled your head with promises of a better life among the Dark Angels. After what you've done, do you think they'll accept you? Or my traitorous wife?"

Raven found her former courage, and her temper, "What do you want from us? Why can't you just let us go? I'm one of hundreds of wives you've had over the centuries. You don't love me. You love no one but yourself."

"Till death do us part," said the Kaiser. "I'm not ready to die, nor do I want to be parted from my wife. I'd like you to put on your ring, Raven, and come back with me." He took a step forward and held up the ring. "We are meant to be together. Forever."

Raven stepped back, afraid, and bumped into Pallaton. He placed his hands on her shoulders to steady her. "You never loved me, nor I you," she replied. "You manipulated me. I will never put that cursed ring back on. Never!"

Her voice echoed in the tunnel. In the distance, a zombie answered with a searching groan. She glanced at Pallaton as Luna snapped at the Kaiser. The guards pointed their guns at the werepuma, prepared to fire. The Kaiser lifted his hand, holding them back.

"Raven and Luna are coming with me," said Pallaton. His gun trained on the Kaiser.

The Kaiser trembled with fury. "I'm not talking to you. I'm speaking with my wife! Come with me, Raven, or I'll kill both of your friends."

"No," said Raven, shaking her head. "I won't go anywhere with you, demon."

The Kaiser gave a shrug and pointed his weapon at Pallaton. "You disappoint me, captain. You were the first human who caught the virus and turned vampire. The first Maker of this age, and I loved you like a son. A wiser man would have accepted my offer. You leave me no choice but to kill you and the cat."

Raven struck the Kaiser's hand, sending the ring flying through the air. She heard it fall somewhere in the tunnel. It was a grave mistake. The Kaiser shook with rage. Hatred burned within him as the shadow danced on the wall. The flesh on his face rippled with darkness and scaled over, while fangs the size of daggers hung from his widening mouth. He grew until his head pressed the ceiling, turning from a man and revealing his true, hideous form. With a snarl, the demon lifted his clawed hand to swipe at her face as Raven cried out.

"I command you to stop, and let us go, Prince Balan!"

For a moment the Kaiser stood shaking, desperate, until he let out a roar. He convulsed in a rage of violence, and froze. His fanged mouth was open wide, releasing foam and drool that streamed onto his broad, scaled chest. He neither blinked, nor stirred, but remained as a statue. Water around his feet rippled as pipes burst through the sewers, expelling a fetid, warm stench. The shadow, likewise, could not move and the walls trembled.

Guards stared in shock at their leader and in that instant Pallaton shot every one of them in the head, landing a second round through their hearts. The echo of gunfire faded and the groans of approaching zombies grew louder.

"My love," cried Raven. She threw herself into Pallaton's arms and kissed him. "It worked. Speaking his real name is the only way to subdue him. But Balan won't stay like this forever."

"We must hurry. Let the zombies have them."

Pallaton, Raven, and Luna ran with vampire speed, passing a group of stray zombies. They ran for what seemed like miles, until they came to an intersection where the tunnel split into four directions. Pallaton led the way to the tunnel on the left and they soon reached metal hand-rails leading to a manhole. Pallaton climbed the rails, pushed the cover aside, and climbed out.

"It's clear. Come up, Luna," Pallaton called, standing back.

The werepuma sprung upward and cleared the opening. Raven took a step back and jumped. Pallaton caught her and pulled her into his arms. He kicked the manhole cover back into place and led them across a city street to a black Hummer.

"We'll drive to Cadence's camp," said Pallaton. "Rose will meet us there. We've helped the survivors enough times that we should be welcome. But I do have one stop."

Eyes scanning, Raven watched for any unwanted followers. As they turned a corner, Luna rested her big head on Raven's shoulder. Raven stroked Luna's face and received a warm, wet lick across her jaw. Pallaton came to a halt at an exit ramp leading to Interstate 25. Raven glanced in the side mirror and spotted the three figures running toward the car. Two humans and a wolf. It was Loki, Cricket, and Red Hawk. Loki opened the back door and stuck his head in.

"Thanks for the lift," Loki said with a wide grin. The scar on his right cheek was visible and looked redder than usual. "We were beginning to wonder if you'd forgotten us."

Pallaton nodded. "Get in. Hurry! We may be followed."

They climbed in, and as soon as the door closed the vehicle was speeding over the highway. They passed a group of zombies standing under a streetlight, staring up at the light in wonder.

"I'm so glad you made it out alive," said Raven, turning to face the three.

A smile appeared on Loki's face. "It's too bad about Monkey and

Skye," he said, though he didn't sound remorseful. "I told them to follow me, but they wanted to protect Nightshadow as long as possible. He was bitten right about the time Lt. Habit was devoured. I grabbed Red Hawk, and Cricket followed her sweetheart."

The sound of a large explosion filled the night, followed by a series of smaller ones. In the distance, a fire could be seen coming from the Citadel. Raven and the others turned to look out the back window as the stadium burned.

"We're not coming with you to Cadence's camp," said Cricket. "Red Hawk and I want to find his tribe. Please give our love to everyone. Tell them we are safe and going to join Chief Chayton." She tapped Pallaton's shoulder. "You can let us off right here, captain. We are close to Cave of the Winds. The tribe may still be there. We'll let your brother know that you two got out."

"Chayton won't care if I'm alive or dead," said Pallaton, "but thank you."

Raven gave Pallaton a worried look. "Bechtel will return to the Citadel. It's not safe for them. Please don't stop. You're coming with us Cricket. You can meet the wolf tribe later. Cadence will know where they've gone."

"Red Hawk can find them," said Cricket. "I appreciate your concern. It's what we both want. Stop the car, Pallaton. Please."

The Hummer slowed and stopped. It was snowing and the moon lit a sign that read 'Cave of the Winds - 3 miles.' Loki opened the door and Red Hawk crawled over him and jumped out. Loki helped Cricket out of the vehicle. When Raven looked in the side mirror, she no longer saw Cricket or Red Hawk.

"Well, that was a short reunion," Loki said. "I should have warned them though. One drop of chameleon blood can kill a vampire and turn a werewolf into an animal forever. It's something I discovered in the arena. Pity about Salustra. I believe she was a Dark Angel."

"Let's not mention it to the others," Pallaton said. "They won't understand and I'd rather not give Cadence or Highbrow another reason to hate me and Raven."

Driving up a mountain road, Pallaton pulled up behind a line of vehicles parked outside the Cheyenne Mountain Complex. Highbrow had brought the entire camp to the bunker. Supplies were still being unpacked and carried inside. Dragon approached the Hummer and Pallaton rolled down the window.

"Leave the vehicle here and follow me," said Dragon. "You're wanted inside."

Chapter Twenty

*H*ighbrow sat at the head of a large conference room table. Picasso, Tandor, Micah, Rose, Pallaton, and Raven had gathered, along with Lt. Sterling, Thor, Star, Dragon, Freeborn, and Luna. Pitchers of water and bottles of synthetic blood dotted the table. As Highbrow discussed tactics, Loki slid into the remaining vacant chair. Highbrow had not invited Loki, but he did not ask him to leave, either.

"Thank you all for coming. I'll get right to business. To attack the Kaiser, it will have to be a ground assault. Long-range warheads aren't an option if we intend to stay here. We have one Black Hawk, and Picasso will use it to fly the Dark Angels in and engage the Shadowguard choppers. Three teams will go in. The Dark Angels, and two divisions of Earth Corps. Team leaders will be Tandor, Thor, and Dragon. We'll send one through the tunnel under NORAD and the second from the mountains. The vescali, according to Picasso, number at least six thousand strong, but we don't know if they'll fight for the prince. Pallaton has confirmed seven thousand Shadowguard. I'll set up position on the outskirts of the Citadel to coordinate our assault once in, and Lt. Sterling will stay here and assume command of NORAD. Since vampires stay inside in daylight hours, we'll attack at dawn."

"I've tried to contact every U.S. military base in North America," said Picasso, "but so far no one has responded. The Bull Dogs are in the control room but I need to get back in case we get a response."

"It can wait. This meeting is more important."

"What about Cadence?" asked Star. "I thought we were going to wait until she arrives? Logan and Rafe will find her. I know it. She's the one who should lead the attack."

Highbrow frowned. "The vampire lords are still here. If we wait until Cadence arrives, if she arrives at all, they may leave. Pallaton said D'Aquilla has a jet at the city airport, which means the other vampire lords have escape methods. If we're going to attack them all, we can't wait, Star. Now, does anyone have any questions that don't involve Cadence?"

Arms crossed, Tandor pushed his long hair back from his face and glared at Pallaton. "Why is Pallaton part of this war council? He's not one of us. Nor is Raven. Just yesterday these two were conspiring against us."

"We discussed this," said Rose, firm. "This is a Dark Angel problem, not Captain Highbrow's or the Earth Corps'. Raven has taken her vows. Both are Dark Angels and as far as I'm concerned that means they are part of this council, Tandor."

"And why isn't Salustra here? Why didn't Pallaton rescue our Maker from the Citadel? Where is Jean-Luc? Shall we overlook their unexplained absences as well?" Tandor's fangs flashed as he spoke.

Loki snorted. Highbrow lifted a hand, waving him silent. The Maker's absence had not been among his concerns, though he noted Tandor's questions produced concerned expressions with both Picasso and Rose. He let them argue.

"An eye for an eye. Is that how it is?" asked Pallaton. He lifted the patch revealing a flesh-covered socket, and lowered it. "You blinded me, Tandor. I could challenge you to a duel to settle our grievances, as we did in the Shadowguard. But have I? No. I had to do unpleasant things to remain at the Citadel and keep the Kaiser satisfied. Killing Salustra and Jean-Luc aren't among them. Both died in service to the Dark Angels, and Raven and I are fortunate to be here. Do you want us to leave? Is that what you all want?"

Micah stood. "Pallaton and Raven have my vote. They stay."

"There is no vote," said Rose. "As the leader of the Dark Angels, I say Pallaton and Raven stay. I'm sure Highbrow and Thor will agree with me. We need everyone."

"Good," said Thor. "Let's get back to battle plans." He pointed at the map spread across the table. "I say we use nuclear missiles and target the vampire strongholds in Los Angeles, New York, Chicago, and Rome. The fallout won't affect us in Colorado Springs, but we will eliminate the Kaiser's allies and their respective forces. As for this camp, I'm not leaving Lt. Sterling in charge of crap. You're a guest, Highbrow. I lead the Earth Corps in Cadence's absence. This is a joint op, and you're not in command."

"I lead the Freedom Army, which you were once a part of," said Highbrow. "There can only be one commander and we're not voting. I'm assuming command of this operation and that's final."

Thor laughed. "We all know you're good at that."

"No nukes. The airport remains intact. I've got Nomad and Sturgis trying to repair a few of those tanks we saw outside. We can agree on leaving someone else in command here but we attack regardless of Cadence."

"Do you want to kill the Kaiser or not?" Thor asked. "We have the means to destroy these bastards at our fingertips."

Luna let out a soft growl. "Skye and Monkey are at the Citadel. I'm taking a team tomorrow and so is Sheena. Skye was in our pride, but both are a priority. If Lotus was in this meeting, she would agree. I know Dragon does."

"I do," said Dragon. "I'll lead the first assault team. Luna, Sheena, and Moon Dog can join me. I'll take Freeborn and Phoenix too. Thor can have Star, Lotus, Smack, Dodger, Xena and Loki."

"You can't be serious." said Loki. His black, lanky hair hid half his face. His scar was exposed, bright red and throbbing. "There are over thirteen thousand Shadowguard and vescali, but you've forgotten the zombie cyborgs. Not just fighters. I'm talking an army. We'll be slaughtered. I agree with Thor, nuke them all and be done with it."

Thor grabbed Loki's arm and jerked him back into his seat.

"Let's get back to discussing the Kaiser," Star said. "What can you tell us, Raven? He must have a weakness. What did you find after I left?"

Raven gazed at Star with true affection. "If you use his true name, Prince Balan, he can be stopped for a few minutes. I don't know about killing him."

"Nukes," whispered Thor.

Micah stood again, excited. "Well done, Raven. You found his weakness. If someone with a pure heart and mind spoke his name, they could control him."

Highbrow rubbed his chin. "That still leaves us with another problem. What about Balan's shadow? Pallaton, you've seen it. How the hell do we kill it?"

"When Raven said his name, his guardian weakened too," said Pallaton. "This thing is a demon that drains the life force of anything it touches. This will not be easy, folks. Balan has fought wars against every immortal god and goddess though the ages, and he defeated them all. They were infected with the same virus that created chameleons. You'll be gods one day, if you live that long, but Balan cannot be killed."

"Not without a holy relic," said Micah, "and we don't have one of those."

Loki laughed. "Oh, that's just perfect. A demon from ancient times has killed every known god and goddess, and you think you can stop him by saying his name?"

"Would you shut up? If you are afraid, Loki, then stay here with the children and hide," said Thor.

"It won't work. We'll all die under you."

Highbrow made a quick decision. "Dragon, please see Loki to his quarters. If he doesn't believe in our cause, he doesn't need to be here.

I'm tired of listening to him. Make sure he doesn't leave his room. I don't want him talking to anyone and getting them stirred up."

"I'll do it," said Freeborn, rising from her chair. "Dragon needs to be part of this meeting. Plus, I'm the strongest." She held Loki by the neck and hauled him to the door. "Come on, Loki."

"If you lock me up, you should do the same with those two killers!" Loki pointed at Pallaton and Raven. "The Kaiser's wife killed Salustra in the arena! And, well, what isn't on Pallaton's list? You might as well call the Kaiser and tell him your plan. These two will. They're on his side, not yours!"

Pallaton's eyes flashed yellow and his fangs protruded as he advanced on Loki. "It wasn't Raven's fault," he said, with a snarl. "It was the ring! A cursed ring given to her by the Kaiser, but she no longer wears it. Raven didn't mean to kill Salustra and you know it, Loki."

"Salustra was my friend," said Raven. "It's not what you think. I wasn't wearing the ring when she died. Zombies had surrounded her. They'd already bitten her and the Kaiser's shadow was moving in on her. I killed her to spare her agony."

"Liar," Loki shouted. "You enjoyed it! I saw your face!"

Freeborn lifted Loki over her shoulder, kicking and screaming, and took him out of the conference room. Tandor stood and moved against Pallaton, but Picasso and Micah interceded and stopped him. Lt. Sterling drew his weapon, and Thor disarmed him as they bickered over command.

Highbrow's temper skyrocketed, and he felt the tips of his ears twitching. He reached up to furry puma ears and realized his fingernails had turned into claws. Luna jumped and reached Highbrow first. She dragged him away from the table and removed his uniform as the seams ripped.

"You're changing," said Luna. "Don't fight it or it will hurt. Just let it happen. I'm right here. You don't have to be scared."

Highbrow tore off his shirt and roared as every muscle ached. Within seconds he had transformed into a towering, dark brown werepuma. Luna shed her clothes, dropped to the ground, and morphed, yet half his size. Aware he still thought like a man, Highbrow looked around the room, unable to speak his mind. He felt his temper abating as Star and Rose calmed everyone down. They all turned to watch Highbrow and Luna.

A moment later, Highbrow transformed back to human form, as did Luna. She wrapped herself in her coat and tossed Highbrow his pants. Luna had grown accustomed to her nudity, but it mortified Highbrow and he spared no time getting dressed.

"You don't expect it the first time," Luna sympathized. "You'll get used to changing and be able to handle it when it happens, if you don't lose your temper. But until you can control your wild side, I don't think it's a good idea that you lead the attack. Your battle plan is sound, Highbrow, but you can't command as a werepuma. One of the team leaders will have to lead in your place."

"I know, I know," Highbrow muttered as he zipped up his pants. His hands were shaking, making it difficult. Luna already had her clothes on and sat, smoothing back her hair, as he laced up his boots.

"You should have told us about this beforehand," said Thor. He turned to Rose. "As camp doctor, you might have mentioned Highbrow was a mutant. Isn't that what you call us, Highbrow? Mutants? How does it feel?"

"Miserable," said Highbrow. "I have Chameleon and werepuma blood in me. Luna is right. I can't command if I can't control this, but your temper is no better than mine. The only two real soldiers are Picasso and Sterling. One of them should lead this mission."

"Picasso will be in a chopper," said Dragon. "Sterling should stay here. Picasso can show him how to run the satellite. Then he can watch the battle from here and respond if we're contacted by anyone in the military. As for a battlefield commander, Highbrow will stay in command. Just because he's some super-werepuma doesn't change things.

I've never known you to lose your temper in battle, Highbrow. You've always been cool under pressure. You'll be fine."

"I agree with Dragon," Star said. "Highbrow, you shouldn't be embarrassed. Your change doesn't diminish your effectiveness as a leader. In fact, it makes you one of us. Luna warned you to be cautious, so you'll be cautious. Control your temper, and lead us to victory."

Highbrow leaned to take a seat when Micah appeared at his side. Luna came over and touched Highbrow's forehead. She gave Micah a knowing look. They each took one of his arms and led him to the door. The group stared, concerned, and Dragon opened the door for them.

"He needs rest," said Micah. "Luna and I will take him to his room. Thor. Dragon. You two sort out details with the rest of the group. We'll be back as soon as we can."

"Morphing has worn him out," Luna said. "He'll be no good tomorrow if he doesn't rest."

Highbrow was dizzy. Luna and Micah helped him sit on the bed. After situating Highbrow, Luna took a bottle of water and a bag of nuts.

"Drink and eat," said Luna. "Eating will help clear your head. Just pretend it's a big juicy steak. You'll need your strength sooner than morning."

While Highbrow devoured the water and nuts, Micah filled a bag with apples, a bag of chips, and a protein bar. He topped it off with a medical kit, a revolver, and a box of ammo. He zipped it up and put it on the bed next to Highbrow.

"What's going on?" asked Highbrow. "Am I going somewhere?"

"It's Cadence," Micah said. "I don't think Logan and Rafe were the best people to send after her. Cadence is vital to the success of the assault on the Citadel. Luna and I think Thor sent Logan and Rafe on the mission hoping they wouldn't make it back. Only an immortal can use the portal. If they don't find Cadence and the others, they can't come back."

"What am I supposed to do?" asked Highbrow. "Thor leads the Earth Corps. He's not going to let me go after her. I need to stay here and concentrate on defeating the Shadowguard. Without his army, we may have a chance to capture Balan and hold him here until Cadence arrives."

Micah gave Highbrow a funny look. "We're talking about Cadence here, the girl you're supposed to love. We're not asking you to do anything we're not willing to do, Highbrow. Luna and I already spoke with Phoenix. She's agreed to take us through the portal to find Cadence."

Highbrow choked. "What? Are you two serious? I'm not even sure I believe any of this yet. And, further, I'm told you need a blood sacrifice to open that thing. This is ridiculous. I'll go after her. Thor needs you guys, but I'm expendable."

"I thought you'd say that," said Micah. "You're a super-werepuma. You can go through the monolith on your own. All you have to do is step through it and once you find them, step through it again. Phoenix has arranged everything."

"You can't wear your uniform," said Luna, "or you'll stick out like a sore thumb."

Luna pulled out tall boots and an altered blue sheet from the closet, made into a tunic for a knight. "I took the boots from Phoenix. She has others, and she has big feet. We don't have armor for you, but you can use Micah's sword. We'll dress you like a knight the best we can and help you get to the stone. Dodger and Xena are on guard duty, so they won't be a problem."

"This is the right thing to do, Highbrow," said Micah. "If Cadence is captured or the monolith is destroyed, wouldn't you rather be with her?"

"This may be the only way to make up after throwing her out of camp," said Luna. "What I said about you not being able to command wasn't true. I said that because you needed a reason to not be able to lead the attack tomorrow. You might not get back in time. Are you sure you want to do this alone?"

"Because we will come with you," said Micah. "We have two black cloaks we can wear. Lotus told us where to find them. She's in, too, and is creating a diversion. She went to the fourth lake before the war council. Tell us what you want to do."

Highbrow felt whiskers sprouting on his face. He was nervous. Luna sat next to him and put her hand on his shoulder, but the whiskers didn't vanish. She made him more nervous.

"You have a chance to set things right. Cadence is in another time and place. Do you want to spend the rest of your life missing her? Or do you want to find her?"

"All right," said Highbrow. "This is crazy, but I'll do it. On my own." If Cadence would ever forgive him, he had to do it on his own and prove how much he loved her.

"If you're questioned," said Micah, "use a bad English accent and tell them Richard Mallory sent you."

"And if it gets ugly, turn into a werepuma and eat them." Luna smiled. "I'm teasing. You don't have to eat anyone. I never have."

Highbrow changed his boots and held out his arms. Luna and Micah placed the tunic over his head and buckled a sword around his waist. They fastened a black cloak around his neck with a silver brooch. When they finished fussing over him, Highbrow went to the mirror and gazed at his reflection. He felt like a knight.

Micah and Luna stood as lookouts while Highbrow ran to the lower level and waited at the door to the lake for the pair to follow. Luna went inside to create the diversion with Lotus, leaving Micah to watch the hallway. The door opened and Highbrow heard the diversion, a heated argument between the girls. Micah walked through the doorway and motioned for Highbrow to make his move. He charged into the cavern, jumped the barrier, and ran straight for the monolith. He stopped at the sight of a dead rabbit on the ground. The blood sacrifice. As Highbrow approached, the rock opened and a blinding, green light hit his face. He entered and vanished from sight.

Chapter Twenty-One

A thick mist blanketed Pevensey Castle. Lit torches created a golden halo at the battlements and spread across the battlefield. The dead bodies of foot soldiers, knights, horses, dog soldiers, and wraiths cluttered the field. Thin forms in rags searched the fallen warriors, sucking blood from the wounded. The creatures fled at the approach of Cadence, Whisper, and Blaze. The three walked with their bloodied swords drawn. They had found Lord Darkmoore's reinforcements waiting in the forest, the delay preventing them from arriving at the castle in time to turn the tide.

Cadence had seen the aftermath of war and had lived a year with walking corpses, dulling her senses. Her sense of smell was not one of them. A stench invaded her nostrils, making her want to gag. The wholesale slaughter of medieval warfare had its own gory allure and morbid fascination. The dead were torn, trampled, and devoured. Body parts scattered across the soggy ground. Among the dead was Sir Thomas Mallory, trapped beneath his slain horse. The evidence showed he died of a broken neck. Cadence stared into Thomas's open, glazed eyes.

"What possessed you to ride out and meet the enemy?" asked Cadence. "You had the superior position with a high wall, catapults to launch fire, archers with silver arrows, and a castle keep to fall back to if the walls were breached. All you had to do was wait for us."

"Cadence, you're creeping me out," said Blaze. "Stop talking to dead people. That's Smack's specialty."

Cadence gazed at the castle. "See if the drawbridge is lowered, Whisper. The enemy may be waiting inside. We need to be extra cautious. It's too damn quiet."

"The dead should be silent," said Whisper.

Whisper ran toward the castle, vanishing in the thick fog. The moon slid around a cloud, and added a touch of silver light upon the slain. Blaze walked ahead of Cadence through the mangled bodies. She stabbed something that gurgled as it died, and then moved on, continuing the process until she came across someone familiar.

"It's Logan," said Blaze.

Cadence hurried over to a body wearing a black cloak, she recognized the former FBI agent despite the sword jutting from his chest and a torn throat. She pulled the sword from his body and tossing it aside, knelt beside him. Placing a hand on his frigid skin, she reached beneath the neckline of his sweater and pulled out a gold chain with a diamond pendent. She ripped the necklace from his neck and slid it into a leather pouch on her side.

"Rose will want this," said Cadence.

"What the hell is he doing here?" Blaze asked, sounding far too intrigued. "Was he part of a rescue team? We need to keep looking. More of our people may be here."

Blaze sped away, examining the dead bodies, moving so fast she covered the entire field within seconds. On her way back to Cadence, she let out a gasp and knelt beside another corpse. She said nothing, and waited for Cadence to join her. They stared down at Rafe's lifeless, pale form. A scaled, bat-like creature enveloped him. The creature was Rafe's final kill. He had ripped out its heart and still held it in his rigid hand.

Cadence shook her head. "How did they get here? Logan was at the Citadel and Rafe was being held prisoner. Yet, here they are. Dead. The thing that killed Rafe must be a vescali demon. Get it off him, please."

Cadence watched Blaze peel the demon off Rafe's body and toss it aside. Rafe was as handsome in death as in life. His eyes were closed and a strange, peaceful smile remained. Rafe had been her first serious relationship. She had kissed Lachlan and could do no less for Rafe. Kneeling, she placed a kiss on his cold cheek. Both vampires who loved her were now dead.

"I'm sorry," said Blaze. "Despite all his faults, Rafe loved you, Cadence."

Not saying a word, Cadence turned to the winged demon and kicked its ribs until she heard bones cracking. Then she thought of Lachlan. She jumped and landed on the demon's chest, caving its ribs under her boots.

Blaze put her hand on Cadence's shoulder. "I think it's dead. There are bound to be more inside."

Cadence thought of revenge as she strode toward the castle. Blaze ran ahead and met her on the drawbridge with Whisper. The gates were open, and there were more dead bodies inside the courtyard. Several vescali lay among the slain castle guards. The bodies trailed their way to the castle's keep. A few small buildings were on fire, but nothing moved. At the sound of a lone wolf howl from outside the castle walls, Cadence lifted her massive sword.

"We need to find the monolith. The priests were guarding it. It must be in the chapel."

"Shouldn't we look for the rest of the rescue team?" Blaze said. "Logan and Rafe might not have come alone. There could be others in the keep looking for us. We need to spread out, Cadence. We can't leave anyone behind."

Cadence stared up at the keep. The banners were hanging flat without a breeze and no lights shone from any of the narrow windows. "Whisper, go to the chapel and secure the monolith if it's there. If it's not, meet us back here in thirty minutes. Blaze, search for any of our people. I'll start with the dungeon and work my way up."

"Gotcha," said Whisper.

Cadence found a side door leading to the dungeon. A flight of stairs descended, the stones were damp and torches were flickering as Cadence walked past. She checked each cell and found a few emaciated prisoners. Without knowing if they were infected, she ignored their cries and left them in their cells. She wound her way up to the kitchen and found it covered with blood. Dinner was still cooking over the fire, bubbling over, and causing the burning logs to sizzle. Mrs. Fulbright and her kitchen staff were dead. One young kitchen boy sat up and looked at her. His mouth opened, screeching.

Cadence gritted her teeth. "Wraith."

Sword held high, Cadence lopped off the boy's head and did the same for Mrs. Fulbright. From what she could see, the vampires left no one alive. Those victims would rise again. She took a torch from the wall and set fire to the bodies. She backed out of the room and tossed the torch onto a table. Covered in flames and screaming, the former staff creatures moved toward Cadence. She slammed the door, locking the wooden plank in place. They beat on the door, trapped.

Cadence went to the top floor where Lord Montagu's quarters were. She entered his bedroom and found the decrepit lord lying on his bed, bathed in blood. A tall knight stood on the far side of the bed. At the sound of her footsteps, he looked up and gasped.

"Highbrow? It's you!" Cadence ran around the bed and stopped short of hugging him. "Did you come with Logan and Rafe? Is anyone else with you?"

"I came alone," said Highbrow. "The battle was over by the time I arrived. I've been looking everywhere for you. The old man was dying when I found him. He asked me to stay with him until he died, so I did."

"Rafe and Logan are dead. So is Lachlan." Cadence looked away before Highbrow could see her tears. "We think we know where the monolith is and how to get back home. Come on. Whisper and Blaze are waiting for us."

Highbrow looked at the dead man. "Lord Montagu told me who he was and the story about the three Mallory brothers before he died. A priest told him to send his forces out to meet the Devil head on and God would spare his life. It was a lie. He also said the vescali are a serious threat and won't stop until they take control of the world, even if you kill Prince Balan. This is what they've been waiting for, a chance to break free from Balan and seize control. Montagu thought the vescali needed him, but a priest killed him. The priests are vescali, Cadence. I found no one else alive and I didn't find the priests. If you're ready, I'll take you back to NORAD. I've relocated my camp there. We're mounting an attack against the Shadowguard, but we can't do it without you."

"Or without this," said Cadence, excited. She held up the spear "I found it guarded by Apollo, a real immortal, but I couldn't free him from his sleep."

"And that is…?"

"The Spear of Destiny. A holy weapon. I believe this is what we need to kill Balan. Lachlan died helping me find it." She looked away. "We need to find Blaze and Whisper, and get out of this awful place."

Highbrow was too much in awe to touch the spear when she held it up to him. Nor could he find the words to express his regret that three of her friends were dead. He took hold of Cadence's arm and pointed her toward the bed. She glanced toward the Montagu.

"You should see this before we go. I thought I smelled something odd about the old man. He's not human. After he died, he grew scales and claws. Montagu is vescali, Cadence, but he wasn't evil. He warned Richard and Leopold not to go through the monolith. They wouldn't listen to him. He tried to keep others from going through it, but the priests were too powerful and they kept him here under guard. They've been using the stone for months."

Cadence gave him a hard look. "What do you mean you smelled something? You saw him change. Montagu smells dead, but it's not that ripe."

"I can smell better than you, Cadence. I'm infected with the virus." Highbrow looked at the ground, embarrassed. "I'm both chameleon and werepuma now. We can talk later. The important thing is getting you back to Colorado."

Smoke was thick on the lower levels. They kept to the stairs and entered the main dining hall, finding more dead servants, guards, the lord's hounds, and several vescali in demon form. The fire from the kitchen had spread, trailing banners and tapestries, filling the room with flames and haze. Exiting the keep, they entered the courtyard and found Blaze waiting beside a fountain, loading her carbine with the last ammunition. A few slain vescali lay nearby. Blaze took one look at Highbrow and smiled.

"Look who came to save the day," she said, laughing. "It's nice to have you back on the team, Highbrow."

Cadence looked around the courtyard. "Where is Whisper?"

"In the chapel." Blaze nodded toward a humble wooden building with a tall steeple. "The stone has to be there. Whisper never came back out. With the fire spreading, these demons keep coming out. I enjoy shooting them."

Highbrow took the lead and reached the door first, opening it up for the two young women. Inside, they found Whisper standing over a half-turned, dead priest. He appeared calm for someone who had just cleaved a demon in half. Candles burned bright, while a bowl of incense produced a fragrant aroma. Highbrow walked over to Whisper and shook his hand.

"Good to see you, captain," said Whisper, offering a lopsided grin. "Once a Tiger, always a Tiger. I knew you'd come back to us. Never doubted it for a minute."

"It just took me a while to figure it out," said Highbrow. "But we can talk about that later. We need to leave before the vescali find us. Montagu said they've been guarding him for years. I can smell them. They're close. Did you find the portal?"

"I did. It's downstairs."

As they turned for the stairs, movement at the door revealed several cloaked figures. More vescali waited outside in the gloom. Throwing off their cloaks, they turned into bat-like creatures and swept across the pews, aiming for Cadence and her friends.

"Get to the monolith!" shouted Cadence.

Swinging her sword, Cadence swatted a demon from the air before Highbrow dashed by with a loud roar. His clothes hung off his body, although he had not fully turned. He had the head of a cat with long teeth and claws. He tore the demons apart, destroying the chapel in the process. Demons continued to file in behind their slain brothers. Cadence shouted for Highbrow and waited for him on the stairs before joining the others. She shut the door and bolted it. Vescali pounded on the door, screaming, but it held firm.

"The stone's over here," said Whisper.

Lit torches, a few hung paintings, and the monolith were all that occupied the chamber. The stone stood in the center of the room, projecting from the earth, glimmering as if the black stone was wet. As they approached the stone, it hummed. An opening formed in the middle, revealing its light. A familiar tug pulled the team closer. As the vescali collapsed the door, Whisper ran into the light, followed by Blaze, Highbrow, and Cadence. The demons closed in heavy.

Raven stood with the Dark Angels behind the barricade, guarding the monolith. Since Highbrow had given the Earth Corps the slip to find Cadence, Thor assigned the Dark Angels to security.

"The Cheyenne Stone is humming," said Pallaton. He sat holding a rifle, and turned to look at a security camera. They had been working since the magnetic net covered the great stone. "Get the Earth Corps in here. Now!"

The portal appeared, swirling in light. Raven slid down beside Rose, peering over the barricade. She noticed Pallaton's eyes glowing yellow. The rest of the Dark Angels' eyes turned violet and their fangs extended as the ground trembled. The portal widened.

Whisper, Blaze, a werepuma, and Cadence rushed through the portal and ran for the barricade. The vescali followed. The Dark Angels fired on the demons as their missing friends joined them behind cover. Raven dispersed available guns and the three chameleons formed at the side of the lake, taking aim at each demon that appeared.

"Where the hell is Thor?" shouted Cadence. "There are hundreds more behind us. We've got to destroy the monolith or they'll get through!"

Bodies piled outside the Roman Stone. The vescali had to crawl over their own dead, slowing their progression. Raven heard the door behind her open and smelled a familiar odor as Thor and the Earth Corps charged in to the cavern. The teenagers lined up behind the Dark Angels and the firing paused as Freeborn dashed toward the monolith.

Raven led three pumas and a werewolf in a coordinated attack against the demons. They held the vescali back as Freeborn approached from the rear of the stone. The portal grew so wide Raven could see vescali waiting to come through.

A thunderous sound filled the cavern, and the light dimmed. Raven looked up as Freeborn slammed her fists against the stone. A few more blows and shards of rock crumbled to the ground. Freeborn raised her fists high and with one last strike, she split the monolith in half.

The light vanished and the portal closed on the vescali before the remainder of the Cheyenne Stone shattered into thousands of pieces.

Cheers filled the cavern. The Earth Corps were the first to reach

Cadence, Whisper, and Blaze. A strong hand gripped Raven's shoulder and she turned to find Pallaton smiling at her. She returned the gesture with a grateful embrace.

"We did right, coming here," said Pallaton. "I feel like I've done something right, something good. I'd give anything to see the Kaiser's face when he hears about this."

"Rafe and Lachlan weren't with them!" Raven kept hold of his hand as she climbed on top of the sandbags and counted heads. "They're missing. So is Logan. Something's wrong. That's two more Dark Angels we've lost."

"Let them celebrate," said Rose, worried. "There'll be far fewer of us after the assault on the Citadel. I need to find out what happened to Logan. I don't see him with the others. He may have fled the moment they arrived, though I can't imagine him enjoying life in medieval England." She swept her hand across Raven's forehead in a motherly manner, then hurried over to greet her returning friends.

Logan could not have stayed behind, not when Rose was waiting for him. Raven had a bad feeling about what really happened. She glanced over at Thor and Loki. They hung back looking unhappy. Raven walked over to her former teammates.

"What's wrong with you two? This is a joyous moment," she said. "Our patrol team never received this welcome home, but that never stopped the Vikings from congratulating other teams for a job well done. This is your team now, Thor. Why are you standing there scowling like an old goat? Cadence can lead the attack now, or is that the problem?"

"Highbrow is lapping it up like the credit is his for bringing Cadence back," said Thor. "I suppose he's made up with Cadence. At least Rafe and Logan didn't make it back. I was counting on that. I say good riddance."

Loki snickered. "You'll never fill Highbrow's shoes, Thor. Why do you even try? He's Cadence's boyfriend."

"Something bad happened, here. Cadence is handling it well enough, but Rose is crying. Baldor and Heimdall wouldn't hold a grudge like you two. They would both be celebrating. Loki, you've never had manners, but Thor is a team leader. Stop being so immature and get over there."

Thor snarled. "Don't tell me what to do. You're not a Viking anymore, Raven, and you're not Earth Corps either. This is complicated."

"It's not," said Pallaton. "With Cadence and Highbrow's return, it makes you third in line for command, Thor. But you don't see Dragon complaining. I believe this is about your team, not individual glory."

A smile appeared on Loki's face as he nudged Thor in the ribs. "Dragon is a follower, he always will be. Second best."

Chatter hushed as Cadence walked over. Pallaton pulled Raven aside, while Loki remained at Thor's side. The commander's chain mail and tunic were covered with blood. Her smile faded as Thor bristled and clenched his fists.

"What were you thinking, Thor?" said Cadence. "Logan and Rafe had no business coming after us. Did you send them or did they come on their own like Highbrow?"

"I sent them to find you," said Thor. "If they didn't make it back, then they weren't meant to come back."

Cadence punched Thor in the jaw. The broad-shouldered hunk tumbled hard into the sandbags, collapsing to the ground.

"Don't be so quick to blame me," said Thor, rising to his feet. He waved off Star when she stepped forward to help him. "Rafe and Logan wanted redemption. I didn't force them to go. Nor did I send Highbrow. That was his idea."

Loki ducked out of the way as Cadence glanced in his direction. Raven held firm as the commander turned toward her, and then faced Pallaton.

"Things have changed since I've been gone," said Cadence. "But if Rose wants you both here, I won't challenge her decision. We need everyone we can get if we're going to defeat Prince Balan."

Pushing through, Rose approached Cadence. Raven had never seen the doctor look so heartbroken. She remembered working beside Rose and Logan in the lab at Seven Falls. She remembered the two getting on each other's nerves. It didn't take a Ph.D. to know they had fallen for each other. That they would never get to say goodbye was unfair.

"Did Logan say anything, before he died?" asked Rose.

Cadence dug around inside of a leather pouch and held out a gold necklace. "I wasn't there when he died, Rose. I'm so sorry. We found Logan and Rafe outside Pevensey Castle, amongst the castle guards, murdered by vescali. We lost Lachlan trying to obtain the spear. They sacrificed their lives trying to help our cause. I swear I'll avenge their deaths by killing Prince Balan and every vescali that gets in my way."

Rose turned toward Micah, sobbing. He held her tight.

The giant werepuma lunged over the sand bags, landing between Thor and Cadence. Highbrow opened his jaws and let out a thunderous roar. Cadence nodded and pulled the Spear of Destiny from her side.

"This is it," said Cadence, her voice filled with emotion. "Thanks to Richard Mallory and his brother Thomas, we found the sacred spear in a crystal coffin that contained the body of Apollo. Whether my blood will awaken him or not, I can't be sure. But the gods and goddesses of old are just like us, infected with the virus. Others may still live. Once we defeat Balan and the Shadowguard, we must turn our attention to the vescali. They are a bigger threat than any of us imagined."

Freeborn stepped out front. "I'm behind you, Cadence. The Earth Corps are, too. I believe you were meant to find this spear and bring it here. You're meant to lead us into battle."

"When you face Prince Balan," said Raven, "say his name out loud. Using the name against him will weaken him for several minutes. Freeborn is right, Cadence. You are meant to lead us into battle. We're all behind you and we'll do whatever is necessary to defeat Balan and the Shadowguard."

The door to the lake opened and Picasso burst in, his eyes violet with excitement. "You won't believe what just happened. It's a miracle! I just got through to Senator Powers, and he's coming to Colorado Springs!"

At the mention of his father, Highbrow morphed back into his human form. He stood up naked and his mouth open. Freeborn chuckled. She removed her Army jacket and tossed it to Highbrow. He tied it around his waist before running a hand through his hair. Cadence, Freeborn, Smack, Dodger and Blaze gathered around him. All former Fighting Tigers united again, as if they were never apart.

"I can't believe it," said Highbrow. "All this time we've been waiting to hear from my father. Didn't I tell you he was still alive? I knew he wouldn't let me down. Is he coming here, Picasso? Did he say?"

Picasso grinned from ear to ear. "I spoke with General Winters, who is in command of the military. Your father intends to come here, but first General Winters is sending the Air Force to take out the Citadel. They're already on their way. You can talk to your father later, Highbrow. We're to launch our attack after the air strike. Our orders are to destroy the Shadowguard and take the vampire lords as prisoners. General Winters asked that we try to take the Kaiser prisoner."

"Not a chance," said Cadence. "He's going down."

"Did my dad give me a message?" asked Highbrow.

"Yeah," said Picasso. "Your dad wanted you to know that he has every confidence you'll defeat the enemy. General Winters also said your dad can't wait to see you and will arrive the moment he hears we've won the battle."

Highbrow laughed. "Of course he did. I can't wait to see him."

"General Winters wants us in position before the bombs hit. They're already in route, so that doesn't leave us much time."

"I can't believe it! He came through!" Highbrow had so many

things he wanted to ask. He had not spoken to his father in over a year. He turned to Cadence. "My dad! He's coming here!"

Cadence smiled. "You always said he'd come through. Let's get ready, folks. We have a battle to win."

Chapter Twenty-Two

Cadence gazed across the smoldering ruins of the Citadel. The five bombers from Cannon Air Force Base leveled the former Academy in seconds, vanishing into the blue sky. Seated in the front of a military vehicle, she watched the teams fan out across the battlefield. Picasso flew overhead, scouting enemy troops that might have escaped the air strike. Buildings were reduced to rubble and several major fires raged through the campus. Twisted vehicles fused to their parking spaces, and whatever may have remained of the stadium after the bombing was demolished.

Smack sat behind the wheel, monitoring communication between the teams. Freeborn and Whisper were mounted in the truck bed, diligent.

Dragon led the first team into the tunnels beneath the Citadel, while Thor's team combed through the rubble of the stadium. Tandor led a third team of vampires and searched through burning buildings. So far, there were no sightings of Shadowguard or vescali. It appeared the Air Force did their job well.

Cadence glanced at Smack. The girl clung to the wheel, chomping her bubble-gum, worried. Cadence touched her slender arm.

"Relax, kiddo. It will be okay. Dodger is with Blaze."

"I see people," said Smack, popping a bubble. "It's the Shadow-guard."

Black forms ran scattered through the destruction. Seconds later,

Freeborn's mounted machine gun whirred and Whisper's sniper came to life. The Dark Angels arrived first. As more Shadowguard emerged from bunkers beneath the ground, the two opposing vampire forces engaged in combat.

Whisper thumped the cab of the truck. "We got zombies."

The explosions attracted the living dead. Every zombie within earshot staggered toward the Citadel, while others descended from the mountain and waded through the burning meadow. A group of rotting corpses ignored the truck and its occupants, attracted to the vampires instead. Whisper picked them off, but they kept coming.

"There are thousands of them," said Smack, scanning her surroundings. "Should I warn the teams?"

"Yes," said Cadence. "Get Dragon and Thor top side. We've got a fight on our hands."

Smack honked the horn. Cadence looked up as a company of zombie cyborgs and Shadowguard marched toward the truck. In the center of the troops, a black limo raced toward their position.

The vehicle came to an abrupt stop only fifty yards from Cadence's truck. Flame-throwing cyborgs marched forward and joined the horde. The Dark Angels continued to engage the Shadowguard as gunfire and groans from the living dead rose to a cacophony.

"I'll bet Balan is in the limo," said Freeborn. "And the vampire lords. We can either wait here and watch or…"

Smack leaned out. "I reached Dragon," she shouted. "He's met resistance. Thor isn't answering."

A zombie with a half-shredded face stared at Smack. Several more joined it. The girl smacked a bubble and pointed at the limousine.

"Yo, zombies! Go kill the vamps in that limo. Tell your friends, too. They're the bad guys. Not us."

The zombie nodded and the small group sauntered toward the limo. More zombies joined them and surrounded the limo.

"Did you see that?" asked Cadence. "They understood Smack! Keep talking. Send them to attack the Kaiser!"

"You got it, Commander!" Smack jumped out of the truck and directed a zombie and its ragtag group to fight the Shadowguard. "They'll do it, Commander! Said that's why they're here. They came to help us!" She found another group and directed them.

The Shadowguard flanked the cyborgs, leveling the zombies surrounding the limousine. Cadence waited to see vescali crawl from the tunnels beneath the ruins, but it was Thor's team that arrived instead. From behind, they engaged the Shadowguard at once.

An immense, ferocious werepuma fought beside Thor. Highbrow was as large as a horse and caught the Shadowguard with ease, shredding prey in his monstrous jaws. Loki was with them, arrayed as a warrior of the arena. He flew above the vampires and landed on top of them, staking them to the ground with his trident.

"Someone is getting out of the limo," said Whisper.

The Shadowguard surrounded the limo and secured it against the zombie lines. A vampire stepped out of the vehicle. He undressed as he stood before them. Cadence thought the vampire insane, until he morphed into something that looked similar to a vescali, but larger and more powerful.

She knew at once this was the vampyr, Prince Balan. The demon lord was colossal. Talons emerged as his bat-like face stretched, revealing dreadful fangs. He reached skyward and screamed. Focusing hellish eyes, he targeted Cadence.

"I'll take care of this loser," Whisper said, lifting his rifle. He fired a round that struck Balan in the forehead. The bullet bounced off his scaled hide. "You better get your spear, Cadence. Here he comes!"

Like a furious banshee, Prince Balan screeched and beat the air with his vast wings and swooped for their truck. A monstrous shadow followed him. Balan moved faster than any chameleon or vampire, giving Cadence mere seconds to employ the spear before the demon lord was upon her. Balan's eyes widened at the sight of the spear, giving Cadence a moment to relish his fear.

That moment was short-lived.

Balan tore at her head and shoulders, cutting her flesh. His shrieks drowned out the shouts from Freeborn and Whisper. They screamed in terror as the shadow guardian enveloped both teenagers, draining energy from their bodies. Freeborn and Whisper crashed to their knees, reeling under a shroud of darkness. Cadence released a savage cry and struck Balan with the spear, which sent him rolling through the air. She jabbed at the shadow. The blackness was sucked into the tip of the spear and then exploded outward, splattering across the sky. Inky tendrils spread through the air, consumed by the sunlight. What remained of the shadow fell to the ground. Trembling with rage and heaving fire from his nostrils, Balan flew toward the truck.

"Are you alright?" asked Cadence, pulling Freeborn to her feet. She yanked Whisper up by his coat.

Both nodded, pale and weak, but eager to fight

The war raged around Cadence as she thrust the spear toward the heavens. She shouted, "Are you afraid of me? If not, come back and let's try that again!"

The demon prince soared by her, followed by a reanimated shadow. Together, the dark lord and his familiar flew over the battlefield, giving encouragement to the bedraggled Shadowguard. A war cry echoed through the air. The troops rallied.

Whisper cleared his throat, lifting his rifle. "Should you really be taunting a demon? I don't think I can handle having my energy zapped like that again."

"Me either, but curse him anyway!" said Freeborn. She lifted her shotgun and took a wild shot at Balan, missing him but striking the shadow. The pellets tore holes in its wings, healing seconds later.

"You shall die, Cadence," snarled Balan, in a thunderous voice. He and his shadow made another pass over the truck. "You and your Earth Corps will be welcomed in the pits of Hell. The Dark Angel's will be my slaves. Cowards, made to suffer!"

"Just think," said Freeborn, "Raven slept with that thing."

Prince Balan appeared above. A blow from the back of his large hand knocked Cadence off her feet and into Freeborn. Freeborn tumbled over the side of the truck into a mob of zombies. The shadow guardian scattered the zombies, and reached for her throat. She scrambled beneath the truck, as the creature pursued.

Balan caught Cadence by her arm, breathing fire into her face. She leaned away, lifting the spear in reflex. Its metal tip deflected the flames and fried a nearby zombie. He retracted from the spear, laughing, as the demon's shadow dragged Freeborn from under the truck. The chameleon blasted the inky familiar, dropping it on top of Cadence. The darkness wrapped its arms around Cadence with a cold embrace. She felt light-headed and sick to her stomach. Whisper swung his rifle at Prince Balan's face, but fell aside with a swipe of the devil's wing. He landed on his side, injuring his dominant arm.

"Leave her to me," shouted Balan. He slapped the guardian familiar to the side, and swiped at Cadence with his talons. She jabbed with the spear and missed, dodging his fist as it crushed the ground where her head had been. She jabbed again and left a bleeding gash the length of his arm. Balan flew back, crying in pain. With his guardian, he circled high and prepared for another attack.

Freeborn appeared at the side of the truck. "That thing nearly sucked the life out of me. A zombie tried to pull it off of me. Don't know why, but I guess the shadow didn't like its touch because it let me go."

"There's nothing you can do to help me," shouted Cadence. "If Balan would hold still long enough, I might be able to stab him in the heart. Take Smack and help the city crawlers finish those cyborgs. Whisper, go with her. I can handle this!"

"I'm not leaving you," said Whisper. He tapped on the top of the truck cab. "Get out of there, Smack. Go kill something. Take Freeborn with you. When he flies down again, say his name, Cadence. You're the one who has to do it."

Smack climbed out of the truck and joined Freeborn. They pushed through the zombies and to the front of the battle. Whisper shouted as Balan and his shadow made another pass. The shadow moved faster and knocked Whisper off his feet. Cadence lifted the spear and stabbed into the dark shadow. Blackness slithered up her arm, and squeezed until she dropped the spear. The familiar sucked life from her body. She felt like the meat was being pulled from her bones, separating in rough tears.

Cadence weakened, unable to break free from her attacker or scream out Balan's name. The demon came for Whisper. They struggled, but the demon lord was stronger and sank his teeth into Whisper's shoulder. The sniper screamed in fear, as a frightened child about to die. It jarred Cadence into consciousness, and she found the strength to raise her voice.

"Balan, stop!"

Cadence felt the shadow release her and watched it slam into the bed of the truck, thrashing. Prince Balan stood in front of her, frozen. He was deadlocked in an immobile arch above Whisper. The truck shook from an unseen force, and Cadence retrieved the spear. With a cry of rage, she thrust the tip into Balan's paralyzed chest.

The truck shook with violence as the spear glided through the demon's tough hide. Cadence gripped the spear tight, speaking Balan's name in rapid succession. The shadow evaporated beneath their feet, vanishing from sight. The truck stopped trembling, as Prince Balan's body hardened. In seconds he turned to stone and Cadence released the spear. Kneeling beside Whisper, they watched the brown scales transform white and porous like limestone.

"Is he dead?" croaked Whisper, massaging his shoulder.

Cadence found Lachlan's sword in the truck. She swung the blade with every ounce of energy and rage she had left. The galloglass shattered the stone and the vampyr's head flew into the horde of zombies, lost. Cadence struck again and again, until she reduced Balan's remains to ashes.

"The Kaiser is dead!" shouted Cadence, embracing Whisper. He groaned in pain and she let him go. "Sorry. That's a nasty gash, Tiger. Stay here and heal, while I go finish the battle."

"Yeah, go do that," said Whisper, smiling through the pain.

Lachlan's sword in hand, Cadence rushed into the heat of the battle and took out several Shadowguard before her army killed them all. Zombies fought beside her, consuming vampires that fell beneath them, while Freeborn helped lay waste to the cyborgs. The battle turned to slaughter and the remaining Shadowguard fled from the Citadel. Dark Angels surrounded the limo, guarding it as Luna and Moon Dog pursued the Shadowguard. Their furry tails streaked through the zombies, catching up with the stragglers.

"Go help them," shouted Cadence, flagging Freeborn.

The chameleon dropped the remains of a cyborg, and joined by Thor's team, she caught up with the shapeshifters. They surrounded the Shadowguard at the main entrance. The enemy laid down their weapons, raising their arms in surrender. Phoenix and Smack laughed as they whizzed by Cadence, joining their friends to take the Shadowguard prisoners. Whisper walked over to Cadence and the Dark Angels surrounding the limousine.

"We were waiting on you," said Pallaton. He nodded at Cadence and opened the door, reaching inside. He pulled out D'Aquilla, who placed his hands on top of his head. "Game's over, Salvatore."

"You might have captured me, but the battle isn't over," said D'Aquilla. He snarled as Pallaton pushed him against the side of the limo. "I see you've changed sides, captain. I'm not surprised. You loyalty is like a pendulum and it will swing back to our side the moment your Cadence looks the other direction."

"I've always been a Dark Angel," said Pallaton, angry. "Consider yourself our prisoner. You won't be going back to Italy, so I suggest you shut up and accept defeat with more humility." He looked inside the limo as Tandor took hold of D'Aquilla. "Commander, there are more vampire lords inside. What are your orders? Shall we shoot them or put them in irons?"

Before Cadence could answer, Thor dashed to the limo. He ignored everyone and gave Raven a bear hug, then walked over and kissed a startled Rose on the cheek. He spun and saluted Cadence, grinning ear to ear.

"We've won," shouted Thor. "The Kaiser is dead, the Shadowguard are dismantled. Victory is ours!"

"This isn't a football game, Thor," said Raven, smiling. She holstered her gun and leaned against the hood. "We still have survivors to look for. Dragon hasn't returned with his team. They could be in trouble."

"Then I'll go and find them. But first, I want to chain up these vampire lords and take a picture standing over them. I don't care what you say. We won and I'm going to enjoy it as long as I can."

A few curious zombies had gathered nearby, watching but not interfering. Cadence watched as Pallaton and Raven pulled the vampire lords out of the limo and lined them up. Rose, Picasso and Micah kept their weapons aimed at the vampire lords as D'Aquilla stood before Cadence and lowered his head. It was a defining moment for Cadence. She felt many things, but most of all a sense of pride that despite the odds, she had done something extraordinary. For herself, her friends, and for everyone threatened by the Kaiser and his vampire lords, the reign of vampires was finished. The only thing that would have made it more complete was Lachlan's presence. She held his sword, felt his spirit, and acknowledged the hole in her heart did not feel quite as large.

"We surrender," said D'Aquilla. "The day is yours, Commander."

"Put them in chains, Pallaton. Rose, take it from here. I want to take some time to savor the moment."

Cadence walked away from the limousine, lugging the sword over her shoulder. Luna padded over, her pink tongue hanging from her mouth, and walked beside Cadence across the battlefield. The only sounds she heard were fires still burning among the buildings. Snowflakes fell, settling on motionless bodies. Zombies continued to feed on slain vampires, and Freeborn dismantled any cyborgs she found. Piles of mechanical arms and legs separated, with torsos in another. Cadence looked away. Not all of war was about glory. The truth was horrifying and brutal. She was glad for Luna's company, not required to speak, but not alone.

Cadence hoped Dragon and his team were having success finding survivors. She remained concerned, and wondered if they needed backup or had things under control. Finding Monkey and Skye remained a top priority. She turned to glance at Luna and found the werepuma gazing across the battlefield. Her fur stood on end as a fierce growl rose from her throat.

Someone was watching them.

Near the stadium ruins, she spotted an ominous figure. It was a zombie cyborg bigger than any she had seen before; a mammoth beast of muscle and machine. The only human skin that was visible was charred black. She recognized the cyborg from a poster promoting the Death Games. Aries of Athens was to have fought Dragon the previous evening. His hatred was palpable, even from a distance. And yet, the sadistic glint in his smile told Cadence something was wrong. This was not a simple cyborg.

With a motion that exuded violence, Aries disappeared from sight. Cadence ran across the field toward the stadium, followed by Luna. The werepuma kept at her side, running hard until they reached the place where the cyborg stood. Expecting to find a tunnel, Cadence gazed at the rough ground unable to fathom where Aries of Athens had gone.

"We have a problem, Luna. Go tell the team that Aries is on the loose. Dragon is down in the sewers. We need to warn him. Tell Thor to gather a team and find Dragon."

Luna sped across the field with a vicious roar, breaking the eerie silence. Cadence gazed up at the sky, letting snowflakes fall on her face. Her optimism disappeared with the rays of the sun. It was Christmas and they had defeated the Kaiser, but something in Aries' mechanical eyes told her a beast had just been unleashed.

She turned and watched Luna race toward her friends, celebrating their victory and the capture of the remaining vampire lords.

Cadence wanted to enjoy the moment; she deserved it. But it was no use. She had been in command long enough to recognize that old familiar feeling that things had taken a turn for the worse.

About The Author

S usanne L. Lambdin is the author of the *Dead Hearts* series of novels. A "trekkie" at heart, she received a "based in part" screen credit for writing a portion of *Star Trek: The Next Generation:* Season 4, Episode 76, titled *Family*. She is passionate about all things science fiction, horror, and high fantasy. Susanne is an expert on the subject of zombies, and is affectionately known by many of her fans as "The Zombie Lady."

She lives in Kansas with her family and two dogs. To contact Susanne and to learn more about her current and upcoming projects, visit www.SusanneLambdin.com.

CPSIA information can be obtained at www.ICGtesting.com
Printed in the USA
LVOW12s0333121114

413151LV00003B/5/P